VIRUS HUNTERS

A MEDICAL THRILLER | PART THREE

BOBBY AKART

INTRODUCTION

Thank you for downloading *VIRUS HUNTERS: Part three* of the
Virus Hunters trilogy by Author Bobby Akart.
For a copy of my critically acclaimed monthly newsletter, *The
Epigraph*, updates on new releases, special offers, and bonus content
visit me online at
BobbyAkart.com
or visit my dedicated feature page on Amazon at
Amazon.com/BobbyAkart

Formatted by Drew Avera

PRAISE FOR BOBBY AKART

PRAISE FOR AUTHOR BOBBY AKART and THE VIRUS HUNTERS

"Only Akart can weave a story that begins so calm, so normal and before you know it, you are at the end of the book with your pulse pounding in your chest and your mind screaming for more! ~ Amazon Hall of Fame, Top 2 Reviewer

"Under MY version of Wikipedia, under 'Insomnia – Causation', is a picture of Bobby Akart. I have learned not to pick up one of his books near bedtime as I will be unable to set it aside for hours!"

"Akart is a master of suspense, keeping us on the edge of our seats. But, he does it with fact-based fiction that would scare even the most hardened readers."

"Mixing science and suspense is something Bobby Akart is a master of—writing character driven stories that will have you on the edge of your seat."

ABOUT THE AUTHOR, BOBBY AKART

Author Bobby Akart has been ranked by Amazon as #25 on the Amazon Charts list of most popular, bestselling authors. He has achieved recognition as the #1 bestselling Horror Author, #1 bestselling Science Fiction Author, #5 bestselling Action & Adventure Author, #7 bestselling Historical Author and #10 bestselling Thriller Author.

He has sold over one million books in all formats, which includes over forty international bestsellers, in nearly fifty fiction and nonfiction genres.

His novel *Yellowstone: Hellfire* reached the Top 25 on the Amazon bestsellers list and earned him multiple Kindle All-Star awards for most pages read in a month and most pages read as an author. The Yellowstone series vaulted him to the #25 bestselling author on Amazon Charts, and the #1 bestselling science fiction author.

Bobby has provided his readers a diverse range of topics that are both informative and entertaining. His attention to detail and impeccable research has allowed him to capture the imagination of his readers through his fictional works and bring them valuable knowledge through his nonfiction books.

SIGN UP for Bobby Akart's mailing list to receive a copy of his monthly newsletter, *The Epigraph,* learn of special offers, view bonus content, and be the first to receive news about new releases in the Virus Hunters series. Visit www.BobbyAkart.com for details.

Other Works by Amazon Top 25 Author Bobby Akart

OTHER WORKS BY AMAZON TOP 25 AUTHOR BOBBY AKART

Odessa (a Gunner Fox Trilogy)
Odessa Reborn
Odessa Rising
Odessa Strikes

The Virus Hunters
Virus Hunters I
Virus Hunters II
Virus Hunters III

The Geostorm Series
The Shift
The Pulse
The Collapse
The Flood
The Tempest
The Cataclysm
The Pioneers

The Asteroid Series

ACKNOWLEDGMENTS

Creating a novel that is both informative and entertaining requires a tremendous team effort. Writing is the easy part.

For their efforts in making the Virus Hunters a reality, I would like to thank Hristo Argirov Kovatliev for his incredible artistic talents in creating my cover art. He and Dani collaborate (and conspire) to create the most incredible cover art in the business. A huge hug of appreciation goes out to Pauline Nolet, the *Professor*, for her editorial prowess and patience in correcting the same writer's tics after forty-plus novels. We have a new member of the team, Drew Avera, who has brought his talented formatting skills from a writer's perspective, creating multiple formats for reading my novels. I was pleased to introduce Stacey Glemboski, another new member of our team of professionals, for her memorable performance in narrating the Virus Hunters. I may have written the dialogue, but Stacey has created the voice of Dr. Harper Randolph.

A special thank you goes out to Christie Garness, a long-time reader, who provided valuable insight into the current state of affairs in Las Vegas as well as its emergency operations. Lastly, there's the Team—Denise, Joe, Jim, Shirley, and Aunt Sissy, whose advice, friendship and attention to detail is priceless.

I'd like to thank our neighbor, Pam, for saying a catchy phrase attributed to her sister—*just land the damn plane already*. It cracked me up when I first heard it. It's an alternative way of saying *wind it up* or *get to the point*. I thought it fit Harper's personality perfectly. Thank you, Pam and Tim, for your friendship and Pam's sister for allowing me to put this line to good use.

Characters come and go, but lifelong friendships do not. Everybody needs that set of friends. You know, the ones that you can call on in a time of emergency, that without a doubt, will be there for you. We have Mark and Kathie Becker. The story of how we met can only be attributed to fate. In early 2017, I posted a photo of my vintage Land Rover, affectionately known as Red Rover, in The Epigraph. I received an email shortly thereafter from a reader that recognized Red Rover as belonging to his new neighbors. We may no longer be neighbors, but we will forever be friends with Mark and Kathie Becker. As you come to love the character of Dr. Elizabeth Becker, eighty-eight percent of what you read in the novels, is the real Kathie. Another eleven percent is Lizzie, a mix between Kathie and her three-year-old niece. And one percent is Boom-Boom Becker. I hope you love the character as much as we love the genuine article.

Now, for the serious stuff. The Virus Hunters series required countless hours of never-ending research. Without the background material and direction from those individuals who provided me a portal into their observations and data, I would've been drowning in long Latin words.

Once again, as I immersed myself in the science, source material and research flooded my inbox from scientists, epidemiologists, and geneticists from around the globe. I am so very thankful to everyone who not only took the time to discuss this material with me, but also gave me suggestions for future novels. Without their efforts, this story could not be told. Please allow me to acknowledge a few of those individuals whom, without their tireless efforts, the Virus Hunters series could not have been written.

Many thanks to Laura Edison, a Doctor of Veterinary Medicine and a Lieutenant Commander in the United States Public Health Service, a Career Epidemiology Field Officer, or CEFO, at the CDC in Atlanta. She has stressed the importance of tracking the vast number of travelers during an outbreak. Her creation of an electronic surveillance system called the Ebola Active Monitoring System helped the Georgia Department of Health keep tabs on travelers arriving at Atlanta's Hartsfield Jackson International Airport during that outbreak.

Colonel Mark G. Kortepeter, MD, has held multiple leadership roles in the Operational Medicine Division at the U.S. Army Medical Research Institute of Infectious Diseases, USAMRIID, the nation's largest containment laboratory dedicated to biological weapons. His expertise in all related fields of infectious disease study from the battlefield to the BSL-4 and to the coroner's office was invaluable.

Eric Pevzner, PhD, MPH, a Captain in the USPHS, who is the Branch Chief of the Epidemiology Workforce Branch and Chief of the EIS program at the CDC Atlanta. Years ago, when I was first introduced to Captain Pevzner, he reiterated that the next pandemic was only a plane ride away. Of course, as we know, he was right. In his capacity as the head of the Epidemiology Workforce Branch, he oversees the Epidemic Intelligence Service, Laboratory Leadership Service, Epidemiology Elective Program, and Science Ambassador Fellowship. He works tireless hours to ensure those within our charge have the tools and knowledge necessary to protect us from infectious disease outbreaks.

The Virus Hunters novels could not have been written without the support of the former director of the Defense Advanced Research Projects Agency, Steven Walker; Janet Waldorf, Deputy Chief of Communications within the DARPA Public Affairs office, and her staff; and the DARPA program managers and contractors who took the time to speak with me by phone or via email.

Finally, as always, a special thank you to the disease detectives, the shoe-leather epidemiologists of the CDC's Epidemic Intelligence Service, who work tirelessly to keep these deadly infectious diseases from killing us all. They are selfless, brave warriors, risking their lives and the loss of their families in order to fight an unseen enemy more powerful than any bomb.

This is why I wrote the Virus Hunters.

Because you never know when the day before is the day before, prepare for tomorrow.

Thank you all!

FOREWORD BY DR. HARPER
RANDOLPH

Spring 2020 - The year we discovered the SARS-CoV-2, COVID-19 global pandemic.

In the story of humanity, communicable diseases play a starring role. From the bubonic plague to cholera to HIV, we have been locked in a struggle for supremacy with deadly maladies for millennia. They attack our bodies with impunity and without prejudice. They're a merciless enemy, just one-billionth our size, and they've existed on Earth longer than man.

In 2020, we were a world under siege. In America, with the whole of the nation in the midst of a declared national state of emergency, most communities were ordered to abide by a mandated lockdown. Infections totaled over a million and deaths were recorded in the tens of thousands. The efforts to protect public health from this novel coronavirus was a striking example of this continuing war. As governments and health authorities battled to stop the spread of the new virus, they considered lessons from history.

As epidemiologists, we strive to understand the exact effects and nature of any strain of virus, a relative of the common cold. Our greatest concern is accepting that this information can remain unknown for months as scientists gather evidence as to its origin, spread, and immunology.

Experts are concerned about the speed at which the disease can mutate. Oftentimes, its presumed that animals may have been the original source—as was the case with severe acute respiratory syndrome, SARS, another virus in the same family as coronavirus—reflecting the proximity that millions in China share with livestock and wild animals.

Once an outbreak occurs and is identified, governments must grapple with a response. Today's strategy of containment—one of the key measures deployed against endemic diseases—would be familiar to civil authorities and medical personnel as far back as the ancient world. The concept of a quarantine has its roots in the Venetian Republic's fourteenth-century efforts to keep out the plague by blocking boat travel.

But the maritime power would have been hard-pressed to institute a *cordon sanitaire* on a scale required in China, where many of these infectious diseases originate. Using the early outbreak of COVID-19 by way of example, the ability to lock down the presumed place of origin, Wuhan, a city equal in size and population to the entirety of Los Angeles County, was a reflection of the power of China's Communist-authoritarian rule. To stop the spread of the disease, every citizen of Wuhan was ordered to stay in their homes. No exceptions for essentials. No excuses to visit a friend. No walks in the park. No mowing of grass. It was a severe measure, strictly enforced.

In 2020, mistrust and politics played a role as well. The Centers for Disease Control and Prevention has always been dedicated to identifying, containing, and eradicating diseases of all types. Too often, however, the CDC had become a political football, but not one handed off or passed from one side of the aisle to the other. Rather, the CDC was often punted, kicked, and fumbled as a result of never-ending budget battles or desires to use the agency's efforts to exploit its findings for political gain.

Misinformation and disinformation are also still prevalent, as they have been in the past. During the outbreak of Spanish flu in 1918–19, conspiracy theories of enemy bioweapons circulated. During an 1853 outbreak of yellow fever in New Orleans, immigrants were to blame. On social media during the COVID-19 pandemic, wild claims were circulating that the coronavirus was exacerbated by 5G cell phone towers. Fear and mistrust may be one of the greatest challenges we face in eliminating infectious diseases.

Technological changes have proved to be a double-edged sword. Modern diagnostic techniques have sped up identification, while data science has made it easier to track the spread of a contagion. But some advances, such as improved modes of transportation, have contributed to the rapid proliferation of infectious diseases around the globe.

Even global health cooperation has been less than straightforward. The conversation has far improved from 1851 when European nations sought to standardize maritime quarantines. Yet the World Health Organization, despite its message of worldwide solidarity and cooperation, continues to exclude Taiwan from key meetings and information sharing, under Chinese pressure. China, one of the most secretive nations on Earth, continues to closely guard information and delay announcements concerning outbreaks for economic and geopolitical reasons. Both of these examples are the kinds of unnecessary risks that create windows of opportunity for infectious diseases to proliferate. Frankly, pandemics and politics do not mix well.

However, perspective is needed. SARS, a disease that spread worldwide within a few months in 2002, gripped the nation's headlines, but killed fewer than 800. The perennial scourge of influenza concerns most pandemic watchers. An estimated fifty to one hundred million died from the Spanish flu during a time when commercial air, rail, and auto travel didn't exist. Even with modern medicine, the CDC estimates an average of 34,000 Americans die from influenza each flu season.

Outbreaks of unidentified diseases demand our vigilance and

study. Novelty does not necessarily make them inherently more dangerous than older foes, only more difficult to establish testing, treatment, and vaccination protocols.

I will leave you with this. Deadly outbreaks of infectious diseases make headlines, but not at the start. Every pandemic begins small, subtle, and in faraway places. When it arrives, it spreads across oceans and continents, like the sweep of nightfall, killing millions, or possibly billions.

Know this. Throughout the millennia, extinction has been the norm, and survival, the exception. This is why the Virus Hunters, the disease detectives on the front lines, work tirelessly to keep these deadly infectious diseases from killing us all.

I am Dr. Harper Randolph and this is our story.

REAL WORLD NEWS EXCERPTS

TIMELINE OF A PANDEMIC

December 31, 2019
MYSTERY PNEUMONIA INFECTS DOZENS IN CHINA'S WUHAN CITY
~ *South China Morning Post*

January 13, 2020
CHINA REPORTS FIRST DEATH FROM NEWLY IDENTIFIED VIRUS
~ *KAISER FAMILY FOUNDATION Global Health Policy Report*

January 21, 2020
FIRST TRAVEL-RELATED CASE OF 2019 NOVEL CORONAVIRUS DETECTED IN UNITED STATES ~ *CDC Newsroom*

February 26, 2020
CDC CONFIRMS FIRST POSSIBLE COMMUNITY TRANSMISSION OF CORONAVIRUS IN U.S. ~ *CNBC*

February 29, 2020

WASHINGTON STATE REPORTS FIRST CORONAVIRUS DEATH IN U.S.

~ CBS News

March 1, 2020

22 PATIENTS IN U.S. HAVE CORONAVIRUS, PRESIDENT SAYS *~ CNN*

WORLD HEALTH ORGANIZATION DECLARES THE CORONAVIRUS OUTBREAK A GLOBAL PANDEMIC

~ CNBC, March 11, 2020

PRESIDENT TRUMP DECLARES NATIONAL EMERGENCY OVER CORONAVIRUS

~ BBC News, March 13, 2020

CORONAVIRUS NOW PRESENT IN ALL 50 STATES

~ NPR, March 16, 2020

NEW YORK CITY DECLARED UNITED STATES OUTBREAK EPICENTER

~ ABC News, March 20, 2020

GLOBAL PANDEMIC CASES HIT I MILLION

~ BBC, April 3, 2020

More than a million cases of coronavirus have been registered globally, according to the latest figures from Johns Hopkins University - another grim milestone as the world grapples with the spreading pandemic.

The disease, Covid-19, first emerged in central China three months ago.

Though the tally kept by Johns Hopkins records one million confirmed cases, the actual number is thought to be much higher. It took a month and a half for the first 100,000 cases to be registered. A million was reached after a doubling in cases over the past week. Nearly a quarter of cases have been registered in the United States, while Europe accounts for around half.

The pandemic is taking a huge economic toll: an extra 6.6 million Americans applied for unemployment benefit last week.

NEW EVIDENCE REVEALS TIMELINE OF COVID-19 DEATHS BEGAN EARLIER THAN THOUGHT – The outbreak spanning the globe began in December, in Wuhan, China
    ~ ABC News, *April 23, 2020*

Officials in Santa Clara County, California, announced last night that at least two deaths in early February can now be attributed to COVID-19.

Until now, the first US fatality from the pandemic coronavirus was assumed to be in the Seattle area on Feb 28, but postmortem testing on deaths from Feb 6 and Feb 17 now confirm that COVID-19 was spreading in the San Francisco Bay area weeks earlier than previously thought.

Meanwhile, another new study finds evidence that the first COVID-19 cases in New York City originated in Europe and occurred as early as February. Researchers traced the origin of New York City's outbreak and found it was primarily linked to untracked transmission between the U.S. and Europe, with limited evidence showing direct introductions from China or other countries in Asia.

THE NUMBER OF GLOBAL COVID-19 CASES SURPASSED 5 MILLION
    ~ *CBS News, May 21, 2020*

Some 5,011,000 cases were tallied as of May 20 – more than 1.5 million of them in the United States, which had more than 93,000 deaths of roughly 328,00 globally. Agence France-Presse says

Europe has been hit hardest, with more than 1,954,000 cases and almost 170,000 deaths.

The numbers are thought by many experts to represent only a fraction of the actual number of cases, with many countries testing only people with symptoms or the most serious infections, AFP notes.

Latin America overtook the U.S. and Europe over the past week as the place reporting the largest portion of new daily cases, the Reuters news agency points out.

SOUTHERN HEMISPHERE WINTER SPURS RISE IN COVID-19 CASES
~ The South China Morning Post, June 13, 2020

New research in Australia suggests the virus causing the Covid-19 disease is spreading faster in lower humidity, supporting evidence that the southern hemisphere will see a rise in infections in the coming winter months.

Lower humidity allowed the virus to stay airborne for longer, increasing the potential for exposure, said Professor Michael Ward, a zoonotic disease expert at the University of Sydney who led the peer-reviewed study. High humidity caused the virus to fall to the ground quicker, he said.

"Our studies, one in the northern hemisphere winter and one in the southern hemisphere summer, confirm the role of climate, especially low humidity, in Covid-19 spread," Ward said in an interview. "With this study, it seems humidity is more of a consistent driver of Covid-19 transmission, while temperature's effect can vary depending on location."

The findings echo recent concerns that the southern hemisphere has yet to see the worst of this pandemic, which has largely peaked in the northern hemisphere.

Ward added that another pointer from the research was that the northern hemisphere still faced infection risk during its summer.

ANOTHER DAILY RECORD IN NEW U.S. CORONAVIRUS CASES
~ The Wall Street Journal, July 10, 2020

New coronavirus cases in the U.S. rose by more than 63,000, another single-day record, as hospitals in Texas, California and other states strain to accommodate a surge of new patients.

Experts are calling for shutdowns as coronavirus infections and hospitalizations spike. Increased testing reveals the number of infected is much larger than previously reported. Cases appear to be inching back up over the last month, concerning health officials.

SECOND WAVE OF COVID-19 CASES? EXPERTS SAY WE ARE STILL IN THE FIRST WAVE
~ Associated Press, July 11, 2020

There is at one point of agreement among politicians and scientists: "Second wave" is probably the wrong term to describe what's happening around the world. Specialists at the National Institutes of Health state "We're in the first wave. Let's get out of the first wave before you have a second wave."

Clearly there was an initial infection peak in April as cases exploded in New York City. But "it's more of a plateau, or a mesa," not the trough after a wave, said Caitlin Rivers, a disease researcher at Johns Hopkins University's Center for Health Security.

Scientists generally agree the nation is still in its first wave of coronavirus infections, albeit one that's dipping in some parts of the country while rising in others.

"This virus is spreading around the United States and hitting different places with different intensity at different times," said Dr. Richard Besser, chief executive of the Robert Wood Johnson Foundation who was acting director of the Centers for Disease Control and Prevention when a pandemic flu hit the U.S. in 2009.

Dr. Arnold Monto, a University of Michigan flu expert, agreed.

"What I would call this is continued transmission with flare-ups," he said.

Flu seasons sometimes feature a second wave of infections. But in those cases, the second wave is a distinct new surge in cases from a strain of flu that is different than the strain that caused earlier illnesses. That's not the case in the coronavirus epidemic.

Some worry a large wave of coronavirus might occur this fall or winter — after the weather turns colder and less humid, and people huddle inside more. That would follow seasonal patterns seen with flu and other respiratory viruses. And such a fall wave could be very bad, given that there's no vaccine or experts think most Americans haven't had the virus.

But the novel coronavirus so far has been spreading more episodically and sporadically than flu, and it may not follow the same playbook.

"It's very difficult to make a prediction. We don't know the degree to which this virus is seasonal, if at all. Only time will tell."

EPIGRAPH

"He who fights monsters should see to it that in the process, he does not become a monster. And if you gaze long enough into an abyss, the abyss will gaze back at you."
~ Friedrich Nietzsche, German Philosopher, 1844 - 1900

"Nothing, but the immediate finger of God, nothing but omnipotent power, could have done it. The contagion despised all medicine; death raged in every corner; and had it gone on as it did then, a few weeks more would have cleared the town of all, and everything that had a soul. Men everywhere began to despair; every heart failed them for fear; people were made desperate through the anguish of their souls, and the terrors of death sat in the very faces and countenances of the people."
~ Daniel DeFoe, English Author, writing about bubonic plague in Journal of the Plague Year, 1722

From the vain enterprise honor and undue complaint,
Boats tossed about among the Latins, cold, hunger, waves
Not far from the Tiber the land stained with blood,
And diverse plagues will be upon mankind.
~ Nostradamus, English Century V, Quatrain 63

It's always too late no matter what we do.
~ Dr. Harper Randolph, Virus Hunter

VIRUS HUNTERS

A MEDICAL THRILLER | PART THREE

by
Bobby Akart

PART I

DELIVERANCE FROM 21,000 FEET

CHAPTER ONE

Dr. Basnet's Home
Lhasa, Tibet, China

Staccato bursts of automatic weapons' gunfire reverberated through the valleys and rocky terrain surrounding Lhasa's Gonggar Airport. Even several miles away, the gun battle was evident to Dr. Zeng Qi and his nephew, Fangyu, who nervously awaited the return of their new friends. Dr. Harper Randolph and her Asian-American partner, Dr. Kwon Li, had been fearless in the face of danger as they traveled across the world in search of patient zero.

Despite the threats to their own lives, Dr. Zeng and Fangyu risked certain imprisonment while assisting Harper as she searched for the deadly virus spreading throughout Western China and that had now made its way into the United States.

"What is happening, nephew?"

"Maybe we should go help them?" Fangyu asked in reply. He wandered away from his elderly uncle and stepped toward the gravel driveway entrance leading to Dr. Basnet Dema's home. The Tibetan physician, who'd been maintaining the disease-stricken corpse of a helicopter pilot in a military quarantine facility, had reached out to Dr. Zeng via WeChat.

Both men shared a common goal—prevent the cover-up by the Chinese government of a deadly viral outbreak. The Americans, Harper and the CDC, were trying to make up for perceived shortcomings in their response to the COVID-19 pandemic of 2020–21.

The doctors concocted a plan to perform an autopsy on the dead pilot with a full understanding of the concept of high risk, high reward. The body would provide valuable clues into their quest for patient zero. However, the plan appeared to be in jeopardy as the sounds of gunfire erupted and could be heard for miles across the rocky terrain.

Then it stopped. The shots ceased, but the wailing sirens of security police vehicles persisted. They also appeared to be getting closer.

Fangyu removed his cell phone from his pocket and studied the display. There had been no communications with Harper or Kwon since they'd pulled out of the driveway, snuggled into body bags, in the borrowed ambulance driven by Dr. Basnet's associate Yeshi.

"It is too risky to message them," muttered Fangyu.

"We must try to help, nephew!" Dr. Zeng was distraught. He'd withheld his opinions regarding the risky endeavor onto the People's Liberation Army facility adjacent to the Lhasa airport. He'd observed the determination on the part of Harper and Kwon to pursue this lead. Now he regretted not insisting they consider other options.

Fangyu swung around with his arms spread apart. His face revealed his consternation. "And fight the police with what? These stupid rocks." He knelt down, grabbed a golf-ball-sized stone, and hurled it in the direction of the airport.

Ding!

His cell phone notified him of an incoming message. It was from a number he didn't immediately recognize.

+ 86 89 1632 3302: We are safe. MSS coming. Go now!

Fangyu studied the message and ran to his uncle, waving the phone in front of him until he steadied himself long enough to reveal the message.

"Go where?" asked Dr. Zeng. "Are they expecting us to leave them behind?"

"I am afraid to call them back."

"Should we go looking for them? We have their car and their things."

Oncoming sirens grew louder, causing both men to take a few paces toward the highway.

"Uncle, the security police are coming closer."

"But—" Dr. Zeng attempted to argue his point, but Fangyu, who'd regained his composure, made a suggestion.

"I have an idea. Come with me."

The two men, leaving the front door wide open, moved briskly toward the CIA-supplied Volkswagen C-Trek. It was a common vehicle driven by those in the mountainous communities of Tibet. Therefore, despite its Xinjiang-issued license plates, it would not likely garner the attention of the police.

Fangyu drove down the gravel driveway, keeping one eye out for potholes and the other on his phone. Using his thumb, he navigated the touchscreen display as he skidded to an abrupt stop at the road.

"Nephew, what are you doing?"

He turned the vehicle to the right and eased onto the road. Driving with his knees, he explained, "This is an mSpy app developed by a group of friends at the college. It gives us the ability to monitor calls, texts, and locations of other Android phones."

"How do you know his phone is Android?"

"A hunch, Uncle. The most popular phones used by young people are Oppo, Vivo, and Huawei. All Androids. Our spy app allows us to track the location of the phone using global positioning just like the police do."

Dr. Zeng looked in his side-view mirror and gripped the grab bar in front of him until his knuckles turned white. "Nephew! Look out!"

Two black sedans sped around the corner and barreled down on them. They were unmarked without lights or sirens but bore the unmistakable appearance of China's Ministry of State Security, or MSS. Their sudden appearance startled Fangyu, who instinctively slowed and pulled onto the shoulder of the road. Seconds later, the two large four-door sedans raced past them. The wind draft created by their speed shook the C-Trek.

"They stopped!" exclaimed Fangyu, who stayed focused on the task at hand—finding Harper and Kwon. "Many miles ahead but not far off the road. I can take us there."

Dr. Zeng began to slap the top of the dashboard. "Go, nephew. Hurry!"

CHAPTER TWO

Sherpas' Retreat
Lhasa, Tibet, China

Harper and Kwon met the rest of the Sherpas. In the distance, they could hear the high-frequency shriek of sirens. Unfamiliar with the area, it was difficult for them to discern the direction the vehicles were traveling. The Sherpas, on the other hand, were more attuned to them. They'd often been chased by the local security police during their nights of street racing.

Ghosh, who, like his friend Yeshi and the other native Himalayans, preferred a single name, gestured toward the west. "They have sought reinforcements. That is good news for our adventure."

"Why?" Harper asked. She was still trying to recover from the highly charged encounter during which she had attacked a man with an autopsy knife and shot at several soldiers during their escape from the Lhasa military infirmary.

"There is only one military outpost between here and Gangga in Tingri County. They will be too undermanned to set up roadblocks. We have to prepare to leave."

Harper took a deep breath and exhaled. She turned to Kwon, who'd remained stoic throughout the conversations with the Sherpas. Harper sensed he was still on edge, too.

"Can we pull this off?" she asked in a whisper.

"If it's necessary to find patient zero, then that's what has to be done. We're putting a lot of trust in the abilities of these guys."

Harper smiled and looked at the group of long-haired, unshaven young men who milled about as they gathered their gear from storage sheds and the retreat huts scattered about the hilltop.

"They're not necessarily awe-inspiring, are they?" she asked with a chuckle. The lighthearted question resulted in both Americans visibly relaxing their shoulders. With the tension eased, Kwon opened up a little more.

"There are so many unknowns. We have to breach this military outpost that we know nothing about. Secure snowmobiles without detection or living witnesses. Then we have to race up the east face of Mount Everest, find a dead body that could be covered in snow, and then escape into Nepal without getting caught."

Harper slapped Kwon on the back. "Piece of cake."

"No, not really."

Harper turned serious as the squall of the sirens racing down the highway drew near. "I watched you in action, Kwon. Those phony Action Jackson superheroes in the movies couldn't pretend to do what you're capable of. I see why my husband trusted me in your hands."

Kwon looked down and shook his head. "Everything fell into place, that's all."

"Aw, shit, Kwon. That may be true, but as I look back on it, you anticipated everything. It's as if you ran all the scenarios through your head during the entire fight and knew the outcome in advance."

"Training."

Harper shook her head and smiled. "You undersell yourself."

"I don't like blindly going into these situations." He gestured for her to walk toward the ambulance. He reached inside and retrieved their weapons. "We know nothing about this outpost, its manpower, or whether there are enough snowmobiles to accomplish our mission."

"It's all we've got." Harper was stating the obvious, but she knew he'd agree with her.

He shrugged and nodded. "Certainly is."

One of the Sherpas shouted, "A car is coming!"

"Did you hear anything?"

Kwon shook his head from side to side. "Stay here." He began running up the slight incline to the top of the rise.

Harper ignored his instructions and jogged closely behind him until she caught up. He glanced over at her and scowled. She immediately picked up on his demeanor.

"I can help."

"I've already put you in enough danger," he shot back. "Please go back. I've got this."

Harper glanced over her shoulders. Yeshi and the Sherpas were scrambling to hide the bullet-riddled ambulance on the back side of their car barn. They continued to shove climbing gear into the trunks of the five street racers.

Harper ignored him. "How many shots do you have left?"

Kwon patted his cargo pants pockets. "Dammit!"

"See, you do need me."

The two topped the hill, and Kwon quickly issued his orders. "Post up behind those boulders on the left. You focus on the passengers. I'll cover the driver."

"Okay." She began to split off from him and run toward the rock pile.

"Let me fire first!" he shouted after her. "I'm gonna take out the tires and then eliminate the driver."

The sound of spinning gravel could be heard, indicating the vehicle was moving at a fast rate of speed up the gravel road leading to the Sherpas' retreat. Harper was in position, but the curve leading to the opening between the rock outcroppings prevented her from seeing the oncoming vehicle until the last moment.

Out of the corner of her eye, she checked to see if Kwon was in position. He was still climbing up the side of the rocky hill when the tires spun again. Louder this time. She readied her rifle and raised it so her sights were on the first available location where the car would be in view.

She slid her finger onto the trigger and flipped the safety. She steadied her breathing, set her jaw, and closed one eye to focus like her father had taught her so many years ago. The vehicle was coming into view, and she would see it before Kwon. She was ready.

"Don't shoot!" she yelled. "It's them. Don't shoot!"

Still cautious, she broke cover and walked into the driveway with her gun pointed at the Volkswagen C-Trek driven by Fangyu. Kwon came bounding down the rocky slope and joined her side. Fangyu waved out of the driver's side window, and Dr. Zeng's ear-to-ear grin indicated they were unharmed.

Harper lowered her weapon and waved them forward until Fangyu brought the car to a stop. Kwon immediately quizzed him.

"Were you followed?'

"No."

"Are you sure? We heard sirens."

"Yes, I'm sure. They didn't follow us."

Kwon was still concerned. "How did you find our location?"

"Yeshi texted me, so I tracked him on GPS."

"How?" asked Kwon.

Fangyu held his phone display up for Kwon to see. "I have an app for that."

Kwon rolled his eyes and stood away from the car. "Follow behind us."

As they rolled slowly down the hill toward the awaiting Sherpas, Harper chatted with Dr. Zeng. She gave him the short version of what they'd been through in order to obtain the samples.

She did not, however, provide him the details of their plans to retrieve the body of the dead climber on Mount Everest. She hadn't anticipated seeing the two men again, so she didn't discuss it with Kwon. But she was sure he'd agree they were better off not knowing what was happening next just in case they were apprehended and forced to speak by the security police or the MSS agents.

When the car pulled to a stop, she waved Kwon over to join her. "I didn't say anything about going to Everest. There is no need for them to know our plans."

"I agree. Very good, Harper. I will keep them both busy for a moment. Let Yeshi and the Sherpas know to keep their mouths shut. It looks like they're almost ready to go."

"Okay. I also have an idea that I want to run by Dr. Zeng. Before I do, how many sample vials of each organ did you prepare?"

"Two, just like you asked."

"Great."

"Why?"

"Well, originally, I wanted each of us to carry a set. You know, just in case we got separated, or, um, whatever …" Harper's voice trailed off.

Kwon understood. "Hey, I get it. It's still a good idea."

"Well, I have a better one. Let me talk to Yeshi and I'll be back."

Harper darted off toward Yeshi and Ghosh, who stood at the back of the street racers. Kwon turned to speak with Fangyu and Dr. Zeng.

"We're not finished here, but you two are."

"Why? We can still help you."

"You've done enough. Now, we need to get you on your way home. May I have the keys?"

Fangyu exited the Volkswagen and turned the keys over to Kwon. Dr. Zeng exited the car as well, and the three men stood at the back of the four-door wagon. Kwon retrieved their duffle bags and set them to the side. Then he showed Fangyu the hidden compartment.

Using the magnetic key card, he released the obscure latch and the lid popped open. He retrieved the additional magazines for the Sig Sauer weapons as well as the remaining boxes of nine-millimeter ammunition. Finally, he revealed the three neatly bundled stacks of yuan. Each stack represented ten thousand dollars US. He pushed two aside and picked up the third.

"These are for you," he stated matter-of-factly. "The remainder will be enough for us to accomplish our purpose. The rest will help you make a new life. I wish I could do more."

Both Dr. Zeng and Fangyu picked up a bundle of the newly minted bills. Then tears streamed down their faces.

CHAPTER THREE

Sherpas' Retreat
Lhasa, Tibet, China

By the time Harper returned, the two men who'd risked so much to help her, as well as their fellow countryman, had regained their composure. They placed the money in the secret compartment and were about to close it when she stopped them.

"Wait, before you do that, I have a question." She held up the yellow fanny pack that held the vials of lab specimens to be examined by the CDC. "Do you have a secure way to ship something out of the country? Without scrutiny, of course."

"The bag?" asked Dr. Zeng, pointing at the fanny pack.

"No, only part of its contents." She carefully retrieved four vials of biological samples from the deceased helicopter pilot. They had all been labeled by Kwon. "I have eight samples to be studied by the CDC. Is it possible for you to send four of these to the United States?"

"Shipments are always scrutinized by China Post," replied Dr. Zeng. China Post was the equivalent of the U.S. Postal Service. It operated as a state-owned enterprise and remained under the watchful eye of the Communist Party.

"That is true, Uncle. However, DHL Global does not have the same inspection methods as China Post. I have a classmate who works part time for Twinkling Star."

"Who?" Dr. Zeng asked.

"They make handbags imitating all the major brands—Louis Vuitton, Prada, and Gucci. The leather is the same, but the price is not. Very cheap."

"How does this help, Dr. Randolph?"

"I can have my friend plant these vials in a shipment to the United States. Customs is too busy to inspect every handbag. Thousands are shipped from Urumqi every week."

"Did you say Gucci?" asked Harper as her eyes lit up. Kwon shot her a look and shook his head in disbelief.

"Yes. Do you have a favorite?" asked Fangyu.

"A Gucci clutch?"

"Yes, of course. However, it is a small bag. I will need to send two."

"All the better," mumbled Harper as she searched through her duffle bag and scribbled the address of her assistant, Dr. Elizabeth Becker. She also hand-scribbled a note to her. It read, *Hey Becker! We're Gucci!*

Harper handed the note and Becker's address to Fangyu. Then she carefully placed the specimen vials in his hands. "Please be careful with these, and if you can, include this note."

Yeshi approached the group. He pointed to the gray, mid-level clouds that gathered on the horizon, portending more precipitation. "We must go."

Harper turned to Dr. Zeng and Fangyu. They hugged as they said their goodbyes. Moments later, the last two remaining male members of the Qi lineage known for their anti-communist activism were driving away.

Ghosh was the first to start the engine on his four-door Honda Civic. The ordinary family sedan had been transformed into a speed demon. The modified exhaust system featured larger diameter exhaust pipes, allowing the gases of the motor to leave more quickly. The result was a near-deafening roar.

He pulled up the hill toward Kwon and Harper, taking care not to spin the tires or drag the bottom of the lowered vehicle. The two Americans looked to one another and Harper shrugged.

"It's all we've got," she said, repeating her statement from their earlier conversation.

The other four vehicles revved their engines and slowly pulled out of the car barn. A Toyota Supra was followed by a candy-apple-red Mitsubishi Lancer Evolution. The Chiclet-green Subaru Impreza was next, and lastly, the canary-yellow Mazda Miata. The colors would shock the conscience of most American car owners, but to the street racers, it defined them. It was their way to express their individual personalities.

"You two can ride with me," said Ghosh as he pulled up beside them. "Yeshi, will you copilot?"

"Yes."

"Let me," insisted Kwon. He raised the suppressed Sig Sauer MPX for Ghosh to see. "In America, we call it riding shotgun."

Ghosh found this to be hilarious. "Oh, yes. Like in the old cowboy movies. Like John Wayne!"

Kwon nodded. "Something like that."

He climbed into the passenger seat, and Harper sat on the opposite side of the vehicle behind Ghosh. Yeshi sat to her right. Once they were buckled in, Ghosh waved the Toyota and Mitsubishi around to take the lead. He turned slightly in his formfitting Cipher Viper series racing seat, the tubular frame restricting his movement, as was intended.

"The security patrols know us," he began to explain. "Those two will drive ahead several miles and warn of us roadblocks or closures. At gas stops, we will alternate positions, but my car will always remain in the middle using the other four as a buffer."

"Very smart," said Kwon with a nod of approval.

"With Yeshi on board, we have ten drivers. We will drive continuously and as fast as safety permits. It will take just one day to arrive with two stops for petrol."

His passengers relaxed and got settled into their seats. Ghosh raised his left arm through the window and created a circular motion as if he were getting ready to lasso a calf, just like John Wayne. A minute later, they were on the road and roaring toward Tingri County and the PLA outpost.

Everyone was still too excited to sleep, so they made small talk. The exhaust system was loud and Ghosh was driving over eighty miles per hour, forcing the group to speak loudly at times to be heard. The modified Honda was built for speed, not practicality or comfort.

Harper leaned between the seats and asked, "You're taking a great risk by helping us. Yeshi said you don't want any money. Why would you do this for us?"

Ghosh leaned back into his seat and sighed. "Many years ago, when the coronavirus pandemic spread, the government shut down the mountain. We all lost our livelihood. My family suffered greatly because the Communist Party chose to cover up the disease instead of warning us all so we could protect ourselves." He sighed again and shook his head before continuing.

"I was a teenager when it happened. My father and oldest brothers were Sherpas. The climbing seasons had been interrupted before due to natural disasters like the earthquake in 2015. The mountain had never been closed for an entire season.

"My family relied on the money my father and brother made to live on the rest of the year. We were starving. It was not just us.

Thousands of porters, cooks, and helpers earned only a meager wage during the season. They also suffered."

The group was quiet for a moment and then Harper spoke up. "I am sorry that happened to your family. I bet your father and brother were glad when the next season came around. China and Nepal didn't suffer from the second wave of COVID-19 like we did."

Ghosh's chin dropped to his chest. "They never climbed Everest again. That summer, they both died on Annapurna in Nepal."

Harper closed her eyes and hung her head as well. She was immediately sorry she'd broached this topic of conversation with Ghosh.

"I'm sorry."

Ghosh explained, "They were desperate for work. As the summer came to an end, they were contacted to lead an expedition up Annapurna. The small group of climbers were wealthy but inexperienced for this challenge. You see, the world knows Mount Everest and considers it to be a dangerous mountain. It is not the most dangerous. Many point to K2 or even Nanga Parbat in Pakistan. That is not the case. There have only been around two hundred successful summits on Annapurna. Dozens have died trying. One in three, actually. My father and brother were among them."

Darkness had set in, and the glow of the dashboard illuminated his face as he continued. "They did it for the money, knowing the risks. My family was paid, but truthfully, we lost everything.

"They would not have risked their lives if the government had told us the truth. The disease would not have been so widespread. The climbing season could have been salvaged. My family would still be together."

Ghosh's cell phone rang, and he immediately picked it up, seemingly glad to change the somber mood in the car. When he finished the call, he relayed the purpose of the call.

"My friends are at the petrol station. It is very quiet ahead of us.

They will wait until we refuel, and then my other friends will take the wheel. It will be Yeshi's turn to drive."

Harper leaned forward and squeezed the young Sherpa's shoulder. The Himalayan man looked into his rearview mirror and smiled. His change in posture allowed the dashboard lights to reflect the moisture on his cheeks.

Harper's mission in life was to protect mankind from deadly pathogens. In the moment, she thought Ghosh's life had been devoted to an equal, if not higher, purpose.

CHAPTER FOUR

Shigatse, Tibet, China

The five cars filled their fuel tanks in Shigatse, a prefecture-level city often referred to as the Gateway to Mount Everest. Known for its colorful monasteries and beautiful views of the surrounding mountains, Shigatse allowed them to take a break, top off their tanks, and prepare for the last leg of their journey to the People's Liberation Army outpost in sparsely populated Tingri County.

During their ten-minute respite, Harper chatted up the Sherpas who spoke English. With Yeshi's help as translator, she learned one of the men, Babu Chiri, had been part of the team of Sherpas leading a group up from North Base Camp just before the accident. It was Babu's information Ghosh and the others had relied upon in determining the whereabouts of the bodies that had fallen off the steep cliffs.

Ghosh agreed to turn his car over to Yeshi, and he allowed Babu to take his seat. This gave Harper and Kwon the opportunity to speak with him for an extended period of time as they traveled to Tingri County.

The conversation was somewhat belabored as the young man

had only a basic understanding of conversational English. However, in addition to his native language, Standard Tibetan, he was fluent in Mandarin Chinese. As was Kwon.

Babu explained in Chinese, "Everyone is in that fine line between life and death when they approach the summit. The climb from the South Face is much easier, but also too crowded. Each year is more dangerous because everyone wants the money.

"As Tibetans, we are limited to the paltry sums the government allows us for scaling the North Face. This year was especially difficult because poor weather at the start of the climbing season meant there was only a very small window of time to approach the summit. In prior years, with better weather, we were able to stagger our teams. There are always lines, but nothing like what we experienced this year.

"My friends and I have learned to stay calm on the mountain. We know the most challenging parts of the climb, and we also have learned to conserve our oxygen. Many climbers are doing it for the first time. Between the excitement and inexperience, they run dangerously low on oxygen at the top. However, this accident was different.

"At the base camp, there was a rumor that two men from Australia were not taking Everest seriously. They seemed more interested in socializing with women than preparing themselves for the climb. They were not part of my group, so I stayed out of it. I simply advised my climbers to avoid their drinking and late-night activities.

"Anyway, as the day grew near for the climb, another rumor circulated that influenza or a cold was circulating through the camp. Again, I kept close tabs on my climbing group and monitored their health.

"I hope you understand, I could lose my life if one of my climbers passes out or loses their balance. It is just as important to me that they remain fully prepared for the climb, just as I am. Sadly, not all Sherpas are this conscientious."

With each point made, Babu would pause and allow Kwon to

translate what he said to Harper. Kwon also asked the young man questions and relayed the answers to Harper as well.

"On the day of the accident, my group was third in line to the summit. There are parts of the climb where I can look ahead and see the progress of the other groups. Nearing the Chinese Ladder is one of those times. I noticed there was a delay at the top of the ladder. I was puzzled because every climber was properly clipped to the safety rope, and none appeared to be trying to reverse course.

"I paused my group and passed the word down the line to rest. I was glad I made that decision. You see, when the queue builds like that, there is great danger to us all. The path is too narrow for the more experienced climbers to unclip and pass the slower ones. If someone loses oxygen or needs medical attention, there is no room to drag a body backwards, and it is unlikely the other climbers would give way. They are in their own survival state of mind.

"I do not know what happened on that final climb to the summit because I could not see the start of the accident. I have spoken to the Sherpa who avoided dying with some of his climbers. He told me the two men, both Australians, had become very ill and were unable to hold their balance. One fell, snapped the rope, causing a chain reaction of people losing their footing.

"The first man who collapsed slid backward and over the cliff toward the top of the Chinese Ladder. He was the one evacuated by the military team. The other man, his friend, fell farther down the mountain, dropping as far as the Kangshung Face would allow. Many thousands of feet." Kangshung Face, translated as East Face, is one of the Chinese sides of Mount Everest. It can be accessed from a remote valley near the side of the mountain closest to the Tibet border.

Kwon interrupted him. "If he fell that far down, how do you know where his body is?"

"Ghosh can help, as can I. There are many vertical, overhanging rock buttresses jutting out from Kangshung Face. The body could be seen from above because of its outer jacket in the white snow.

Unless an avalanche swept it farther down the East Face, it will still be lying there."

"Let me ask again. This is an enormous mountain. How can you both be sure where the body is located?"

The young Sherpa chuckled. "It is big, but it is ours. Since we were able to walk as young children, our fathers took us on every route from top to bottom and side to side. Just as their fathers had done with them."

Kwon explained to Harper, but before he finished, Yeshi interrupted them by raising his phone into the air. He'd received a text message.

"Stay calm. We are going to have company."

CHAPTER FIVE

CDC Headquarters
Atlanta, Georgia

The Centers for Disease Control and Prevention, like any other government agency, had a hierarchy. Being aware of turf wars and backstabbing was a part of the job, and Dr. Berger Reitherman understood how to play the game. He didn't like it, but his survival instincts had served him well since arriving in Atlanta.

From the moment Harper had left for Beijing, he kept in contact with her husband, Congressman Joe Mills. He'd promised to give Joe updates on Harper's progress as information came into him. Thus far, there had been complete radio silence, and he was growing increasingly uneasy.

Truthfully, he missed his days as a program manager within the infectious disease group at DARPA, the Defense Advanced Research Projects Agency. The comradery there resembled a unit of the military rather than highly educated stuffed suits looking to climb the government's equivalent of the corporate ladder of success. At DARPA, problem-solving through unconventional methods was the norm, an outside-the-box way of thinking that wasn't appreciated as much at the CDC.

So it came as no surprise to Dr. Reitherman when his superiors lost their collective minds after they learned he'd sent Harper to China on her undercover mission to locate patient zero. The revelation came purely by accident. Four days after the Chinese sent the epidemiologists from Europe into the Great Khingan Mountains in the northernmost region of Inner Mongolia to search for diseased yaks, Dr. Reitherman's counterpart overseeing the U.S. contingent from the CDC in Beijing gained approval to send Dr. Eloise Blasingame as part of a second expedition. Only, he learned from the CIA station chief in Beijing that she was ineligible to travel because her credentials had been *loaned* to Harper.

Within hours, Dr. Reitherman had been called to the woodshed. He argued that the decision to send Harper to the Far East was not only necessary but within his authority. Further, he appropriately made the case for handling such an important matter on a need-to-know basis. One mistake, one slip of the tongue, could've compromised Harper and Kwon.

He was threatened with future discipline and warned against withholding any information regarding Harper's activities. He was also shadowed by his boss, who seemed to make an extraordinary number of visits to his department throughout the day.

When Dr. Elizabeth Becker notified him first thing that morning that she'd received autopsy results and specimens from Las Vegas courtesy of Dr. Wolfgang Boychuck, the medical examiner, his spirits lifted. He decided to get his hands dirty, figuratively speaking.

"Okay, Elizabeth, are you ready to do this?" he asked as he approached Becker, who was studying Dr. Boychuck's notes in the dressing area of the biosafety level 4 laboratory.

"Are you sure about this, sir?" she asked politely. "This is kinda grunt work, if you know what I mean."

He did, but he didn't care. He was ready for a change of pace, and he thought it might be good for his soul to conduct a little research therapy. The serene environs of a BSL-4 was just what he needed at the moment. Besides, his boss couldn't come around to check on him when he was suited up and tucked away in the sterile confines of the submarine-like space.

In separate areas, they dressed in positive-pressure suits made of a material resistant to the virucidal chemical showers required to destroy any deadly pathogens that had attached to it in the lab. It also had to be sufficiently mobile for them to work. The suit was equipped with an in-line HEPA filtration system connected to a breathing air system using the same kind of quick connections available to astronauts aboard the International Space Station in the event of an emergency.

In order for scientists and epidemiologists to safely study the most dangerous biological agents, laboratories were created with certain levels of biocontainment precautions established. The lowest safety level was a BSL-1. The highest was the BSL-4, where most of the CDC epidemiologists performed their work.

True BSL-4 facilities were extremely rare. There were only eleven countries in the world with BSL-4 facilities until years ago when the one in the Central African nation of Gabon had been destroyed by terrorists.

To enter the BSL-4, Becker and Dr. Reitherman passed through two stainless-steel doors into an airlocked chamber. They were able to feel the air pressure change in both spaces through an automated system that ensured high-pressure air in the airlocked chamber flowed into the low-pressure laboratory, effectively preventing any airborne pathogens from escaping.

Once inside, they were immediately immersed in sterile surroundings. The walls had a glistening sheen from the many layers of epoxy compound creating a continuous seal across every surface. Light fixtures and electrical outlets were housed in airtight boxes and lathered in protective epoxy to prevent pathogens from escaping through the wall penetrations. Even the electrical wiring was stripped of insulation and coated with the epoxy.

"It's been a while since I entered your domain, Becker," quipped

Dr. Reitherman as he dutifully followed the young epidemiologist. "The precautionary measures taken never cease to amaze me."

"These boogers don't mess around. Sometimes it's hard to fathom a deadly bacterium or virus that are many millions times smaller than what our eyes can see. All it takes is one to escape and we've got a pandemic on our hands."

"Well, I'm glad to see the results of your work firsthand. You know, Dr. Randolph speaks very highly of you."

Becker motioned for Dr. Reitherman to follow her deeper into the BSL-4 toward a series of microscopes. "She has to."

"Um, why's that?"

"Blackmail, sir. I know things."

Dr. Reitherman slowed his pace and dropped behind Becker. She sensed he was stopping, so she slowly swung around.

"Sir, I'm just kidding. Seriously."

"Okay, sorry, Elizabeth. It's been a rough couple of days."

She motioned for him to stand at a microscope adjacent to her workstation. She pressed her protective helmet up to the bug-eye-shaped eyepiece of the microscope and studied the sample provided by Dr. Boychuck.

"I heard. Word has been going around that you're in the doghouse."

"Really?" he asked.

"Yes, sir. It's a small office, sort of. Anyway, sending Dr. Randolph was the right thing to do, and we all support you."

Becker couldn't see Dr. Reitherman's broad smile. Neither Becker nor the other epidemiologists under his command at the CDC could save his job if Harper's undercover mission went public, but it was good to know his team approved of his decision.

"Okay, Elizabeth, show me what you've got."

CHAPTER SIX

CDC Headquarters
Atlanta, Georgia

"The best way to start is for you to take a look at this killer, and as you do, I'm going to explain what we've found," said Becker as she pointed toward the microscope in front of Dr. Reitherman. He leaned in to get a view of the virus.

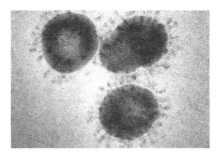

"Looks familiar," he mumbled as he studied the virus particles.

"A decade ago, the whole world saw images of COVID-19 under an electron microscope. When the world experienced the SARS outbreak in '03, it didn't have a meaningful impact on the U.S., so the media didn't cover it as much as the pandemic of 2020."

"Well, this guy certainly has the distinctive crown indicative of a SARS-associated coronavirus. But there is something about these proteins that seems different from COVID-19."

"Very good, Dr. Reitherman," said Becker, who was clearly enjoying the opportunity to interact with the *capo di tutti*, the Italian term for *boss of bosses* often used in discussion of Mafia crime families. It was another of her pet names for Dr. Reitherman that she would never say to his face for fear he might take offense. "Those crowns, or proteins, live on the surface of the virus and determine which cells it can infect. Do you notice how they are varied in size and shape?"

"Yes," he replied without taking his eyes away from the microscope. "Yes, they are ill-defined compared to what we observed of SARS-CoV-2 or even its predecessor, SARS-CoV-1."

"Exactly. Would a rose by another name smell as sweet? In other words, they are similar in that the target receptor is ACE2. Our novel virus particle is in the same family, and it also targets the ACE2 receptor."

Dr. Reitherman stood and studied the other microscope, which provided him a view of COVID-19. The crown was more defined and crisp. He stood again to address Becker.

"Okay, I see the difference, but I sense there's more."

"Yes, sir," said Becker. "The difference has to do with the nucleocapsid proteins. Both CoV-1 and CoV-2 had an abundance of N proteins. This new virus particle does not. As you know, the N protein of coronavirus binds to viral ribonucleic acids that led to the herd immunity achieved after the 2021 flu season. After the first wave, we were able to determine that the N proteins in COVID-19 contributed to the potent immunity after patients contracted the disease."

"Where are you going with this, Dr. Becker?" he asked.

"Well, it appears, at least for some patients, that the N protein of this particle has the ability to neutralize the immune response of the host. Basically, it acts as an antagonist to the action of interferon gamma proteins, resulting in a cytokine storm." Cytokines were a category of small proteins making up a body's immune system. These molecules mediate and regulate immunity and inflammation in the body.

"A cytokine storm?" he asked.

"Yes, sir. Basically, this virus particle antagonizes the body into a deranged immune response. The blood samples of the deceased patients we've studied indicates their veins were teeming with high levels of these immune system proteins."

"The body is overreacting and attacks its own cells and tissues rather than fighting off the real predator. H1N1 was similar."

"Yes, sir. That's correct. In the victims, I would characterize the size of the cytokine storm as gale force and unstoppable. The virus appears to be capable of copying itself very quickly once it infects a cell. That places an inordinate amount of stress on the body. As the cell senses there is something foreign, its immediate response is to kill itself."

"It's a protective mechanism," interjected Dr. Reitherman.

"Based on the autopsies we've studied, you have many cells doing this at the same time. However, like most respiratory diseases, the lungs are the first to go. As the tissue breaks down, the walls of the lungs' air sacs become leaky and fill with fluid. The natural result is pneumonia and the patient's blood is starved of oxygen."

Dr. Reitherman wandered away from Becker and stared aimlessly at the thick glass windows lining the BSL-4. CDC staff members traveled in both directions along the long corridor at a hurried pace. It was all hands on deck.

"Why are some of these patients subjected to the cytokine storm and others are not?"

Becker joined his side. "Before she left, Dr. Randolph set me on this course of research. Here's what I've learned from the autopsies, the blood samples and the patient histories. Unlike COVID-19, which primarily affected the elderly and those with a predisposition to respiratory illness, this novel virus tends to feed on young adults who appear to be the picture of health."

"Why is that?"

"I'm still trying to put together a pattern."

"Tell me what you need. More resources. I can pull personnel from another branch. Name it."

Berger shook her head before she responded, "Sir, it's simple. In order to model the progress of the disease and define all of its traits, we need patient zero. It's up to Dr. Randolph."

CHAPTER SEVEN

Gangga, Tingri County, Tibet

Babu slowed the street racer to avoid unwanted attention from the oncoming vehicles. The first Shaanxi six-by-six troop carrier rounded a bend in the highway. As it lumbered past, half a dozen members of the PLA who were huddled under the olive drab green canvas top peered through the rear opening. Seconds later, an identical truck approached. Followed by another.

"They are sending everyone, it appears," said Babu. "This outpost is small compared to the Lhasa Airport base. I believe they are planning a house-to-house search."

"They will be looking in the wrong place," Kwon commented dryly.

The last of five trucks passed, and Babu picked up the pace to catch up with the lead vehicles. Thirty minutes later, they were entering the small township of Gangga in Tingri County, Tibet. The Himalayan village, population 523, used to be an important trading post where Sherpas from Nepal would bring rice, grains and iron to exchange for Tibetan wool, livestock, and salt. Over time the

Nepalese Sherpas took up residency, and a few of the Sherpas accompanying Harper were of Nepalese descent.

In the region, the Sherpas didn't look at one another as being from China or Nepal. They were Himalayans who'd been caught up in political struggles in the regions for many centuries. The inhabitants of this desolate, challenging part of the planet looked at each other as one people. Their loyalties were to each other, regardless of the nationality imposed upon them.

They resented the PLA outpost built just outside Gangga. The soldiers who occupied the facility were arrogant and looked down upon the Tibetans with disdain. Babu was one of the young men who'd grown up in the small villages that dotted the Tibetan landscape around Gangga. His family, like so many others, lived by farming and ranching. Apart from the great priesthood, these were the main occupations of the locals. They weren't subjected to the stress and strain of city living. They rarely traveled to Lhasa, relying upon the land and one another for sustenance.

Few were politically active. The younger people aligned with the Free Tibet movement. They believed Tibet to be an independent state under illegal occupation by China's Communist government. However, they would never say that in the presence of a stranger for fear of imprisonment and loss of their family's rights to farm.

Babu directed the others to the westernmost side of the small village town while he parked the car behind an open-air market. The temperatures were considerably cooler in Gangga than they were in the lower elevations of Lhasa.

Harper immediately noticed the moist chill in the air as she exited the vehicle. She joined Yeshi and Babu at the back of the car as they opened the trunk. Kwon had already wandered off, anxious to get started on the task at hand.

"We have clothes for you," said Babu as he rummaged through the trunk space. There were sweaters, down-filled jackets, wool tights, and waterproof climbing apparel.

Harper studied the hodgepodge of apparel and smiled. "Nice stuff. North Face. Eddie Bauer. Athleta. Do they sell this in Lhasa?"

Babu reached into the trunk and pulled out a black cable-knit sweater and held it up in front of Harper to check it for size. "No. These are throwaway clothes. The new climbers always bring too much gear. They find themselves loaded down and begin to empty their packs as they climb up the mountain. We pick up after them on the way back. Sometimes, we sell the clothes in the village to other climbers. However, with the mountain closed, there are no customers."

"Lucky for me," quipped Harper, who took the sweater from Babu and slipped it over her head. "It's a great fit. I'm going to need another layer." She glanced into the truck in search of a down-filled jacket.

Kwon reappeared and approached the group. "The outpost is much bigger than I expected. The complex sprawls into the hills behind the main road."

Babu gestured for Kwon to pick from the clothing. "Yes. The snowmobiles and Arctic Cats are stored near the maintenance depot at the back. It provides direct access to the valleys leading toward the mountains. The machines are rarely used except for training by the Siberian Tigers."

Kwon glanced at Harper. She picked up on his reference. Another connection to the four dead men in Las Vegas.

"Babu, are you sure of this? Are they here now?" Kwon was concerned that his foes might be more formidable than the PLA soldiers regularly assigned to the remote region.

"Not likely," he replied as he handed Kwon a jacket. Kwon declined and reached for a vest instead. He would need a full range of motion for what he had in mind. "They come for training under the most extreme conditions during January and February."

"Is it possible to walk the perimeter of the outpost without being detected?"

"Yes. There is a yak trail used by my people to travel to the monastery located up the mountain. The trail circles both sides of the outpost and then joins at the back."

"Let's get started," said Kwon.

"Not yet. We cannot go dressed like this. The patrols will be suspicious. Stay here. I will get my friends and one more layer of clothing."

Babu closed the trunk lid and rushed to get into his car. He pulled away in the slushy snow, spinning his tires slightly, leaving Yeshi and the two Americans standing alone.

Harper turned to Kwon, who handed her the Sig Sauer rifle along with two magazines. "I need to see everything to come up with a plan. We're going to need a distraction, and it can't be one that threatens the outpost."

"Whadya mean?"

"If they suspect they're under attack, then those trucks we passed earlier will be back. It has to be more of an annoyance, one that pulls their attention away from the back of the outpost."

"Like what?" she asked, wandering away from Kwon to get a look at the main street of the village.

"We'll ask Babu and the others when they return. Maybe there's some type of public interaction with the outpost we could take …" His voice trailed off as the low rumble of a truck approached. The tires crunched the ice and snow as it turned toward the back of the building.

"This way!" said Kwon in a loud whisper. The three of them raced behind a lean-to shed full of oil drums and wooden crates.

The truck entered the open space behind the market. Kwon peered through the wooden slats of the lean-to and immediately recognized Ghosh behind the wheel. He, like the group of young men in the back of the large farm truck, were dressed in oversized furry coats.

Harper recognized them as well. "Look at those fur coats!" she exclaimed as she broke cover and rounded the shed.

"Yak wool," offered Yeshi. "They are made from the wool the yaks shed naturally each spring. There is nothing warmer."

"I want one," said Harper as she led the way to greet Ghosh and Babu, who waved from the truck bed.

"Yeah, me too," added Kwon. He saw the coat from a different perspective from Harper's fashion perspective. The coats would allow them to blend in with the locals while providing a way to conceal their weapons during their surveillance of the outpost. Apparently, Ghosh and Babu had had the same idea.

The group of eight young men exited the truck along with two local girls, who turned out to be relatives of Babu. They presented Kwon and Harper with their own yak coats, who immediately slipped the voluminous jackets on over their existing clothes.

"Now you are true Himalayans!" exclaimed Ghosh.

Harper lifted the sleeve up and sniffed it. She reflexively wrinkled her nose.

Babu laughed. "It smells like yak, yes?"

Harper managed a smile. She suddenly had fond memories of playing in a friend's barn as a child. They'd built forts out of hay bales, and she'd helped groom the horses for a few dollars an hour.

"I don't mind," she said, taking another whiff.

Kwon turned to Ghosh. "Can everyone here help us?"

"That's why Babu recruited his cousins. We will be your army."

Kwon slowly nodded as he surveyed his *soldiers*. They were loyal, but certainly not fighters. He looked toward the sky. Clouds were building again, and it was apparent snow was on the way. There was plenty of daylight left, but a sense of urgency had pervaded his psyche since they'd stepped off the plane in Urumqi.

"Good. Here's what I want to do first."

CHAPTER EIGHT

PLA Outpost
Gangga, Tingri County, Tibet

Babu led Harper and Yeshi around the east side of the PLA outpost while Kwon, Ghosh and one of Babu's cousins traversed the rocky cliffs overlooking the compound to the west. Kwon had received assurances from Ghosh that all of the Sherpas were willing to take considerable risks to help the Americans, although they refused to use weapons or violence. Subterfuge was fair game, and one they'd enjoyed playing since they were children.

"We have always enjoyed taunting the soldiers," Ghosh explained to Kwon as they made the final climb to the back of the outpost. "Once America and the United Nations took an active role in protecting the human rights of all Tibetans against the Communist Party, we learned they would not retaliate out of anger."

"Weren't you concerned with retaliation?" asked Kwon.

"Yes, at first. Then we learned the soldiers suffered severe punishment for violating their orders. They were instructed to maintain discipline and not react to us. Honestly, after we learned that our efforts to aggravate them did not produce a reaction, we stopped."

"Oh." Kwon's utterance reflected his concern. He wondered if the young Himalayans had lost their edge.

The streetwise, astute Ghosh picked up on his change in demeanor. "Do not worry, friend. As you Americans say, it is like riding a bicycle. You never forget."

Kwon nodded and pointed ahead to where Harper and Babu waited. A minute later, the group was exchanging their observations. There were two roving patrols of two men who followed the inner perimeter of the outpost. The facility was completely surrounded by ten-foot-tall chain-link fencing except where the rocky cliffs created a natural wall. However, because the rock outcroppings were nearly vertical, they would be nearly impossible to climb out.

"Getting into the outpost using the rock cliffs will not be a problem for us," suggested Babu. "We can use our rappelling gear to drop down, and the others can retrieve the ropes after we are in."

Kwon stepped away and studied the back of the compound. The metal fabricated buildings were open on both sides. He counted a dozen snowmobiles pointing toward the rear gate, the only other point of ingress or egress into the camp other than the main entry.

"How many of you are necessary to climb the East Face in order to reach the body?"

Ghosh glanced from Kwon to Harper. "Are you both coming?"

"Yes," Harper firmly replied, simultaneously with Kwon's likewise adamant response of no.

"No. Just me."

"Kwon, I need to examine the body," argued Harper.

"We'll bring it down to you."

Harper turned to Ghosh. "Can you guarantee that?"

"Maybe. I don't think so. It is a very dangerous climb. I am not sure either of you can do it." He turned to Kwon to gauge his expression. As was typically the case, Kwon's face revealed nothing.

"I'm capable of making the climb and obtaining the samples if we can't retrieve the body," he said matter-of-factly. His tone of voice indicated the discussion was over. "How many of you are necessary to get to the ledge where the body is located?"

"Three."

Kwon thought for a moment. "Which of you are willing to use a weapon? Anyone?"

Yeshi raised his hand. "I will to defend myself."

Kwon pointed to Harper. "Will you defend her?"

Yeshi made eye contact with her. "Yes, absolutely. Without fear."

The group concocted a plan and took up positions around the perimeter. The PLA soldiers, it appeared, were lax during the patrols, most likely because their fences had never been breached. They began their rounds like the opposite hands of a clock. Like a clock that's right twice a day, the patrols, who began their rounds from the front gate at the same time, left the same location unprotected twice. After they both passed the most vulnerable parts of the compound, the unfenced cliffs, there was plenty of time for Kwon and five Sherpas to rappel down the rocks and drop into the compound.

Harper and Yeshi were instructed to take up secured positions on the cliffs at the rear of the compound to provide cover fire as the group of six escaped with the snowmobiles.

Babu's two female cousins and the last two Sherpas got to have all the fun at the main entrance protecting the outpost's administration building.

They waited for their moment, and then with the efficiency of experienced climbers, the Sherpas set up the rappelling equipment and dropped down the thirty-foot cliff one at a time. Kwon was the next-to-last to arrive at the bottom, impressing his new friends.

"We have a job for you if you would like to enjoy the simple life," quipped Ghosh as he disconnected the gear and gave the signal for the Sherpas at the top of the cliff to retrieve it.

"Sorry, too cold," Kwon was quick to respond. He removed his silenced weapon from off his shoulder and pointed to a series of buildings in the center of the compound. "This way."

Ghosh was confused. "The snowmobiles are at the rear."

"We need to hide from the patrols as they come back around. Also, something caught my eye. Let's go."

The six men raced across the open and immediately sought cover in between several transport trucks and pallets of crates marked with black and red stenciling. Kwon approached the crates first and ran his hand along the slightly snow-covered wood.

"What are these?" asked Ghosh.

Kwon responded by reading the sides aloud. "PF-97, 93 millimeter. Type 93, 60 millimeter. Type ninety-ones."

"They are coming," one of the Sherpas whispered loudly.

Kwon and Ghosh lowered themselves to a crouch. They rushed around the stacks of crates and hustled toward the nondescript concrete building at the center of the outpost.

Kwon issued his instructions. "Wait here. Listen for their radio and watch the movements of the guards."

"Where are you going?"

"Shopping," he replied as he dashed across a clearing toward the entrance to the building. Kwon reached a block half-wall that created a semicircular courtyard. In the center of the building was a steel-door entrance flanked by bar-covered windows. He slowly rose out of his crouch to check for movement inside the building. Through the windows, he observed a single soldier sitting behind a desk just inside the entrance.

Kwon shouldered his weapon and pulled out a hunting knife given to him by Babu. He walked low to the ground, keeping his head below the half-wall. Then he waited for the ruckus to commence.

CHAPTER NINE

PLA Outpost
Gangga, Tingri County, Tibet

Babu's cousins ditched their yak jackets and changed into body-hugging sweaters and tights. Each of them carried an open can of chhaang, a Nepalese and Tibetan beer brewed from rice. The Himalayan people considered chhaang to be the best remedy to ward off the severe cold of the mountains, as well as having healing properties for the cold and accompanying fever. Its alcohol content was also potent, creating the perfect accessory for two inebriated young women.

They wandered up and down the street opposite the outpost's main gate. As they drank, they became increasingly boisterous, eventually garnering the attention of the two bored gate guards. The women immediately became flirty.

They stumbled across the road, which was devoid of traffic, and began a conversation with the guards. Then, by design, their pretend jealous boyfriends suddenly appeared from down the street. They immediately called for the women to join them. As planned, the girls laughed at the guys and called them names before swigging more of the chhaang.

"We have new boyfriends!" one of the women shouted.

"Yes. They both have real jobs and uniforms."

One of the women stumbled toward the soldiers, who were now standing next to the movable blockades. She drunkenly waved at them and came closer, pretending to sniff them.

"Awww. Clean and fresh. Not like river dogs!" She said it loudly so their co-conspirator boyfriends could hear her.

"I will show you how a river dog makes love!" one of them shouted angrily as he crushed his beer can and tossed it against the perimeter fence. He began to storm toward the woman, who inched closer to the guards.

"Please protect me. He is brutish."

"Me too. I want a real man for a boyfriend," said the other.

The soldiers swelled with pride. They turned toward the young men, who were walking with purpose, fists balled up and jaws set. The soldiers were very much aware of their limited rules of engagement and had strict orders not to engage the locals in the event of a conflict.

The Sherpas knew this as well. The girls cowered near the soldiers. Their boyfriends marched closer. Then the yelling between the four of them began in earnest. As planned, it was designed to draw the attention of the other soldiers remaining at the outpost—including the perimeter patrols and the unsuspecting desk clerk of the camp's munitions depot.

Kwon heard the desk clerk's radio squawk to life. He eased his head above the wall to observe the young man's movements. The baby-faced soldier stood and placed the radio closer to his ear to listen. He had a single holstered sidearm strapped to his utility belt. Frustrated, he began to adjust the dials on the handheld radio before slamming it down on his desk.

The chaos at the main gate grew louder as the women's shrill shouts filled the valley. Kwon inched closer, waiting for his opportunity. He didn't want to waste time, but he hoped to find a weapon that might provide him an edge.

The soldier emerged from the building and Kwon pounced, catching the young man off guard. With a stunning blow, he smacked the back of the soldier's head with the butt end of his knife, knocking him unconscious. Leaving him lying on the snow, he rushed inside the building. His eyes quickly searched for his next target.

He switched weapons, sheathing his knife and leading his search with the silenced MPX. Satisfied that the building was empty, he retrieved the soldier and dragged him inside and shoved his unconscious body under the desk. Kwon doubted the soldier would report what happened when he awoke for fear of punishment. He took the soldier's radio and clipped it to his belt.

Kwon raced through the munitions depot, searching for useful weapons. The Sig Sauer rifles were bulky and therefore not easily concealed. He located a cabinet full of pistols and chose two QSZ-92s chambered in nine-millimeter ammunition. He shoved them in his pockets and then made his way to the deepest recesses of the building. That was where he found his most important prize.

"Arrggh!" the soldier groaned loud enough for Kwon to hear him. He bolted for a side door he'd observed as he approached the entrance. With the Sig Sauer in his right hand, he shouldered his new weapon and burst into the cold air caused by the increasing cloud cover.

Ghosh was already positioned at the back of the munitions crates, and he waved to grab Kwon's attention. The group met up and then began to dash to the rear of the compound.

As they moved rapidly through the parked vehicles and utility sheds, Kwon monitored the radio communications. The PLA patrols were now at the front gate, observing the confrontation between the four Sherpas. The young people were careful not to make any form of threatening gesture toward the soldiers, confident the men wouldn't get involved.

During their reconnaissance, Kwon confirmed that the storage area for the snowmobiles and Arctic Cats was unmanned. The key to success was getting through the back gate quickly before they were discovered. He arrived at the storage building first and ensured there were no guards or mechanics. Satisfied they would not be interrupted, he led the group into the garage part of the building.

As they stood staring down at the Russian-designed but Chinese-made Irbis T150 snowmobiles, Kwon shook his head and managed a slight grin. It conjured up visions of the murder hornets that had plagued the Western United States a decade prior. Shaking the odd, random thought out of his head, he issued his orders.

"Locate the keys and ready six machines. Fuel them up if they are not already. Plus, add full gas cans in the compartment behind the seat. Hide the keys to the others and disable their throttles. I'll be right back."

Kwon turned toward a steel-mesh-covered wall that held a variety of tools hanging on hooks. He quickly scanned his options and grabbed a tire iron. While the Sherpas got ready for his return, he took off for the rear of the outpost, where he used the tire iron to break the undersized chain securing the swing gates. By the time he returned, the guys were standing next to their chosen ride. They'd worked together to push the snowmobiles out of the storage building and pointed them toward the back of the compound.

"Everything is done," announced Ghosh. "They will hear us leave. These machines are very loud compared to other brands."

"We won't look back," said Kwon. "I'll lead us out the back to retrieve Harper and Yeshi. Then you take us to the drop-off point for the two extra riders before we continue to the East Face." Kwon looked skyward as snow began to fall. The sun was setting behind the Himalayas, prompting him to confirm the machines were equipped with headlights.

As if choreographed, the Sherpas swung a leg over their seats and got settled in. They studied Kwon as he gazed upon the cockpit of the T150 and learned the controls. He nodded to the others, slung his new weapon firmly over his shoulders, and pressed the ignition button. The hundred-and-fifty-cubic-centimeter engine screamed to life. He goosed the motor, put it into gear, and lurched forward onto the hard-packed snow.

Just thirty seconds later, they'd arrived next to Harper and Yeshi. Harper climbed onto the back of Kwon's seat, and Yeshi joined Babu. As they raced away from the compound, Harper yelled into Kwon's ear, "What the hell do we need this for?"

Kwon shrugged as he leaned a little forward in his seat. He didn't respond because he honestly didn't know the answer. He hoped he wouldn't have to use it.

CHAPTER TEN

Fremont Street Experience
Las Vegas, Nevada

Dr. Wolfgang Boychuck had been working long hours examining every corpse that had passed through the medical examiner's office. He disregarded the official cause of death listed by the hospitals or attending physicians. He was devoting his efforts to finding evidence of the mysterious disease that had surfaced at the Gold Palace.

During a rare break in his office, he'd glanced at the local news covering the quarantine at the Fremont Street Experience in downtown Las Vegas. Mayor Carol Ann Silverman was granting an interview to a reporter, in which she discussed the troubles Las Vegas faced if the quarantine continued, or extended to the other casinos.

"Our slot machines are powered down. These casinos are boarded up and barricaded courtesy of the governor's actions. Sidewalks are deserted and our glorious electronic marquees that once flashed inviting guests into the gaming establishments, nightclubs, and magic shows are off.

"It breaks my heart to see what has happened to the downtown casinos, and my fear is the same thing is spreading to the Strip."

"But, Mrs. Mayor, the governor has specifically stated the quarantine will not apply to the other casinos on South Las Vegas Boulevard. In a statement—"

Mrs. Mayor raised her hand and cut him off. Her anger toward the governor oozed out of her with every word. "He has proven himself to be a liar and nothing but a stooge for the president. The first time a single suspected case of this disease rears its ugly head in the Venetian, or Trump, or Caesar's, he'll be moving to shut them down, too.

"It's having a chilling effect on our tourism. Visitors are cancelling flight and hotel reservations by the thousands despite the fact their destination may not be affected by the quarantine. Quite frankly, folks are concerned they'll be placed on lockdown like the hotel guests stranded in the hotels here on Fremont Street."

Mrs. Mayor stood in the center of the Fremont Street Experience on a stage used by musical performances. The Nevada Guard had cleared a perimeter of thirty feet in all directions and were preventing anyone from accessing the stage without approval.

Dr. Boychuck continued to listen to the interview until he noticed a group of people standing behind the stage fully clothed in white personal protective equipment. Two of them were holding devices that resembled a drone-operator's controls. As the interview with the mayor continued, his curiosity took hold and he bolted out of his office, hastily slinging his lab coat off until it landed on Squishy, the anatomical model.

He drove the mile and a half to Fremont Street in just a couple of minutes. He used his coroner's office credentials to get past the guardsmen blocking the South Casino Center entrance to Fremont Street. This put him just a few feet away from where Mrs. Mayor was winding up her interview.

"Can you tell us what is happening here this morning?" the reporter asked.

"Yes. Only after considerable pressure, mind you, the governor will be releasing any visitors or personnel who've been quarantined since the beginning and who can pass the basic physical, which includes temperature checks and a minimally invasive respiratory exam. Everyone stuck here for the last twelve days can begin to make an orderly exit this afternoon. Our office is coordinating with local travel agencies and hotels to accommodate our visitors as much as possible."

"Then what?" the reporter pressed.

"Well, I refuse to allow our fair city to struggle economically like we did in 2020 and '21. Without tourism, we all suffer. Our visitors should feel like it's safe to return, and casino workers should not have to choose between their paycheck and their lives. Toward that end, as soon as the last person leaves this afternoon, we are going to begin the cleanup process."

"Are you referring to those devices lined up behind us?" asked the reporter as both she and Mrs. Mayor looked toward the west end of Fremont Street where it ended at South Main Street.

"Yes, indeed. The CDC acquired the technology for these in the years following the COVID pandemic. Basically, they are remote-controlled mini tanks used to disinfect streets, sidewalks, and the fronts of buildings.

"The mini tanks were originally designed for cleansing prisons and can cover up to half a million square feet in just a couple of hours. I guess if you are looking for something to compare them to, think about the mosquito spray trucks used in neighborhoods around the country. This does the same thing with disinfectant, except the machines are smaller and easily navigated into tight spaces."

"What about the inside?" the reporter asked.

"The restaurants and casinos are ready. Using the CDC's guidance on cleansing properties exposed to these kinds of diseases, they've created teams that will systematically give the interiors a scrubbing like no other. Years of bacteria, germs, and viruses will be eliminated, making the Fremont Street Experience one of the cleanest places on the planet to visit!"

Mrs. Mayor's voice rose to a crescendo as if she were making a campaign speech to her adoring constituents. On that high note, she abruptly ended the interview, a tactic she'd learned from her famous husband, the former mayor and accomplished attorney. "When dealing with the media, always end on a positive," he'd told her. "Even if it means you get up and walk out in the middle of the interview." It was a tactic she'd used before, oftentimes leaving the interviewing reporter in stunned silence.

She walked off the stage toward where the Clark County medical examiner stood. "Woolie! Did you see the interview?"

"Yes. Yes. Yes," he replied, nodding his head vigorously as he spoke. "I caught a glimpse of these most intriguing machines."

"Let him through," she demanded of the guardsmen who blocked Dr. Boychuck from squeezing through the narrow opening between two barriers. "He's our medical examiner and has every right to be here. More than you two, I might add." She was extremely bitter about the governor's actions and let anyone who'd listen hear about it.

Dr. Boychuck entered the cordoned-off area to join the mayor's side. He analyzed the mini tanks before addressing her. "Mrs. Mayor, I continue to study every case that is sent to the morgue, as you requested. I am trying to establish a pattern on my own, and naturally, I feed my results to the CDC."

"What does Dr. Randolph say?" the mayor asked.

He grimaced. "It's odd, actually. I haven't been able to speak with her. All of my contact has been through her aide, Dr. Becker."

"I imagine she is busy," interjected the mayor.

Dr. Boychuck wasn't sure that was the reason. "Yes. Yes. Yes. However, a simple email providing me an update on her investigation would be appreciated."

"Are they not being responsive? I can make a call."

He held up both hands. "Not necessary. Their communications with me have been excellent, and I see they are providing you these machines to utilize. It's just odd because she and I had a good working relationship. Then, suddenly, she disappeared."

"Well, I'm sure there is a good reason. You and I will continue to stay the course until we can once again fill these casinos with players and workers."

CHAPTER ELEVEN

Tingri County, Tibet

The trip to the East Face of Mount Everest from the central part of Tingri County in Tibet was an exhilarating mix of seclusion, wildlife sightings and physical challenges. In addition to the six-thousand-foot rise in elevation from Gangga, the terrain became increasingly more difficult to travel across. The new snow accumulation helped add to the existing base in the valleys, but Ghosh and Babu had to be careful of hidden rocks jutting through the white powder.

They raced away from the outpost until their fuel tanks were nearly empty. The twenty-plus-mile ride was tense and required a single detour to drop off the two excess passengers. By the time they refueled, it had turned dark, but the group agreed not to stop until they'd reached the base of the Kangshung Face. There, they'd camp for the night in the single, six-person tent strapped to the back of Babu's snowmobile.

The cover of darkness helped them. They doubted the PLA soldiers could quickly fix the damage they'd caused to the remaining snowmobiles. In addition, the keys to the machines would never be found, as they had been dropped into the stench-filled toilet of an outdoor latrine. A good mechanic could devise a way to bypass the key, but the time required gave the group a nice head start.

Fortunately, the fresh snowfall helped cover their tracks while making their trek safer. The springtime snow, however, was damp and wet, immediately soaking their clothing. When they arrived at the base of the East Face, the Sherpas quickly set up the tent, and everyone huddled together inside to keep warm. Using their body warmth to survive, they were able to avoid building a fire, which would act as a shining beacon to the PLA helicopters if they were performing a nighttime search. Before they drifted off to sleep, Ghosh introduced the two Americans to the Kangshung Face.

"Kangshung is like two mountains stacked on top of each other," began Ghosh as he tried to describe the daunting task ahead of them. "The lower part, the base, is made up of steep vertical ridges separated by narrow valleys. Imagine a mighty kapok tree found in Guangzhou. The roots rise out of the ground and support the limbs of red flowers. Only, Kangshung supports the glaciers.

"These are no ordinary glaciers as found on the South Col. They hang, perched on the edge of the rocky buttresses, ready to fall if Everest is shaken."

"Shaken?" asked Harper.

Ghosh nodded as he answered, "Oh, yes. Many years ago, a very large earthquake struck Nepal and impacted Tibet. Twenty-two people died when an avalanche broke apart the glacier, dropping snow and ice on South Base Camp.

"The earthquake activity is common on the East Face of Everest. This is the reason very few outsiders have attempted to climb Kangshung Face. Most Himalayans are fearful of dying here."

"But you're not?" asked Harper.

"No, because we respect Kangshung," he replied. He turned to his other Sherpas, studying their serious faces in the light provided only by an illuminated cell phone display. "You see, fear does not exist except in the mind. There is only *chi*. All else is only illusion."

BOBBY AKART

"What do you mean by *chi?*" she asked.

"Chi is the energy of life itself. It flows through everything in creation. It is not defined by science. It is derived from your core beliefs. Here, in your mind and soul." He touched his forehead and then patted his chest.

"It requires meditation and understanding," added Babu. "You must learn to block out all external thoughts. Do not possess in your mind and heart what others seek to force upon you. Your chi is just as important as the air you breathe and the water you drink. But, most importantly, it is yours and yours alone. When you accept this, you will be invincible."

Harper was scientific minded although she'd been a practicing Catholic since she was a child. She'd learned to find inner peace by filling her mind with scripture and the presence of the Holy Spirit. There were times of turmoil in her life in which the only way she could let go of anger, worry, and fear was by turning to God. She totally understood the Sherpas' explanation of chi.

However, she didn't believe herself to be invincible, and she wasn't prepared to accept that these young men were either.

"Have you successfully climbed this part of Mount Everest?"

"All of us have made it to the glacier, but only I have scaled Kangshung to the summit. There are two options for us to reach the cliff where the body rests.

"As you will see at sunrise, the deep gullies are filled with drifts of soft snow from the avalanches. We can use the snowmobiles to ascend the East Face as far as the snowpack will allow. At some point, it may become too soft to support our weight and we will sink."

"Then what?" asked Kwon.

"We will begin the climb up the overhanging rock formations. This part is far more dangerous than being swept up by an avalanche. The buttresses are full of ice towers and, because of the unexpected snowfall, unsteady drifts. You must be very careful of your footing. One mistake, and you will die. It is that simple."

Harper asked, "What about me? Will I follow you up the valleys?"

54

Kwon thought for a moment before answering, "Let's make an assessment at first light. My inclination is to leave you and Yeshi here to act as lookouts. If the PLA sends a team to find us, you can either lead them away from the valley entrance or, if you can, neutralize them."

Harper nodded. The term *neutralize* was a kind way of saying kill. Kwon's suggestion also made sense. If she and Yeshi rode up the valley with them, everyone would be trapped with no escape.

Two of the Sherpas had drifted off to sleep and were blissfully snoring. Harper wondered if the tent full of men would be too loud to get any meaningful sleep. Or would her anxiety over the next day's risky endeavor keep her up all night? Eventually, fatigue overcame her and she joined the chorus of snoring men.

CHAPTER TWELVE

Kangshung Face
Mount Everest
Tibet Autonomous Region
People's Republic of China

Harper was the last to emerge from the tent that morning. The Sherpas, despite their propensity for hard and fast living, were extraordinarily disciplined when it came to the mountain. She wiped the sleep from her eyes and found the men a hundred yards away, staring up at the impressive Kangshung Face, which was awash in an orangish glow from the sun peeking up behind them.

Mount Everest occupied a rare spot in the collective imagination of anyone who stood before it. Most onlookers were filled with a mix of wonder, reverence, and trepidation. Over time, thousands of climbers had successfully and safely reached the summit and returned home with inspirational stories of conquest and perseverance.

Too often, however, the mountain conquered man. Heartbreaking reports of tragedy were commonplace. At home, distraught families begged for assistance in bringing the remains of their dead loved ones home. Despite the costs and the risk of life to those who undertook the arduous task, the retrieval of dead climbers was the only chance for the families to attain some semblance of closure.

It was a part of the job that the Sherpas despised the most. Their goal in leading climbers to the summit of Mount Everest was to achieve success, for failure most often meant death. Each of them had been a part of the scenes at base camp following a fatal climb in which survivors begged them to help. To do something. To find a way to recover their dead friend's body, the grieving family or friends of the climber not realizing that some parts of Mount Everest were not meant to be conquered.

Kangshung Face, the East Face, was not meant to be climbed. Yet the Sherpas, the Himalayans who'd grown up looking up at the massive mountain every day, had done it several times.

Kwon approached her with his usual serious look on his face. "Good morning."

Harper's first inclination was to respond *need coffee*, but she sensed Kwon wasn't in the mood for lighthearted chatter.

"Mornin'," she said. She broke eye contact with Kwon and returned her gaze to the mountain. She was asking a great deal of this extremely intelligent, physically gifted man. He'd never undertaken a climb of this magnitude. Everest wasn't for rookies, even the closest thing to a superhero like Kwon. "Um, listen. I was thinking …" Her voice trailed off. Maybe it was time to scrap this ridiculous idea and scoot across the border into Nepal before the weight of the Chinese army dropped on their heads.

"Don't think. Just do."

"What?"

"Harper, I see your mind second-guessing what needs to be done. You can't look at the entire climb at once. There are stages to what we have to do. Steps. And we'll take them one at a time."

"Kwon, this is crazy. I don't know what the hell I was thinking."

Kwon reached out to her and gently nudged her so she focused on him rather than the Kangshung Face. "We both know this is a critical point in our investigation. We've been fortunate to find someone who could connect the dead pilot with the body studied by Dr. Zeng. Now we have an opportunity to learn who he was and where he came from by bringing down the remains of his friend. So many questions will be answered today."

"Will they?" she asked, second-guessing herself further. "If this man is patient zero, we still won't know how he contracted the disease in the first place. Maybe we should simply rely on the genetic aspects and help develop a vaccine that way?"

"That's the reactive approach," he began his reply. "From what I've learned about you, that's not your nature. You are very proactive. Balls to the wall. In fact—"

Harper cut him off with a laugh. "Hey, Navy SEAL, you're talking to a lady, you know."

Kwon's face almost broke into a smile. "Those are Joe's words, not mine. He was trying to warn me."

"Warn?"

"Harper, he was very straightforward with me. Joe loves you and is concerned for your safety, which is why he asked me to join you. There were words like headstrong, impetuous, and impulsive."

Harper set her jaw and began to contemplate the ways she'd punish her husband for speaking of his wife in such a manner. "Really?"

"These are admirable traits and typical of people who get things done. You have to put yourself out there to succeed. The key, and I've come to believe you realize this, is to take managed risks. Well-thought-out impulse actually works. Not looking before you leap gets you killed."

Harper turned away from Kwon again and noticed the Sherpas were growing impatient. They had a long day ahead of them. She pointed at Mount Everest then chuckled.

"And you call this managed risk?"

"I do and here's why. The key to pulling this off is having an experienced team who is unafraid. Do you have any doubts about these guys?"

Harper shook her head, so Kwon continued.

"Neither do I. I'm putting my life in their hands so we can save millions. Risky? Yes. Necessary? Absolutely."

Harper sighed and then spontaneously hugged Kwon. She held him and said, "Go ahead, you damn fool. I know you just want to play with the boys anyway."

"Thanks, mom," he said, almost smiling again. "Now, you and Yeshi be ready. Break camp and take up a position on the high ground overlooking the valley. Stay out of sight and only fire upon the PLA if absolutely necessary. No risks. Understand?"

"Sir, yes, sir!" Harper responded with a snappy salute. "See ya later."

Kwon began to walk away, and the Sherpas readied their snowmobiles for the ride up the valley to the exposed rocks.

"Don't forget to take a few selfies!" she shouted after him.

She stood alone as Kwon and the three Sherpas roared up the mountain until they were out of sight. She called upon a higher power to protect her protector. *God, be with them.*

CHAPTER THIRTEEN

Kangshung Face
Mount Everest
Tibet Autonomous Region
People's Republic of China

In 1921, George Mallory, an English mountaineer who took part in the first three British expeditions to the summit of Mount Everest, said of the Kangshung Face—"*Other men, less wise, might attempt this way if they would, but, emphatically it was not for us.*" It wasn't until 1983 that an American team scaled the East Face on their way to the summit of Mount Everest. Since then, only a handful of climbers from outside the Himalayans had successfully reached the top via the Kangshung Face—a vertical climb of nearly two miles. Fortunately, Kwon and the team of Sherpas only needed to reach the halfway point to retrieve the remains of the dead climber. Still, it was a physically demanding task that portended death with every reach and step.

The sun was shining, but the air was dangerously cold and thin as they made their ascent up the East Face. A plume of snow clouded the ridge toward the summit of Mount Everest—so close above them yet just over a mile away.

The Sherpas were conditioned to climbing at these extreme elevations, generally waiting until an elevation of eighteen thousand feet to use their portable oxygen to prevent high-altitude sickness. Kwon, despite excellent physical conditioning, began taking draws on the portable air canisters much earlier. Their supply was limited, as they'd had to reduce the weight they carried on the snowmobiles.

Ghosh and Babu led the way, masks on their faces, oxygen tanks tucked inside their jackets. The wind occasionally swept up the face, causing their down-filled outerwear to flap in the whipping wind.

With Kwon strategically placed in the center of the four climbers, they were able to make steady time up the face, using a route well known to the Sherpas. Their destination was a rock shelf that spread from the South Col connecting Lhotse, the fourth highest mountain in the world, to neighboring Mount Everest. The rock shelf was referred to at times as *Pakrā'u*, *The Catcher*, by the Sherpas for its natural propensity to prevent fallen climbers from dropping an additional mile to their rocky graves.

Another hour of hard climbing had passed, and the group had entered the death zone where the rock shelf was located. The unexpected spring snowfall had accumulated along the rock outcropping that jutted away from the East Face, roughly fifty feet at its widest point but narrowing to just a few feet as it stretched toward the north.

They began their horizontal climb around the mountain, being cognizant of their footing as they maneuvered the treacherous terrain. The snowdrifts created by the blowing wind made the shelf appear deceivingly flat. For that reason, the Sherpas resisted the urge to hike along the center of the shelf, where they could easily sink into a crevasse. Instead, out of precaution, they used their rope and spike system to hug the rock wall.

Along the way, they came across another fallen climber. Ghosh and Babu easily stepped over the twisted man, his remains contorted from hundreds of broken bones. His body was still affixed to a portion of a rope and reclined on the slope as if he might continue climbing after waking from an awkward nap. Apparently, he'd succumbed to the elevation in his quest to reach the summit of Everest and had been cut loose by the Sherpas to prevent injury or death to others.

Kwon numbly treated the body as an obstacle, a muted embodiment of his own suppressed fears. Putting on a brave face for Harper to ease her guilt was one thing. What he felt in his gut was another. *This is madness.*

He inadvertently stepped on the man's arm and apologized profusely. There was no crunch. No spongy give. It was as solid as the rocks beneath it. Frozen over time. Thawed slightly in the summer. And refrozen again.

Soon, another body blocked their path. It was from a more recent climb. Unlike the first one they encountered, some of the climber's clothing was still intact. As was her hair. What were once long, flowing locks had turned into stringy wisps of matted blond strands covered with ice crystals and sticking up in all directions as the wind undertook some kind of cruel hairstylist's revenge.

Kwon shook his head and continued. He lost track of time as he dutifully followed his guides, trusting them implicitly to provide him the safest foothold and grip. Just as he thought he couldn't move forward anymore, he noticed Ghosh and Babu had stopped. They stood over a body that was partially submerged in a drift as if it were seated at a dining table when a flood of snow had washed over it. It was as inanimate as the boulders sticking up through the snow around them. They removed their face coverings so they could talk to one another without obstruction.

"This is the man," began Babu, gesturing as he spoke. "He accompanied the first man to fall off the gravel parking lot before the summit. Once his friend fell back toward the Chinese Ladder, the rest lost their balance."

Kwon asked a logical question. "How can you be sure this is the same man? The friend?"

"It is my job to identify my climbers by their clothing. I make a mental note of each person I come into contact with. This man wore a black outer shell. Very unusual. Most climbers prefer bright colors."

They surrounded the corpse and removed their pickaxes from their small backpacks. Each of them began to swing at the ice and snow around the body's edges, working carefully to pry it from its icy grave. They systematically knocked chunks of frozen snow away, sending the shattered pieces down the gentle slope leading to the edge of the Catcher.

At twenty-one thousand feet, the men took frequent rest breaks, and concerns were raised about the levels of oxygen in their tanks. Like a race car burning through its fuel toward the end of the last lap, the Sherpas questioned how much longer they could fight the ice to free the man's body.

Kwon was the one who made the call. "We can't continue doing this. We know it's extremely risky to carry the body down the mountain anyway."

"We will do as you ask," offered Ghosh.

Kwon shook his head and waved the men away from the body. After retrieving his knife from his pack, he dropped to his knees and began to tear open the dead man's frozen jacket. He cut open the dead man's facial covering, revealing a ghoulish, bone-white face. Its eyes stared upward as if they were still seeking help from above.

He tried to close the frozen eyelids to no avail. He pulled out the CIA-issued cell phone and took several pictures of the dead man. He did not take the selfies jokingly requested by Harper. It would've been irreverent to say the least. He put away the phone, glanced at the onlooking Sherpas, and took a deep pull of oxygen through his mask.

"I'm sorry, friend," muttered Kwon. He drew the knife over the body and attempted to plunge his knife into the middle of the man's chest. It barely pierced the corpse's frozen skin. He gripped the knife again, this time with both hands, and drove it a little deeper this time.

Kwon closed his eyes, begging forgiveness from anyone who loved this man. He was going to have to mutilate and desecrate his corpse in order to get the minimal amount of tissue samples for testing. A blood sample was out of the question unless it happened to be contained in the tissue samples he was able to carve off the corpse. Blood, which is a mix of many components, behaves like other saline solutions and begins to freeze in a corpse at twenty-six degrees Fahrenheit.

Kwon looked up at the Sherpas. Their eyes were dull and sad. The young men had not expected this, and he regretted that he had to do it. But they were out of time as their oxygen became depleted. He stopped looking at the corpse as a human being, steeled his nerves, and finished the job. He reached the lungs by hacking through the rib cage. Then he carved off pinky-sized slivers of tissue and pressed them into the empty vials in his pack.

It wasn't until he was done with the brutal form of autopsy that he searched for the man's identification. After rummaging through the man's clothing and gear, he found a wallet, a passport, and a hotel room key with no identifying location. It simply read *xiang Fu Lou*. He crammed them into his backpack, apologized to the dead climber, and nodded to the Sherpas.

Kwon was ready to get off the Kangshung Face and its snow-covered graveyard.

CHAPTER FOURTEEN

Kangshung Face
Mount Everest
Tibet Autonomous Region
People's Republic of China

Immediately after Kwon and the Sherpas left for their climb, Harper and Yeshi broke down the tent and began carrying their excess gear to a rocky ridge a thousand feet up the valley. They located a crevasse that divided the ridge in half. It was ideal to stow the snowmobiles out of sight while giving them two exits away from the base of the mountain.

As they'd discussed, they didn't want to lead any pursuers to the vertical base of Kangshung Face, resulting in the group being trapped. It took several trips to get the partially filled fuel cans, the tent, and their weapons to a secure place. As a result, the snowmobile tracks left behind were obvious to any passersby.

The warming sun had begun to expose some of the plant life located just below the tree line, or alpine zone, of the eastern Himalayas. At fourteen thousand feet, the lack of oxygen prevents trees or shrubs from growing. Junipers and a smattering of rhododendron appeared through the slowly melting snow.

With their moving task complete and the gear safely hidden away, Harper suggested they use the plant material to smooth over the snow in an effort to cover their tracks. Ideally, the unexpected snowfall would've done them the courtesy of a light dusting to fill in the T150s' ruts created by the fifteen-inch-wide composite tracks at the rear, which propelled the machine and the two front skis used for steering.

Wanting to do something to help the brave team of climbers who were risking their lives to retrieve the body, Harper and Yeshi worked together to sweep the snow into the grooves. Then, with a little luck, the wind would blow the new powdery snow over the top and leave the appearance of a pristine, undisturbed valley.

It took the entire morning to accomplish their goal. They made their way back to their perch atop the rocky ridge leading to the base of the rock wall. They waited, sitting in silence for the most part, dividing their attention between their surroundings at the lower elevations and the East Face.

By early afternoon, both she and Yeshi were relieved they hadn't been pursued by any snowmobiles deployed by the PLA outpost. Their attempts to disable the remaining T150s had provided them a head start, but a good mechanic could make repairs on the machines in a matter of hours.

Also, Harper surmised, the Himalayan region surrounding Mount Everest might have been too vast to be searched by the remaining soldiers, especially since their ranks had been thinned by the activity at the Lhasa Airport. What she didn't consider was an eye in the sky.

Harper had created a swale using soft snow as a cushion. Although the temperatures were well below freezing, the full sun provided plenty of warmth. She stretched out in the snow, allowing her face to bake to the point of a mild sunburn.

Her mind had wandered to the trail of evidence. The key part of the puzzle, assuming the body Kwon went to recover was patient zero, was which species of the animal kingdom had passed the novel virus into its human host.

Harper was on the verge of drifting off to sleep when Yeshi called out her name.

"Harper, do you hear?"

Yeshi had heard it first. The unmistakable *thump, thump, thump* of a helicopter's rotors. Coming from the east, the sound reverberated off the rocky cliffs of the East Face and echoed through the valleys. The helicopter was coming towards them at a high rate of speed.

Harper immediately wished she had binoculars to get a better view. She and Yeshi stood and used their eyes to shade them from the bright, overhead sun. The noise grew louder and then it seemed to multiply.

"Aw, shit. There's more than one. Come on. We need to find cover between the rocks."

Harper took off and Yeshi scampered along behind her. He eventually passed her and helped her down a part of the rock outcropping where the footing was unstable. They were almost to the bottom when Harper stopped their descent.

"What is it?" Yeshi asked.

"My jacket. I left it in the snow. They'll see it." Harper pulled away from Yeshi and began to claw her way back up the ridge.

"There is no time. We have to hide."

Harper stood frozen in her tracks. Her mind raced as she tried to make a decision. The threatening sounds of the choppers approaching made the decision easy. She'd have to hope for the best. She joined Yeshi at the bottom, and the two of them shimmied between a snowdrift and the ridge. The sound of the rotor blades was deafening, and the force against the ground was so strong that large pieces of snow slid off the ridge and landed in the space between the rocks where they'd stashed the snowmobiles.

The two of them held their breath, mentally making every effort to avoid detection. They listened, fully expecting the choppers to land atop the ridge and dispatch armed soldiers to apprehend them, if they were lucky.

However, that didn't happen. The helicopters continued on their path, racing along the Nepalese border northwesterly toward India. After several moments of returned silence, they emerged from their hiding spot and walked into the valley. They cautiously surveilled the valleys and adjoining ridges. There was no sign of a threat.

Harper breathed a sigh of relief and immediately thanked God for giving them a break. They'd been through enough, and Kwon certainly didn't need the distraction. She and Yeshi returned to their observation post at the top of the ridge, convinced they had avoided being seen. However, they continued observing the ground and the skies with a heightened state of awareness.

Kwon and the Sherpas were completely exposed as they ascended the East Face of Mount Everest. There was no cave to crawl into. It wasn't possible to change the color of their clothing, which stood out like neon beacons against the gray-white granite wall. They were over a thousand feet above the valley, so jumping was clearly not an option. All they could do was continue moving in hopes the helicopter's crew didn't think to look for them there and overlooked the four snowmobiles, which had no place to hide.

When the helicopters zoomed out of sight toward the North Face of Mount Everest, Kwon presumed it was on a routine patrol of China's border with Nepal. The Chinese had engaged in a number of border skirmishes with their former ally, India, over the prior decade. Nepal was caught in the middle of the geopolitical conflict as those two nations fought over Ladakh to the north of Nepal and Arunachal Pradesh to the east. India claimed the territories, and China wanted them back.

After the two helicopters disappeared from view, the men continued toward the valley. The final hour was grueling. The entire day had taken a toll on their bodies, and their minds, which worked as hard as the muscles that kept them from falling, were exhausted as well. When the last of the four men placed their feet on the packed snow, the next best thing to solid ground under the circumstances, they nervously burst out laughing and exchanged high fives.

Their jubilance was short-lived.

CHAPTER FIFTEEN

Kangshung Face
Mount Everest
Tibet Autonomous Region
People's Republic of China

"I hear the snowmobiles!" exclaimed Harper, and she spun around, diverting her attention from the valley below toward the East Face. "I've been on edge since those choppers buzzed over our heads."

"Me too," Yeshi agreed. "Let's get our things ready. We need to move east toward the border to get you both safely—"

Harper interrupted his sentence. "Stop! Listen! Something's not right."

She wandered back up to the top of the ridge and surveilled the base of Mount Everest. It was getting darker as the sun dropped behind the massive mountain range, so Harper couldn't identify any movement in the distance. However, her sense of hearing sent warning signals to her brain—these snowmobiles were coming from a different direction.

She removed her weapon from her shoulder. Holding it in front of her, she focused her attention toward the direction they'd traveled from the PLA outpost. Yeshi quietly walked past her toward the edge of the cliff.

"We have to get ready," he said. "Follow me."

He didn't hesitate as he took long strides, each foot placement finding an exposed rock as if he were walking on lily pads floating on a country lake. Harper was slow to catch up, and her sense of urgency caused her to stumble, landing hard on her right knee. She moaned in pain, causing Yeshi to pause.

"Are you okay?"

"Yes," she said, lifting herself off the snowy rock. Just as she stood, she swung around toward the mountain. "Yeshi! They're coming!"

"I know!" he hollered back. He'd reached the pile of granite rubble they'd identified earlier as an ideal spot to fire upon anyone pursuing them. "They're less than a mile away. I see at least four, maybe more!"

"No, I'm talking about our guys! They're coming down the valley!"

Harper ignored the pain in her knee, which was beginning to swell, and moved quickly down the slope to join Yeshi behind the boulders. He stood up from his crouch and looked up the valley.

"They have no idea," he muttered.

Harper finished his thought. "They're on a collision course, and they're only armed with pistols."

Yeshi prepared his rifle. Harper had taken some time throughout the day to teach Yeshi what she'd learned from Kwon. He'd assured her that he might not be the best marksman, but he wouldn't freeze under pressure.

"The helicopters must have alerted them," Yeshi observed.

"Okay. We've got this. We need to hold them out of the valley until Kwon and the guys can join us. Then we'll slip through the ridges and at least have a head start."

Yeshi and Harper locked eyes. Their determination oozed out as they turned toward their pursuers. Then they waited until they could get a clean shot.

Harper's voice lowered. Her tone was taunting. Inviting. Almost wishful.

"Come on. Come on. I dare you."

She got her wish. Four snowmobiles, riding two by two, slowed at the entrance to the valley. After a brief stop during which the men appeared to be studying a map, the leader stood on the running boards and pulled binoculars out of his jacket. He stared up the valley.

The high-pitched sound of the snowmobiles carrying Kwon and the Sherpas could now be heard by Harper. And apparently, by the PLA soldiers, too. They shouted to one another and turned their machines uphill to intercept Kwon.

They were just into range when Harper and Yeshi opened fire. The suppressed gunfire went unnoticed by the approaching soldiers as the first pieces of snow and ice began to spit into the air all around them. Their heads swiveled from left to right, searching for the source of the gunfire. They instinctively slowed their machines, providing Harper and Yeshi an easier target.

The two fired again, this time peppering the four matching T150s with bullets. The ricocheting rounds forced two of the men off their machines in search of cover. The other two drew their weapons and sprayed the ridgeline where Harper and Yeshi hid behind the granite outcropping.

Harper rose first and returned fire. The men shouted at one another in Chinese. None of the soldiers had been wounded, and they scrambled back onto their seats. One by one, they retreated to the bottom of the ridge and behind the rocks.

"Well done, Yeshi!"

"Yes! But they are not gone."

"I'll watch for them to return," said Harper before issuing her instructions. "Hurry, go to the cliff and wave to our people. I'll hold off the soldiers in case they return. Go!"

Yeshi adeptly ran along the ridge and disappeared from sight. Harper focused on the last location where she'd seen the four riders. She couldn't hold them off alone, especially if they split up. She waited several minutes until Kwon and the Sherpas arrived. Yeshi came running for her.

"Kwon said we will escape to the east and not engage the soldiers. They may be waiting for reinforcements."

Harper smiled. *Good*, she thought to herself. *While you guys wait for your buddies, I'm goin' to Kathmandu*. She couldn't help herself. She hummed the classic Bob Seger song as she followed Yeshi along the ridge.

When they joined the group, Kwon's appearance spoke volumes. He was weary and fatigued. His normally erect stature had turned into somewhat of a slump. Yet his mind was fully engaged. His eyes darted between Harper, who dropped the short distance from the rock ledge to the snow, and the open valley where the PLA soldiers had attempted to enter.

"We don't have any time to explain," he said without uttering a *hello* or *good to see you again*.

Harper glanced at the Sherpas and their snowmobiles. She didn't see the dead climber. "Where's the body?"

"We couldn't get it out. I have samples." Kwon motioned to the others to get on their snowmobiles. "We've got something."

Harper grimaced. She felt his sense of urgency. At the moment, they had bigger problems. She climbed onto her snowmobile as Ghosh was relaying his escape plan.

"We will lead you to the border as far as we can. Each of us will take a different route back to Tingri County. The many tracks will confuse the soldiers."

Kwon fumbled through his jacket in search of the Blackberry. He was about to pull up the GPS app installed on the old device when Ghosh stopped him.

"That will not be necessary. I will be the last to leave you, but I will point you in the direction of the border when I do. There is no other way."

Kwon nodded and shoved the phone back into the jacket's pocket. He took the gun from Yeshi, and he nodded to Babu, who would be leading the pack, followed by Ghosh and then Harper.

Yeshi took one of the handguns to lend assistance if they were followed.

Ghosh held up his left hand high so all could see. He splayed his fingers apart and slowly counted down from five to one.

Lady and gentlemen, start your engines!

CHAPTER SIXTEEN

Kangshung Face
Mount Everest
Tibet Autonomous Region
People's Republic of China

Kwon fired the snowmobile's ignition and the machine came to life. He pushed the shifter level into forward and revved the engine. The others did the same simultaneously, and seconds later, Babu and Ghosh raced into the adjacent valley and into deeper snow. At full throttle, these machines emitted sound levels over a hundred decibels. The six of them roaring along the snow in a bunch was near deafening. Certainly, the sudden break in the quiet surroundings grabbed the attention of the Chinese soldiers.

The group had a head start of half a mile, at best. They'd barely exited the adjacent valley and were on a direct, southerly route toward Nepal when the soldiers reacted. The group of four snowmobiles rumbled around the lower end of the ridge toward them. The men in matching navy blue parkas skimmed across the packed snow with a gracefulness and speed that surpassed Kwon's group. It was a testament to their experience driving the T150s under all types of conditions. It clearly gave them an edge, and they were slowly gaining ground.

The soldiers wore face masks to prevent themselves being pelted with ice and snow like Kwon was at the rear of his pack of six machines. It threatened to cloud his concentration, and he found himself drooping slightly in his seat to avoid the stinging pain.

They were in an untenable position. He was used to being the pursuer. Whether on a motorcycle or in a car, it was always easier to drive with your weapon pointed forward, especially on an uneven, unpredictable surface like this combination of snow and ice.

He turned and released a barrage of bullets in the direction of the soldiers. They easily avoided the rounds, which missed wildly. The men reacted by splitting their group apart. Now they were four targets instead of one.

Two of them returned fire, also missing their targets, as they were out of range and wrestling with their steering as well. The trained soldiers on both sides knew they'd have to get closer to one another to get an accurate shot.

Kwon ignored his pursuers and focused on catching up to Harper and the Sherpas. He leaned over the handlebars of the snowmobile to make his body as small and streamlined as possible. It helped him gain speed to catch up, but the soldiers kept pace with him.

More gunshots rang out, splattering the short end of the ridge to their right. A gust of wind kicked up the snow, blowing the white powder into a series of eddies and swirling mini-tornadoes.

Ghosh turned and waved the third Sherpa toward the left. He broke off from the group and rushed down the valley between the ridges and toward the open plain. Kwon continued to glance over his shoulder to gauge their pursuers' reaction.

They didn't bite.

They raced on. Their Chinese hunters were growing impatient, releasing the fury of their automatic weapons, which grew more intense as they closed the gap. Kwon began to feel they were fighting a losing battle. He had to make a decision on how to end it. He just needed the right opportunity.

Several more minutes passed, and Babu waved as he steered his machine toward the left and took off down another valley separating two fingerlike ridges. Kwon suspected they were getting closer to the Nepalese border, or their companions were bailing on them to save their own lives.

A sudden gust of wind rushing down the South Col and blanketed the group with snow. Kwon turned toward the ever-closing group of snowmobiles behind him. They remained undeterred as they closed the gap. Darkness was setting in, and visibility was becoming poor. He was running out of time.

Suddenly, Ghosh raised his left arm and waved. He was leaving. They must be close. But would the PLA stop at the border? Would they risk an international incident in pursuit of two unknown subjects whose crime was stealing snowmobiles? Or did the PLA suspect Kwon and Harper were behind the melee at the airport?

By the time Kwon glanced to the rear and forward again, he was alone with Harper leading the way through a narrow gap in a ridge that loomed large in front of them. Kwon assessed the opening and the thick drifts of snow on the right side of the ridge. It was going to be his best shot.

He ducked as a bullet whizzed by his head. At first, he struggled with the twenty-four-pound weapon he'd grabbed at the outpost's munitions depot. It wasn't one he'd specifically used before, but its operation was simple. He had one chance.

Driving with his left hand, he pulled the Chinese-made Norinco LG5 automatic grenade launcher over his shoulder and rested it on the console of the snowmobile. He expertly engaged the fire-control system and the laser rangefinder.

Despite the fatigue in his right arm and shoulder, Kwon raised the weapon and pointed it ahead of him. He took a breath and considered his timing. Too soon, and he'd cut himself off from Harper. Too late, and he would have wasted his one opportunity to create separation from their pursuers.

Harper raced through the gap, and Kwon calmly gauged the time and distance. At less than fifty yards, he squeezed the trigger.

The blast of the forty-millimeter grenade was deafening, but it was the LG5's kick that almost got him killed. The low-velocity, high-impact grenade found its mark—the underside of a rock outcropping jutting out from the ridge.

The weapon flew out of Kwon's right hand and over his head. The momentum caused by the grenade being propelled forward almost knocked him off the snowmobile. He wrestled the steering with his left hand in an attempt to keep from being thrown off. Like a bull rider with his arm raised high, he rode through the rock chute just as it exploded into thousands of pieces of rock and debris. However, it was the avalanche that sealed their escape.

As he regained his balance and settled into his seat, he turned to view the results of his efforts. The view of the gap was obliterated by snow and rock sprayed in all directions. He applied the brakes and slid to a stop, turning the snowmobile sideways to provide himself cover against their attackers. He readied the Sig Sauer MPX and stood fearlessly, ready to shoot the first of the soldiers as they cleared the debris.

He never got the chance. He waited, scanning the two disconnected ridges. Scanning the debris for any human movement. Half a minute passed and they never emerged. Another half minute later, he realized why. The grenade had struck the side of the opening so hard that it had collapsed into the gap and then filled with snow. Their pursuers were either cut off or buried in the rubble. Either way was fine by Kwon.

He mounted the snowmobile and raced forward toward the border. To Harper's credit, as instructed, she didn't wait to watch the destruction unfold. If he got the chance, he'd have to be sure to tell Joe, who most likely would respond with something akin to *that's a first.*

He continued on for half a mile, and as he cut through another pass, he found himself rapidly descending a slope toward a sharp turn to the left. He slowed the snowmobile to maintain control as the bend in the trail left him blind. When he followed the curve, he found Harper standing alone, with her snowmobile nowhere to be seen.

He pulled his machine to a stop next to her and turned it off. It was eerily quiet again. Harper managed a smile as he joined her.

"I see you got to use your new toy."

Kwon glanced backward just to confirm the soldiers didn't manage to go around the ridge or through the rubble.

"Yeah," was his simple response as he rolled his neck on his shoulders to relieve some tension.

Harper scowled. "Well done. Except, we have a problem."

Kwon furrowed his brow and studied Harper's face.

"What?"

She turned and pointed down the slope. "Look."

CHAPTER SEVENTEEN

CDC Headquarters
Atlanta

As the days passed and the number of people infected by the mysterious novel virus multiplied, an enormous amount of political and media pressure came to bear upon the CDC. Over the weekend, a senior adviser to the president had appeared on ABC's Sunday morning show *This Week with David Axelrod*. During the interview, he was pressed by Axelrod whether the president still had confidence in the CDC to lead the outbreak response.

Although the senior advisor deferred that specific question to the president, he did go on to say, "Early on in this outbreak, the CDC, whom the world considers to be the most trusted organization to deal with infectious diseases, really let the country down in its efforts to inform the president, and the public, about the threat this virus posed for us all. I anticipate changes in the CDC's approach in the future."

The senior advisor's response sent shock waves through the CDC campus in Druid Hills. A decade prior, the CDC had been roundly criticized for dropping the ball from the beginning of the

COVID-19 pandemic with regards to testing. Many public health experts had condemned the CDC for failing to ramp up testing quickly enough to track and control the epidemic.

To make matters worse in 2020, early tests were delayed due to a scientific breakdown at the agency's central laboratory. Faulty test kits were sent to public health labs across the country. It was later determined those tests were problematic and didn't deliver accurate results. It set back the agency's response to COVID-19 by nearly a month.

Following the novel coronavirus pandemic, the CDC took measures to prevent this type of fiasco in the future. However, as was so often the case, politicians and the media had a short memory. As the twenty-four-seven news cycle continued to be dominated by every individual case in which a patient was deemed a presumptive positive of this new disease, comparisons were being drawn to the CDC's response to COVID-19.

At seven a.m. that morning, the director of the CDC himself gathered everyone under his supervision, including Dr. Berger Reitherman. The agency's public relations team had worked overnight to fashion a response. The two-hour meeting was filled with expletives, fists slamming the table, and newspaper articles being ripped apart before being thrown about the room. The director was furious and vowed his people would not be the whipping dog for the media.

The CDC was going to go on offense to defend itself before it got out of hand. Unlike 2020 when mistakes were made by the agency, they were on top of this outbreak, and the director wanted to let the world know about it.

Surprisingly, at least to him, anyhow, Dr. Reitherman would be the first batter up. He'd not conducted that many media interviews in the past. Following 2020, when many public officials spoke out on the pandemic, the CDC and the National Institutes of Health agreed to allow any interviews and messaging to be generated out of Atlanta. This would prevent confusion for the public and stop the media from playing the gotcha game by pitting the two agencies against one another.

The director of the CDC chose Dr. Reitherman because he was considered the point man on the new outbreak. The disease detectives were under his purview. The accumulated data was analyzed by his team. And genetic analysis, the last important step before pharmaceutical companies could begin working on a treatment protocol and a vaccine, fell squarely on Dr. Reitherman's shoulders as the director of the Center for Surveillance, Epidemiology, and Laboratory Services, or CSELS.

WSB-TV, channel 2 in Atlanta, was the local ABC affiliate. For more than eighty years, WSB had been a highly respected news station for Atlanta, and a friend of the CDC. To interview Dr. Reitherman, the news station sent a production crew led by Jorge Estevez. Estevez had joined WSB after spending nearly ten years as an anchor with WFTV in Orlando, Florida.

Estevez began the interview in Dr. Reitherman's office. With the assistance of Becker, Dr. Reitherman organized his workspace to make a better impression on viewers. She also spent every available moment bringing him up to speed on their investigation and prepping him for possible questions.

Naturally, Dr. Reitherman was abreast of all aspects of the novel virus, but he rarely watched the never-ending supply of pundits and Monday morning quarterbacks who permeated the airwaves. He'd had enough of that during the COVID-19 pandemic.

Becker, on the other hand, had to watch the news. Harper, like Dr. Reitherman, rarely watched, so she tasked Becker with keeping her up to speed. As the young epidemiologist reminded her boss before he went on air, the questions would be based one-third on factual information and two-thirds on speculation or hyperbole.

She suggested a basic rule, something she'd learned from her younger years of competing in beauty pageants. Before you answer, take a deep breath and formulate a response in your mind. The key was to do this every time. The interviewer will pick up on this as being your nature rather than an attempt to equivocate.

The interview began with a series of smooth questions. Estevez had chosen a series of questions geared toward walking Dr. Reitherman through a chronology of events. This was the fact-based part of the interview. Then came the pointed inquiries designed to either make headlines or create a sound bite that would be circulated around the nation, if not the world.

Estevez had noticeably changed his demeanor after they'd taken a short break. Dr. Reitherman was caught off guard.

"Doctor, the president has been critical of the CDC's handling of the outbreak. In particular, he has openly pointed the finger of blame at your team for what happened in downtown Las Vegas. This morning WSB's Jamie Dupree, who has many contacts with Washington insiders on Capitol Hill, reported when the crisis abates, the president will be making sweeping changes at the CDC. In particular, he plans on demanding Senate hearings into the handling of the outbreak and the delay in providing the administration details on a possible vaccine. How do you respond?"

Dr. Reitherman bristled. Once again, Harper and the CSELS were going to be blamed for the Nevada governor's decision to quarantine the Fremont Street Experience. Naturally, the president had disavowed any involvement in the decision. Dr. Reitherman forgot Becker's advice and fired off his response.

"If the crisis abates, as you say, it'll be due to the tireless efforts of the people in this building and the dedicated disease detectives around the world who will not rest until all the facts are gathered. These investigations take time.

"Identifying patient zero, conducting the contact tracing to supplement existing patient data, and then applying principles of genetic engineering to develop a vaccine requires weeks and months of study. Let me give you some examples.

"In 2009, when a strain of the H1N1 influenza virus emerged in early April of that year, causing the first global flu pandemic in many decades, it took six months to administer the first of the newly developed trial vaccine. Even then, because the nation was entering flu season, a second wave of H1N1 activity peaked by

November. It wasn't until mid-December of 2009 that the first one hundred million doses were available for ordering. That was eight months later. Also, keep in mind, we'd already had an influenza vaccine in place since the 1940s thanks to Dr. Jonas Salk, the man who stopped polio."

Dr. Reitherman caught his breath and decided to continue. Perhaps it was time to educate the public and the president with some cold, hard facts. He was defensive and it showed.

"Now, fast-forward to 2020, Jorge. This agency took a lot of heat early on regarding testing and its efforts to stem the spread of the pandemic. I want your viewers to let something soak in for a moment.

"We were in the throes of a global pandemic. Pandemics are capable of killing everyone. Do you realize that? Loss of life is never acceptable for our disease detectives, but they are realistic, science-based members of a team, who try to separate emotion from fact.

"The number of deaths in the United States was far lower than the initial models predicted. Actually, by a factor of a hundred. Early models showed several million deaths could be expected from COVID-19. The actual numbers were less than one hundred fifty million, and that included counting presumptive positives as well as those patients who died during the pandemic from other causes who happened to be COVID-positive.

"Now, did the CDC receive credit for keeping the death toll to a minimum? No. Were the genetic scientists credited with creating a vaccine made available by the end of the year—a timetable in line with the 2009 H1N1 vaccine for a simple mutation of the influenza virus as opposed to the novel coronavirus? No.

"Jorge, here's my point. Novel viruses, like H1N1, which caused the pandemic of 1918 and COVID-19, have never been seen before. Hence, the term *novel*. We are facing the same situation here. Our team at the CDC—scientists, epidemiologists, and public health officials, are working as quickly as possible to find answers to key questions about how this disease is transmitted and why some cases are more severe than others. At the same time, we are working with physicians around the country to establish treatment protocols, and our geneticists are studying the virus to create a potential vaccine."

Rant over.

Dr. Reitherman took another deep breath and took a quick swig of water from a glass Becker had set on the desk for him. The inside of his mouth had become dry as he gave his response without taking a breath.

Estevez studied his notes. There were many questions left for the director of the CSELS, but he considered this to be an opportune time to ask a whopper.

"Sir, where is Dr. Harper Randolph?"

PART II

MY ADVENTURES AS A DISEASE DETECTIVE

When you have eliminated all which is impossible, then whatever remains, however improbable, must be the truth.
~ Sherlock Holmes through the creative mind of Sir Arthur Conan Doyle

REGIONAL MAP

CHAPTER EIGHTEEN

Chukhung Village
Khumbu Region, Nepal

Harper and Kwon took in their surroundings. It was deathly quiet as they stood in the midst of the enormous ridges leading up to the tallest mountains on the planet. The springtime temperatures on the South Face of the rising peaks turned the snowy conditions they'd used to evade capture and cross the border into rock. They slowly turned in all directions, observing nothing but rocks of varying sizes and shapes. They'd run out of snow and had to continue their journey on foot.

"Now what?" asked Harper.

"We walk."

"Duh," she sarcastically fired back. She was slaphappy after the ordeal they'd been through. Her demeanor was more reflective of the sense of relief she felt rather than teasing the man who'd saved her life more than once. "What I meant was where do we go from here? I don't see any street signs or tour guides, do you?"

Kwon shook his head disapprovingly. He retrieved the Blackberry from his jacket pocket. Despite the beads of sweat pouring off his forehead, he kept his jacket on in case they had to sleep in the mountains that night. Darkness was approaching and it was a very real possibility they'd need to seek shelter in a cave.

Harper grew impatient with Kwon's lack of conversation, so she continued to badger him. "Are you gonna call an Uber? LifeFlight? Beam me up, Scotty? What's the plan?"

After searching for a cell tower signal, which he expected was a pointless exercise, Kwon navigated to the GPS app on the Blackberry. Global positioning satellites were constantly raining signals down from low-Earth orbit. Cell phones were able to connect to them without reliance on cell phone towers.

"There is a village seven miles to our southwest," began Kwon. "We'll need to be careful if we are going to walk there in the dark."

"I'd rather keep moving than sleep out here under the stars, cowboy," said Harper. "Let's go. Besides, I can feel it getting colder already."

Kwon slowly zipped up his jacket. "It feels like the upper forties. I suspect we'll see below freezing before we make it to this village."

"What's it called?"

"Chukhung."

"Great. Hotel accommodations?"

"With a little luck," Kwon replied.

Harper shook off the cold and shoved her hands back into her pockets. "I've slept in the jungles of Africa and the mud houses of Syria. Not to mention last night when I was huddled in a tent with five snoring and farting men."

"What?" asked Kwon as his head snapped in her direction.

"Yeah, somebody had gas. Mainly, I was just making sure you were paying attention to me. Are you gonna tell me what happened on the side of Everest?"

Kwon sighed and explained the difficulty in dealing with the frozen body. He tried to avoid the gory details of the butchering of the dead climber, but he assured Harper that he had been able to retrieve several cultures for analysis.

"I wasn't able to label the vials like we did in Lhasa."

"They'll figure it out. I may enlist the medical examiner in Kathmandu if Dr. Reitherman gives me clearance. Most likely, he'll want me to send them to Atlanta undisturbed."

Kwon reached into his pocket and handed Harper the man's passport. "I found several things to identify him by and possibly his travel itinerary. He had what looks like a hotel room key with *xiang Fu Lou* engraved on a key ring."

"What does that mean?"

"Literally, *missing your happiness on the floor.*"

Harper erupted in laughter. "It's a hoochie mama house!"

"We don't know that, and highly doubtful in China."

Harper couldn't stop laughing. "Oh, puhleeze. I guarantee there are hookers in China."

"Hong Kong, maybe. But not in the West."

"Well, mister hooker-denier, how do you know he came from Western China?"

"They had a rental car from Tibet Vista. Their identifier was also on the key ring."

Harper was impressed, although she still thought the man had been staying in some kind of flophouse. She held the passport close to her face so she could read the text in the dimming light.

"Trent Maclaren. White male. Australian. Issued in Melbourne. Thirty years old." She thumbed through the pages to look at his travel stamps.

"Is he a frequent traveler?"

Harper shrugged. "It's hard to see, but there are many entries. Hey, this is a start. I'll get Becker on this to find out what he was doing in a hoochie-mama house in Tibet, and to see who his pal was who caused the disaster on Everest."

Kwon reached for the passport and replaced it in his pocket. "There's a river up ahead. That's a good sign."

"Did it show up on your GPS?"

"Yeah, plus we appear to be following it downstream. Do you see the lake?"

"It looks cold."

"According to the GPS, that's Imja Lake. Chukhung should just be another couple of miles."

Harper picked up the pace, finding her second wind. It was completely dark by the time they reached the western edge of the lake. The terrain had continued to slope downward toward a lower elevation, and as they passed the earthen dam holding back the melted glacial water, a few flickering lights could be seen in the distance.

"Hey, they have electricity!"

"Don't count on it," said Kwon, dampening her spirits. "This is probably a base camp or intermediary stop for Mount Everest climbers. My guess is we're looking at campfires of some kind."

"I was hoping for a hot bath," she mumbled. What she really wanted the most was the opportunity to talk with her husband.

Forty minutes later, they wandered onto the crushed-gravel main street of Chukhung, although it was nothing more than an eight-foot-wide trail. There were no vehicles of any kind in sight. No cars, trucks, bicycles, motorcycles, or scooters. There were a couple of horses tied up to a tree near the front porch of a plain block building known as the Khangri Resort.

Harper immediately picked up on the fact it was labeled in English. "Are you sure we're in Nepal?"

"It's for the climbers, many of whom are either English-speaking or can read it," said Kwon.

He approached the wood-carved entry door and pulled on the handle. It was locked. He stretched to peer inside a small, three-foot-by-three-foot window. The building appeared dark and empty. "I think they're closed."

Harper wandered toward the horses. "There's a small fire down around the side of that barn. Let's check it out."

Kwon raced off the porch and got in front of Harper. "Me first and I'll do the talking."

"Do they speak Chinese here?"

"No, Nepali. It's closer to Chinese than English."

Kwon stopped to remove his jacket. He tucked his rifle around his back and put the coat back on. Harper did the same. Kwon also readied his pistol and placed it in his jacket's right pocket. Generally speaking, the Nepalese were a friendly people and their relationship with America was a good one. However, he wasn't going to take any risks after what they'd been through.

They arrived at the bonfire built in the middle of a rock formation. Several locals were huddled around it, sitting on boulders that had been carved into cubes. They were passing a bottle around and took turns drinking from it.

Kwon engaged them in conversation the best he could. Using a combination of English and Chinese, he learned the village was indeed a rest stop for climbers making their way to the summit of Mount Everest. The two hotels were closed due to an avalanche on the South Col. However, in a nearby town, there were a variety of accommodations ranging from hostels to a small hotel-and-restaurant combination.

Kwon negotiated a taxi ride of sorts. Despite the darkness, the men agreed to pull them down the trail in a yak-drawn wagon in exchange for the rest of the money in Kwon's possession less the cost of the hotel and some food.

Harper readily approved the transaction, as she could now envision a phone call with Joe and that hot bath she desperately needed.

CHAPTER NINETEEN

Dingboche
Khumbu Region, Nepal

It was near midnight when the yak-driven wagon and its slightly inebriated driver pulled to a stop in front of the only hotel in the small town of Dingboche. The driver and his companion waited while Kwon confirmed the hotel was open and had two rooms available. He paid for a single night and set aside some money for snacks and breakfast. Then he thanked the driver and gave him the equivalent of four thousand dollars in Chinese yuan. The men briefly complained about the form of currency because they'd hoped for U.S. dollars, but in the end appreciated the generous payment equal to half a year's pay for the retired sherpas.

When Kwon returned to the lobby, Harper was grinning. "Seriously, this place is called the Yak Hotel and Restaurant. Are we ever gonna get away from these yaks?"

Kwon raised his eyebrows. "I don't know, have you checked out the restaurant's menu?"

"Eww!" complained Harper. "Give me my key. I want a bath and my husband on the phone, not necessarily in that order."

Kwon turned over a single key with the number 1 engraved on it. He was staying in room 2.

"I'll check in with our friends," he said, tapping the top of his left forearm where the tracking chip was inserted. This town is only slightly bigger than the last one. I doubt they have taxi service. I'll try to arrange for transportation to Kathmandu. The desk clerk said there is a helipad at the west end of town."

"What about the embassy?" asked Harper.

"I thought about that, but I can't be sure the CIA station is located there," replied Kwon. He pointed toward the hallway leading to the guest rooms. "I'll figure it out. Get some sleep, and if you need something, pound on the wall adjoining our rooms. I'll come running."

Harper spontaneously hugged the DARPA operative. "Thank you for, um, well—everything. I don't think I can ever say that enough."

Kwon patted her on the back and pulled away out of respect. He shyly looked down and then made eye contact. With a shrug, he said, "It's what I do. Good night."

He stood in front of his door and waited until Harper was securely inside her room. Kwon nodded to himself and entered the dark room alone, wishing he had a loved one to call.

Harper had no idea what time it was in the States. It took her a moment to realize she was a day ahead of Atlanta and Washington. She walked around the hotel room, which was spartanly furnished with bunk beds and a queen-sized fold-out sofa bed. Clearly, this room was designed to cram mountaineers into for a quick night's stay before they hiked to the next point on their journey to the summit.

She stripped off her clothes except her jeans and the Netizen tee shirt she'd worn for days. She couldn't help herself as she raised her right arm to see how bad the stench was.

"Pretty bad," she said with a laugh. Her first stop was the bathroom, where she enjoyed peeing in a real toilet for the first time since Dr. Basnet's house. She then grabbed a washcloth and soaked it in warm water. The brief refresher was all she needed to stay up another hour to speak with Joe and then to call Becker.

She took a deep breath to steady her nerves. She needed to appear calm as she spoke to Joe. He'd been against her trip to China and only acquiesced after adding Kwon as part of the mission. Harper was glad he'd insisted upon Kwon. Still, she didn't want to unduly worry her husband. She wasn't certain she was done yet.

She dialed Joe's cell phone number and immediately grew concerned when it was answered by Joe's chief of staff, Andy Spangler.

"Andy?"

"May I help you?" came the response.

"Andy, this is Harper. Is Joe all right?"

She heard a gasp on the other end of the line. "Holy shit. Harper, is that really you? Where are—?" He purposefully cut himself off. "No, don't answer that."

"Andy, you're scaring me. Did something happen to Joe?"

"No, no. No worries. It's just, well, I'll let him explain. Listen, he's chairing a committee hearing right now, so—"

"No, don't interrupt him. I can call back."

"Forget it!" he whispered emphatically. "He'd string me up if I didn't get his attention. Besides, it's kinda contentious right now. He can stick a needle in the ranking member's eye by calling an abrupt recess. Plus, it'll get the damn reporters buzzing again."

"Again?" she asked. "About what?"

"Hold on," he responded and pressed the phone against his clothing. Harper could hear him speaking to Joe even as his starched shirt rubbed against the iPhone. "One minute, please, General."

Harper laughed. She loved political subterfuge, at least when it benefitted her husband. She gathered all the pillows from the other beds and propped them up against the wall in the bottom bunk. She heard the gavel pound the block and the uproar of the gallery as Joe called a recess. Seconds later, she heard his voice, causing her body to quiver and the tears to flow.

"My god, I've missed you. Darling, tell me you're safe."

"I am. Promise. Kwon, too. It's been a heckuva—"

"Honey, stop. I'm sorry, but listen to me. We can talk but only generally. Do you understand?"

Harper wiped the tears away and exited the bunk bed. She paced the floor as she walked, rubbing her temples with her free hand. Her mind began to race, immediately filling with speculation of nothing but bad things.

"Um, yes. Can you tell me anything?"

Joe hesitated before responding. She could hear the general chatter of staffers in the background, indicating he'd exited through the rear of the hearing room into the hallway. Seconds later, the chatter stopped and the sound of cars filled her ears. He was outside.

"Beijing is embroiled in geopolitical shitstorms on several fronts. It's really exploded in the last forty-eight hours. They are about to go to war with India on their western border. Hong Kong protests have resulted in a massive crackdown on dissidents. They're buzzing the Taiwan Straits with their fighter jets. And, to top it off, they've got it in their heads that the U.S. Embassy in Beijing is harboring two American fugitive spies. They've threatened to expel everyone in the embassy unless they find these nonexistent spies first."

Harper's eyes grew wide. She wasn't sure what to say. "That certainly is a shitstorm. Sorry for their luck." She thought for a moment and then asked, "Does any of this involve your committees?"

It was her indirect way of asking if he was taking any heat for her actions. Joe immediately picked up on her intentions.

"You know the media. They're always trying to find fire where there isn't any. Listen, I need to get back in there shortly. The minority member was apoplectic when I interrupted his soliloquy with the unexpected recess. I may have to add a minute to his time."

"You're so generous," said Harper with a chuckle. "I love you and I miss you. Um, Kwon is working on a ride for us. I suspect tomorrow I'll have access to a phone with a better connection. How does that sound?"

"Perfect. I'll let your friends know you'll be calling them as well. In case you're wondering, it's three o'clock Thursday here. You can do the calculations from there."

"Got it. Joe, are you sure everything is okay with you?"

"Nothing I can't handle, especially after hearing your voice. I love you so much. Please be careful, and I'll watch for your call, no matter what time. Okay?"

"I love you more."

Harper disconnected the call and fell back onto the bed. She tried to process everything Joe had relayed to her. Her imagination ran wild as she envisioned an army of hackers sitting in a windowless building in the heart of Beijing, monitoring phone calls and pouring through electronic messages as they searched for the two American spies. She chuckled as she chastised herself for having such an overactive imagination. As the scenario played out in her mind, she drifted off to sleep without the hot bath she craved so badly.

In her dreams, the hacker army continued its search for her and Kwon. She slept fitfully, waking several times throughout the night. She tried to make light of her dreams, not realizing there was more truth to them than fiction.

PLA Unit 61398, the military's own hundred-thousand-man army unit, had, in fact, been tasked with finding Harper and Kwon. They were listening and watching everywhere.

Including Nepal.

CHAPTER TWENTY

Kathmandu, Nepal

Harper was jolted out of her sleep by the sound of a helicopter hovering nearby. The thumping of the rotors frightened her as she recalled the PLA choppers sailing over her head at the base of Mount Everest. Oddly, she immediately searched for her weapon rather than look outside the window to find the source of the commotion. As she became fully awake, she found herself gripping the Sig Sauer until her knuckles turned white.

Her mind recovered and she remembered that Kwon had mentioned a helipad. He'd likely arranged for transportation to Kathmandu. However, it was her initial reaction that troubled her. Was this going to be her default response to danger? Reach for the nearest weapon?

She'd never carried a gun while treating patients in Africa. Despite the fact she frequently investigated infectious diseases in war-torn regions, Harper had never found it necessary to be armed. Even in Syria, when she'd investigated a deadly MERS outbreak in the midst of a civil war, Harper had relied upon the militia comprising the Syrian National Coalition.

Kwon was knocking on her door. "Harper, are you awake? Our ride's an hour early."

"Yeah. Um, hold on."

She rushed into the bathroom and did her business. While she did, she glanced to her right and rolled her eyes at the disheveled woman in the mirror who returned the favor.

Aren't you a vision of loveliness?

Then she turned her head toward the unused shower-bathtub combination. *A lot of good you did me.* Harper silently cursed herself for not taking five minutes to shower before she'd crashed last night.

"Harper?" Kwon persisted.

"Yeah, coming!"

She flushed, quickly washed her face with cold water, and after making a lame effort at fixing her bedhead hair, she suited up for the trip into Kathmandu.

The flight only took forty-five minutes in the French-made Eurocopter. The machine rattled and shook as if it was out of balance in some manner. The interior was worn and several seats were missing. Even Kwon appeared concerned as to whether the single-engine utility chopper had the ability to get them to the city without crashing.

The United States enjoyed friendly relations with Nepal although the extent of U.S. military support was largely through the United Nations. The Nepalese Army helicopter had been dispatched from the UN Training Barrack located halfway between Dingboche and Kathmandu.

Out of an abundance of caution, the CIA station chief located within the U.S. Embassy in the city arranged for Kwon and Harper to be delivered to the Nepal Police Headquarters rather than to the heliport located on the embassy grounds. He'd advised Kwon during their brief conversation that intelligence chatter out of Beijing indicated finding the two American spies was of the highest priority.

At the police station, a black Tata H5 SUV greeted them, driven by an attractive Nepalese woman. Harper couldn't help but notice Kwon's change in behavior in speaking with her. While the two chatted continuously during the twenty-minute ride to the embassy, Harper took in the sights.

The Nepalese capital was home to over a million people, but it was nothing like the large cities found in the United States. The driver, who was constantly checking her mirrors, was friendly but also on alert. She clearly was taking a circuitous route to the embassy in order to avoid any vehicles tailing them. She navigated the small SUV into the old city, a place of narrow cobblestone streets, overhanging brick buildings filled with colorful flower boxes, and a variety of garments strung across balconies with clotheslines.

There were also endless crowds of people. Many of the women, like their escort, were dressed in colorful saris. The men wore traditional tunics and baggy pants. A few were dapperly dressed in Western attire. What struck Harper the most about the locals were the children. Most appeared poor and unkempt. They scampered through the old brick streets in their bare feet, playing chase or kicking a soccer ball when an open space presented itself. Despite their outward appearance, the children were happy. It caused her mind to wander.

Were children, despite their circumstances, happy because their view of life hadn't been tainted by the trials and tribulations of the adult world? She thought back to her days in Africa. To her *young miracle*, the baby she'd saved from Ebola, Harper had given the child an opportunity to grow up, but toward what kind of life? Would she live to be six years old, or would the raging unrest in Central Africa take her life? Would the *young miracle* ever get the chance to play soccer or hide-and-seek like the kids of Kathmandu?

Then Harper grimaced and her mind wandered back to her childhood when she thought life as she knew it was over. The unexpected death of a father. The loss of a mother to mental illness because she couldn't cope with her husband being taken from her.

Harper turned her head to avoid her face being seen by Kwon

and their driver. She wiped away her tears as she cried for the innocents. The ones who got dealt a bad set of cards in the game of life. Yet, as she tried to gather herself, all she saw was exuberance. And laughing faces. And playful bundles of energy racing among the adults on cobblestone streets that would've been ripped up and paved over long ago in America.

"Here we are," the driver announced as she navigated through the open iron gates leading to the parking lot. Unlike Beijing, where security was tight, a uniformed guard nonchalantly waved them inside without checking for credentials or deploying bomb-sniffing dogs.

Harper tried to snap herself out of her melancholy mood. Her mind conjured up visions of being in her husband's arms, and then, oddly, she was able to inhale the scents of Southern-style home cooking served up by the two women who'd rescued her from despair as a child—Ma and Mimi. In that moment, she vowed, when this was over, she'd find time for a little R & R at Randolph House.

For now, her level of excitement began to build as they cleared security and entered the main building at the U.S. Embassy. She thought of her conversation with Joe from the night before. Her eyes searched for a clock. She found an even better tool. A wall of LED digital displays provided the current time of every major city or every time zone in the world. It was only 5:30 in the afternoon, eastern time.

She loved her husband, but the first order of business was to catch Becker at the office, although she had little doubt the energetic epidemiologist would still be there for hours.

CHAPTER TWENTY-ONE

United States Embassy
Kathmandu, Nepal

Harper and Kwon were escorted into a large conference room, where they were immediately served coffee with a variety of pastries. The two weren't shy as they gobbled up apple strudel and cinnamon raisin buns. Apples were plentiful in Nepal and a staple of their diet. Their coffee choices included Bourbon and Typica, both organically grown in the region because of the suitable climate of the Himalayas. Harper didn't care for the somewhat bitter taste, but her body appreciated the caffeine coursing through it.

Three casually dressed men entered the conference room and closed the door behind them. The oldest of the three introduced himself.

"Welcome to Kathmandu. I'm Karl Hughey, chief of station here. These are my associates, who'll be available to get you squared away."

Harper smiled at the two men of Nepalese descent. They never formally introduced themselves, so Harper, staying true to the *modus operandi* of the CIA agents she'd met in Atlanta, mentally assigned each man a fictitious name. *Mister Kath* and *Mister Du.*

"Nice to meet you, Mr. Hughey. Listen, I really need access to a telephone to get in contact with the CDC."

"Yes, Dr. Randolph, I know you do. Two things. First, Dr. Reitherman and your assistant, um, Barker, is it?"

Harper laughed. "Becker." *Oh, how I wish I had this on tape.*

"Okay. Anyway, they're expecting your call. I have to bring you up to speed on a few things. As you know, we've been actively tracking you across China. Our recon birds were able to view the activity at the Lhasa airport, although not in real time. In any event, sometime shortly thereafter, your true identities were ascertained by Beijing. Well, pardon me. Dr. Randolph was ID'd. Dr. Li was not, of course."

"I was ...?" she began to ask before pausing, immediately showing her concern. "Was Dr. Zeng captured? Or Dr. Basnet?"

"I'm sorry that I don't have a definitive answer for you. We do know that shortly after your tracking devices were shown leaving the area, MSS agents swarmed the compound where you were located for a brief time. Satellite imagery showed the ambulance being loaded onto a flatbed and returned to the PLA installation at the airport."

"Probably prints," offered Kwon.

"Agreed. Regardless, Beijing blew a gasket. They identified Dr. Randolph. Learned she'd traveled to Urumqi using a fake passport. And then eventually discovered your connection to Congressman Mills."

Harper wandered away from the group, which had remained standing throughout the initial conversation. She rubbed her temples and addressed the men.

"I spoke to Joe last night. He alluded to a problem and warned me to be careful as to what I said until I got to a secure line."

Hughey took a deep breath and nodded. "We know, Dr. Randolph. I'm sorry about the intrusion, but our team here at the embassy monitored the call, per my instructions. I wanted to give you the opportunity to make contact with your husband, but if the conversation went in a direction that might compromise your safety, I'd instructed our agents to terminate the call."

Harper grimaced and nodded her head. "I understand. Is this a problem for my husband?"

"I know of your husband and have the utmost respect for him. Without a doubt, he'll be able to handle it. Besides, the agency has a way of diverting attention. Besides the usual vehement denials, we outed a few things related to the CDC's investigation, which placed the Chinese on the defensive. Make no mistake, they are still searching for you, but their chest-pounding in the media has ceased."

Harper smiled and mouthed the words *thank you*. She finished off her coffee and promptly poured another one.

Hughey winked at her. He was a grandfatherly sort who appeared empathetic. "The other thing I need to advise you about is the situation between China and India. Hostilities exploded over the last several days. There were multiple skirmishes along their shared western border, resulting in deaths on both sides."

"A hot war?" asked Kwon.

"No, not yet. Hand-to-hand combat. Very brutal. You would've thought Sun Tzu was back with his army."

"Will that impact our ability to return home?" asked Harper.

"No. That said, the MSS has operatives throughout Nepal and especially here in Kathmandu. Now that you're here, we're contemplating flight options, including private transportation. That might take a day or two to arrange."

One of the agents added, "There is a concert in several days for World Refugee Day. They have a chartered Boeing 737 to carry the band members, their instruments, and a smattering of media types. We might be able to fly you out under press credentials."

"A concert? Who's playing?"

"Sam Tsui. Phoebe Ryan. Talisco. A few others."

"Oh-kay," Harper stretched out the response, showing her complete lack of recognition of the artists' names.

"Alternative music," the youngest agent explained. "Anyway, their next stop is Tokyo. From there, we can get you on any number of flights to DC or even Atlanta."

Hughey stepped forward. "I know you're anxious to make phone calls. Let me add that we have room accommodations for you in the complex. They're not fancy, but I suspect they're better than what you've experienced in the last week. Each room has a telephone and, of course, a full bathroom with a shower." He looked directly at Harper when he said it. She reflexively scowled. *Watch it, buddy. I'll sick Barker on ya.*

Kwon removed his jacket. "We checked our weapons at security. Do you have someone who can clean them for us?"

"I'm not sure you'll need them, Dr. Li. If you leave the embassy compound, you'll be escorted by armed personnel with diplomatic credentials."

"We have some tissue samples to examine," interjected Harper. "What kind of relationship do you have with the local hospital? Do they have a pathology department?"

The other agent answered her question. "I anticipated this, Doctor. We have been in contact with Dr. Keyoor Gautam with Samyak Diagnostic. He is the nation's expert in clinical pathology and will willingly assist you. More importantly, he can be trusted not to reveal his findings to others."

"Good, thank you," said Harper. "Also, I need help researching the background information on a climber who died on Everest. We believe he is one of the first humans to contract the new disease I'm investigating. Can someone help me with that?"

"Yes, Doctor," the youngest agent replied. "That's one of the things the agency does best—fill in the blanks."

Harper and Kwon provided the agents the documentation found on Maclaren's body. They also were escorted to a secure area accessible only by CIA personnel to store the tissue samples until Harper could decide what to do with them. Part of her was anxious to study them, but she knew the right thing to do was to securely ship them back to the CDC.

Finally, they were escorted to small, but efficient, apartment-style rooms, where she was finally able to make her way into a shower. To top it off, she was furnished a variety of jeans and sweatshirts to wear while her clothing was being laundered. She couldn't resist choosing the goofiest one, featuring a cartoonish yak accompanied by the words *yak swag*.

Squeaky clean, dressed and refreshed, she called Atlanta first.

CHAPTER TWENTY-TWO

United States Embassy
Kathmandu, Nepal

"Did you miss me?" Harper was grinning ear to ear when she heard Becker's voice on the other end of the line. The response she received was not what she expected.

"I'm sorry. Who is this?"

"Aw, shit, Becker! Don't mess with me. I had to sleep in a yak hotel!"

Becker began to laugh. "Gak?"

"No, yak!"

"What's a yak?"

"You know, it's like ..." Harper's voice trailed off. She really wasn't sure whether it was more cow or ox or just its own kind of critter. She came up with her best description. "It's a really hairy cow with curly horns."

"Oh, like my aunt Ouiser?" asked Becker with a chuckle.

Harper was genuinely confused. "Weezer? Who?"

Becker dodged the question. "Never mind. Welcome back to the free world."

"I guess. I'm kind of locked down in the embassy until they can figure out how to get us out of the country without the Chinese catching us first. I guess we stirred up the pot a little too much."

Becker was not surprised. "I heard a little something about that from the Bergermeister. He had to give an interview to ABC the other day, and he got blindsided with a question that he couldn't answer."

"What was it?"

"They wanted to know where you were."

"Did he tell them?"

Becker laughed. "Nope, it was the first time he followed my advice. He demurred."

"Huh?" asked Harper, who was confused. "Demurred?"

"Yeah, it's a new word I learned from the *Washington Post*. You know, those reporters really are smarter than the rest of us common folk. They use hundred-dollar words like *demurred*."

Harper laughed. "That's legalese, isn't it?"

"For lawyers maybe, but not *WashPo*. Demurred means he took issue with the question."

"Why didn't they just say that?" Harper was amused by the whole conversation. The two epidemiologists had a lot more important matters to discuss, but somehow, in this moment, the two best friends needed some playful banter to reconnect.

"Beeecause it sounds a whole lot worse than *took issue with*. The whole interview was designed to make the CDC, and especially you, look bad. Anyway, the Bergermeister got fussy with the reporter, defended your honor like a good boy, and then began to talk about something ABC had no interest in."

"Which was?" asked Harper.

"Genetic markers and such."

Harper burst out laughing. "Yeah, I bet that shit sailed right over the head of the hundred-dollar-word crowd. So tell me what's new."

"Um." Becker paused for a long moment. Harper waited and then asked if her assistant was still there.

"Becker?"

"Yeah, still here. I'm eating dinner."

"Something good, I hope," said Harper.

"M&M peanut. I'm branching out." She paused while she finished eating the two piles of three blue M&M's, her new favorite.

Harper shook her head and smiled. She missed Becker. "All right then, me first. Listen, some of this has to be between us. I'll tell Joe in my own way, and I sure as heck don't want Reitherman to know what I've been through."

Becker was still chomping when she spoke. "Maybe you shouldn't tell me the deets? If I don't know, the Bergermeister won't be able to torture me for answers."

Harper ignored her silliness. "Let me just say that we got lucky. A whole lotta lucky. But, when it was all said and done, I think we located patient zero."

"That's great! Are you sending us the body?"

"Well, not exactly. Parts. Kinda small parts."

Becker lowered her voice to a whisper. "Crap. Incoming."

"What?"

Then she spoke louder than necessary. "Perfect timing, Dr. Reitherman. I have Dr. Randolph on the line. Let me put her on speaker."

The ambient noise coming through her phone's earpiece immediately changed to a hollow, airy sound.

"Good evening, Harper. I trust you're safe."

"Yes, sir. Thanks. I'm on a secure line, so I can speak freely. I'm at the U.S. embassy in Kathmandu, Nepal. The CIA has provided us a place to stay until they can figure out a way to get us out of the country. It appears our cover was blown along the way."

"So I gather. Don't care. They shouldn't hide things from the world health community. Otherwise, we wouldn't have to go to such extreme measures. You may have covered this with Elizabeth already, but will you fill me in on what you've found?"

"Yes, sir. To begin with, we located the doctor who first began releasing information on the disease through their social media. The trail actually led us into Tibet, where I met a military doctor, sort of, who had a corpse stored in a refrigerated locker at this medical facility. The deceased was an army pilot who'd flown a rescue mission to Mount Everest."

Harper heard Dr. Reitherman shut the door and slide a chair across the linoleum floor. "Is there a connection to our four index patients in Las Vegas?"

"Yes, sir. They were part of a team that had to deal with a gruesome accident near the summit on the Chinese side of Everest. Two men became ill. Check that, possibly several people suddenly got sick, causing a chain reaction. The four soldiers, our Las Vegas patients, brought one of the dead men back to the hospital in Tibet. The corpse was sent to a hospital in Xinjiang for study, which is where this Dr. Zeng got involved.

"Let me also mention, I have four vials of tissue samples in my possession; plus I have another four vials being shipped to Becker via DHL Express. They're coming to her home as part of a handbag purchase."

Becker perked up. "Really? Presents?"

"For both of us. I don't know if the samples will help, but I needed to try another means to get them to you, just in case."

Neither Becker nor Dr. Reitherman commented on Harper's statement. They understood the meaning.

"Have you identified the deceased?" asked Dr. Reitherman. "We can get started on contact tracing."

"Nothing yet, sir. However, I do have a lead and a theory. The second man, a possible companion of the first climber who fell, also died in the accident. We'd hoped to retrieve his body, but it was frozen and too dangerous to recover. We did get several samples of lung and organ tissues. I have them refrigerated and ready for transport."

"Could you identify him?"

"He's Australian. White male. Name is Maclaren. We turned over his identification and other personal effects to the CIA guys here to conduct a full background check as well as a reconstruction of his travel itinerary."

"Good, let me know how we can help. When will you be returning to the States?"

"As soon as the CIA guys give me the green light. If it looks like it might be a few days, then I'll pack these vials in dry ice and get them to you overnight if I'm stuck here."

Becker and Dr. Reitherman spoke to one another for a moment before addressing Harper again. He asked, "If you don't have anything to add, we can bring you up to speed on what we've learned."

Harper breathed a sigh of relief. She wasn't going to be pressed on the blow-by-blow details that led to her discoveries. She wouldn't get off so easy with Joe.

"What've you got?" she asked.

Dr. Reitherman replied, "First of all, this Dr. Boychuck has been a tremendous help on the ground. Our people were experiencing some pushback from the local hospitals. Woolie stepped in and made things happen."

Becker blurted out, "He's weird."

"Eccentric," said Harper. "Weird is a little harsh."

Becker couldn't help herself. "To-may-to. To-mah-to. He's weird."

Dr. Reitherman continued. "There have been several more victims of the disease, although indirectly. You know how it goes. The patient's weakened immune system from another illness allows the novel virus to invade their respiratory and cardiovascular systems."

"That was nice of him to send the bodies to us for study," said Harper.

"It was a package deal," interjected Becker. "They arrived yesterday."

"Boychuck is there?" Harper asked.

"Yes. Yes. Yes." Becker was sarcastic in her reply. "Weird, I tell you."

"In a brilliant sort of way," added Dr. Reitherman. "His ability to cut to the chase, pardon the pun, is extraordinary. I like him."

Harper could visualize Becker rolling her eyes and crossing her arms as she sat back in her chair. She broke the awkward silence by changing the subject.

"I understood the subject of genetic markers has become introduced to the public. Tell me what you've learned."

"Once again, our team, with an assist from Woolie, gained approvals from the patients and loved ones to access their pharmaceutical records. A pattern started to develop."

"What was it?" asked Harper.

"I'll let Elizabeth explain since she was the one who created the working theory," he replied.

"This virus has similar functional host-cell receptors to SARS. Specifically, angiotensin-converting enzyme number two."

Harper added, "I can see that. The ACE2 enzyme typically attaches to the outer cell membranes of both cardiovascular and respiratory organs."

Becker continued. "Through our analysis, we learned the protein coding gene was prevalent in patients whose immunities were compromised by other illnesses. However, here's the odd part. Many of the elderly patients, those most susceptible to things like influenza or even COVID-19, have managed to fight this thing. It's the healthiest patients who've succumbed to the disease."

"You'd reached that hypothesis before Harper left for China, am I right?" asked Dr. Reitherman.

"Yes, sir. That's why I suggested Becker study the pharmaceutical records of the infected."

"We did and found a common thread although there's a lot of work to do before its conclusive."

"Spill it, Becker," demanded Harper.

"Most, although not all, of the survivors were taking ACE-inhibitor medication like lisinopril or enalapril."

Harper's body tensed as she took a deep breath. "The medications are slowing the activity of the ACE enzyme, which decreases the production of angiotensin II. The blood vessels widen, raising flow capability, thus increasing the amount of blood the heart pumps."

Dr. Reitherman finished the concluding thought. "It lowers the heart's workload, giving the patient a longer period of time to fight the virus."

"Wait," said Harper. "Are you implying the ACE inhibitors don't prevent the spread of the disease?"

"Correct," replied Becker. "They simply slow the progression. We're still missing the genetic markers from the original host and any intermediary host. Even if your dead climber was patient zero, it doesn't mean the disease started with him. We're still lacking that one critical piece of evidence to completely define the genetic traits."

Harper, deep in thought, was startled by a firm rapping at her door. "Hold on, please," she said into the phone. She cupped the mouthpiece and addressed the person in the hallway. "Yes?"

It was Kwon. "The CIA has a dossier on the dead climber for us to review. You're gonna want to see this right away from what they just told me."

"Okay!" Harper returned to the call. "Hey, there might be more news later. Sorry. Gotta run." She hung up and bolted out the door.

CHAPTER TWENTY-THREE

United States Embassy
Kathmandu, Nepal

Harper and Kwon rushed back to the conference room where they were first greeted upon arrival. The CIA contingent was larger this time. It included Hughey, the two agents Harper had labeled Kath and Du, as well as several other analysts, who were poring over reports and photographs. The door was immediately closed behind them, and they were directed to seats at the side of the table.

"You guys work fast," quipped Harper as she got settled into her seat. One of the analysts offered them bottled water, and they both readily accepted.

Hughey wandered the large room wrapped in acoustical wall tiles. He shoved his hands in his pants' pockets as he spoke.

"We do have a vast network of resources to tap into. There are times when our agents need information on the fly and waiting isn't an option. Fortunately, your subject was an ordinary citizen with no nefarious intentions. Other than a drunk and disorderly charge outside a Melbourne bar years ago, this Aussie kept his nose clean."

"So he was just another climber?" asked Harper.

"Yes, to an extent," replied Hughey. He pointed at two identical file folders in front of Harper and Kwon. "Those are for you but cannot leave the embassy compound when you leave. I will forward them to your stateside offices, if you wish."

Harper opened the file just as Kwon did the same. Their eyes darted up and down the pages and quickly moved into the meat of the research. Kwon was the first to comment.

"He was traveling with his friend and coworker Mooy. They are both from Melbourne, worked for an outfit that does archeological digs around the world. I suppose they had a love of climbing, right?"

One of the analysts responded, "Yes. Maclaren more so than Mooy. His passport was recently reissued, so you wouldn't have been able to see the prior travel stamps. Our guess is that this was a bucket list item that he took advantage of since he was working in the region."

Harper focused on his employment history. "Would that be this TPE Program referred to here?" She tapped the paperwork and looked around the room.

"Yes, ma'am," replied another analyst. "Our cursory research revealed that two climatologists co-created the Third Pole Environment program, or T-P-E. The program's purpose was to study the climatology of the Tibetan Plateau. According to their research papers online, the plateau contains the Earth's largest repository of ice outside of the North and South Poles, hence the reference to a Third Pole."

Another analyst joined in the discussion. "The Tibetan Plateau and the Himalaya Mountains hold thousands of glaciers whose meltwater feeds seven different countries. From what we can determine from their online research papers, they believe there is evidence of drastic changes in these glacial areas contributing to climate change."

"Maclaren and Mooy were scientists?" asked Kwon.

"No. they worked for a subcontractor that conducted core drilling. The company name is Black Diamond Drilling, an

Australian outfit that services mineral exploration and the geotechnical sectors of the drilling industry."

Kwon asked, "Where is this TPE program located?"

"The facility is located in Gar County, a fairly small community in Ngari Prefecture. It's in the far western part of the Tibetan Plateau at the base of the Himalayas not that far from the Indian border."

"I wanna go there," Harper said.

Impulsive.

"That's not really possible," Hughey said, shaking his head.

Harper shot back, "Anything is possible for you guys. We need to make it happen."

Impetuous.

"Dr. Randolph, it's entirely too dangerous under the circumstances, especially in light of its proximity to India's border."

"Mr. Hughey, either you help us or we'll go it alone. We managed just fine in China before. This will be much easier, I'm sure of it."

Headstrong.

Kwon stepped in. He stood and reached his hand under Harper's arm to urge her out of the chair. "Would you please excuse us for a second?"

Nobody responded.

Harper, surprised by Kwon's forcefulness with her, willingly stood and followed him into the hallway. She wandered away from the conference room door and then turned on Kwon.

"You know I'm right! The answers are at this Third Pole place, whatever the hell it is. I don't see why we can't make a quick—"

Kwon cut her off. "Harper, you don't know that they came in contact with the host animal there. This place could be nothing but rock and ice. The usual zoonotic suspects most likely aren't found there."

She wasn't backing down. "Then we'll follow the next lead. We can't stop now, Kwon. We're too damned close!"

Her outburst had attracted the attention of several embassy personnel. First, they noticed Harper's determined look, and then they took in the yak swag tee shirt. A few shrugs and whispers accompanied their assessment of her actions.

"Please calm down. I get it. Let's go back and take in the rest of their research before we discuss going back to China. Don't forget, they're looking for us. We barely got out of there the other day."

Harper's shoulders slumped as she fidgeted with her feet on the shiny tile floor. "Let's just see if it's possible, okay?"

"Fair enough."

The two reentered the room, but Hughey had cleared out the analysts, leaving only the two agents assigned to assist Harper and Kwon.

"Dr. Randolph, please don't misunderstand," began Hughey. "Yes, it's possible to sneak you back into China, and yes, we are prepared to make it happen. However, I cannot in good conscience allow it. This remote part of China is ordinarily forgotten about by Beijing. There is a single military outpost in westernmost Ngari Prefecture near the border where the conflicts have arisen. Our fact book lists four dozen regular army and support staff. It's much smaller than the one you entered at Tingri County."

"That's good, right?" she asked.

"I said ordinarily," Hughey explained. "Because of the increased hostilities between the two nations, the PLA has greatly increased its presence along the border. I'm talking heavy artillery, helo gunships, and lots of troops."

"How far away is the TPE facility from the border?"

"Fifty miles," replied Hughey.

Kwon shook his head and turned to Harper. "If we get exposed, they'd be on us in a flash. There'd be no way to outrun them this time."

Harper stood her ground. "Why? You did a great job on the snowmobiles."

"Harper, this is different. Trust me."

She turned to Hughey and the two agents. "Can't you create some new documents for us? Like they did at the Beijing embassy. Call us glaciologists or environmental something-or-others. Hell, the roto-rooter man. I don't care. Just get us across the border and to this Gar City."

One of the agents corrected her. "County. Gar County."

"Fine. That place. Don't you have your own passport printing press?"

Hughey was exasperated. "That's not the problem, Dr. Randolph. We have a route to get you back and forth across the border without detection. I assume it's still workable." He turned to the analysts, who both nodded. One of them spoke up.

"They have their prints. If they're captured, all the docs in the world won't get them out of it if they're printed."

Harper turned to her partner. "Then we won't get caught. Right, Kwon?"

All three of the agency personnel looked to Kwon, who threw his hands up. "She's relentless."

"I can't guarantee your safety, but I can provide you the best possible tools to get you in and out."

Harper spontaneously clapped. "We'll take it. What's next?"

CHAPTER TWENTY-FOUR

Annapurna Conservation Area
Nepal-Tibet, China Border

Harper and Kwon's return trip into China was far more surreptitious than their relatively routine flight into Beijing of over a week ago. Outfitted with a Mahindra Roxor, a cross between a vintage Willys Jeep and an old Ford Bronco II, the Roxor was an off-road enthusiast's dream. The boxy vehicle was designed with short overhangs to make rock climbing easy. It had a reinforced undercarriage with components that were near impossible to break. The ten-thousand-pound, front-mounted winch supplemented the Roxor's ample torque to pull it out of the most difficult of situations.

The extended back end allowed the CIA agents to load the vehicle with camping and climbing gear, as well as weapons with ample ammunition. Kwon agreed and understood that if they were to get apprehended, they'd most likely disappear forever or become the poster children for a major international incident. They both accepted the risks and agreed to take every tool available to prevent capture.

It was just after dawn when they slowed to the designated point on the Garmin Aera 760 portable GPS navigator. Almost the size of an iPad Mini, the device was designed as an all-in-one aviation tool, giving pilots a portable alternative to their cockpit-installed devices. Because of its advanced technology relative to topography, the CIA provided it to their operatives who undertook to cross the Nepal-China border through the mountains rather than the closely monitored highway checkpoints.

An hour northwest of Kathmandu was the Annapurna Conservation Area, Nepal's largest protected area and home to some of the world's highest peaks and its undisputed deepest valley created by the Kali Gandaki River.

They'd left the embassy just after midnight and traveled the road from Pokhara, the nearest town, until they reached a series of mountain trails leading to the river. The Garmin became essential at this point. CIA operatives had planted beacons in the rocks and soil that were visible on the device. Even in the dark of night, trekkers or vehicles, following the preferred route suggested by the agency personnel, could make their way to the shallowest, most narrow part of the river. Just beyond the river lay a series of valleys zigzagging through the Western Himalayas into China.

It was imperative that Kwon stay on schedule and not attempt to enter China during the daylight hours. At another designated point during the journey, an alarm sounded on the Garmin, indicating they must douse the vehicle's lights and switch to infrared navigation using the AGM night-vision goggles they were provided. Again, they were a favorite of the CIA operatives entering China because they did an excellent job of illuminating the terrain and preventing the flattening effect of lower-quality models.

Once into China, Kwon and Harper exited the vehicle to change license plates. The Nepalese plates were ditched and replaced with Chinese plates issued to a construction company in Xinjiang. Once in the country, they'd avoid the scrutiny of patrolling police vehicles. However, if they were pulled over and searched, it would be game over. For that reason, both Harper and Kwon kept their silenced Sig Sauer MPX weapons hidden under blankets next to the center console of the vehicle.

"Thank you," Harper said after they reentered the Roxor and began the final stretch toward the highway. It was the first words they'd spoken since they pulled off the road and began to bounce their way along the woodland trails. "I know this is more than you signed on for."

"Harper, you don't know much about me," said Kwon, his face only visible by the light provided by the full moon. "At the end of the day, I'm a soldier and a patriot. I love my country and will do whatever it takes to protect her and all Americans from any threat. You and I both know a deadly microbe is just as capable of destroying our way of life as a Chinese nuke."

"We agree on that, but the risks you're taking to indulge me are above the call of duty."

Kwon shook his head. "Listen, as a soldier, a physician, and a man, I believe in certain core values, including loyalty, duty, respect, and selfless service. When I'm called on to serve, I do it without regard to myself, and I try to do it with honor. Fear never enters my mind because I have the courage to face any adversary. It's a mindset that few people understand."

"Kwon, are you afraid of dying?"

He didn't hesitate. "No. Do I have a death wish? Absolutely not. I train, study, and prepare to give myself the best possible advantage going into any situation. Sometimes, circumstances dictate I undertake a mission flying by the seat of my pants."

Harper sighed. "Case in point—my whims."

"You're wrong, Harper. This is not a whim. If it were, we'd still be back in the embassy. This is just another step in a quest for the truth that began when we met at DARPA. Not moving forward would mean failure in my mind. Don't doubt that."

They bounced along quietly for a while as Kwon carefully navigated the Roxor through narrow gaps in the ridges and then up and down inclines. Harper continued the conversation.

"I firmly believe we are going to save lives. It's why I'll pick up and fly around the world on a moment's notice to investigate these mysterious diseases. It's all about containment and preventing a much larger outbreak. Not just for our country, but for all of mankind."

Kwon understood. "What you do is dangerous on many levels. It's like you're trying to extinguish hundreds of thousands of hot sparks in a pile of dried leaves. Diseases spread so rapidly, they could overtake a community, or a country, before the appearance of symptoms. That's why time is so critical in your investigations, and that's why I'm here shaking the fillings out of my teeth on a return trip to China. Some might consider it insanity. I say it's just part of the job."

Harper chuckled. "I love my husband for making sure you were with me. I'm gonna miss you when this is over, Kwon."

Kwon soaked in her statement, and then he asked, "By the way, how did Joe take the news that we were going back in?"

Harper closed her eyes and laid her head back against the headrest, allowing the terrain to beat it repeatedly against the cushioned seat. It was a form of self-induced punishment. *Well-deserved*, she thought to herself.

"I didn't tell him."

CHAPTER TWENTY-FIVE

China National Highway 219
Gar County, Ngari Prefecture
Tibet, China

Despite the fact that Kwon was maintaining the speed limit as he and Harper drove west along China National Highway 219, they soon found themselves stuck behind a convoy of military vehicles heading toward the India-China border. They had just entered Ngari Prefecture in Western Tibet, approximately forty miles south of Gar County, where the Third Pole research facility was located, when Kwon ran up on the tail vehicle of the convoy. He immediately slowed to back off in an effort not to draw attention. Thus far, their second incursion into the Communist country had been smooth. He didn't want to derail their efforts by making themselves known to the PLA, who were possibly looking for them.

Ngari was known for some of the holiest tourist attractions in the world—Mount Kailash and Lake Manasarovar. Religious sites from the Zhangzhung civilization of four thousand years ago were frequented by visitors from around the world.

The CIA analysts had provided Harper a briefing package

embedded in the Garmin Aero GPS device. Armed with the local knowledge of interest to tourists, she and Kwon might be able to talk their way out of a routine traffic stop without raising suspicions.

After she covered the basic points of interest in Ngari, she turned her attention to the TPE facility. "These guys are all about the environment and climate change. Just to summarize what we learned before. The Third Pole refers to the high mountain region centered on the Tibetan Plateau. It covers two million square miles.

"According to this, the entire area stores more snow and ice than anywhere on the planet outside the Arctic and Antarctic. One spot in particular, the Guliya Ice Cap ..." Harper's voice trailed off. She paused as she turned in her seat and rotated the Garmin slightly before continuing, "... which appears to be due north of where we are now, is the largest ice cap in the Himalayas. Guliya seems to be the focus of the TPE's study."

Kwon slowed to a near stop as brake lights appeared on the convoy's trucks. "They're stopping."

"Or turning," added Harper. "According to the GPS, there's a highway that leads west toward India. Gar County is just ahead about fifteen miles."

Kwon was intense and focused. "Good. I'm ready to find out about these guys, Mooy and Maclaren, and then get the hell out of here."

Harper set the Garmin in her lap and watched the convoy disappear down a narrow, two-lane highway.

"Well, this is all good stuff and should allow us sufficient information to make conversation when we get there. The scientists here are from all over the world, including the U.S. One of the founders is from Ohio State."

"You have our cover down, so I'll let you take the lead. If Chinese is required, I'll jump in, but I suspect English is spoken by most."

Harper sat a little taller in her seat and messed with her hair. She vowed to work on her acting skills after she returned to Atlanta.

She'd pretended to be more people on this trip to China than someone suffering from dissociative identity disorder.

As they entered the outskirts of Gar County and its main city of Shiquanhe, Harper was amazed at the primitive construction of the buildings and the frontier-like living conditions. The area's population of twelve thousand people appeared to live simply. Many were dressed in traditional garb reminiscent of what she'd observed in the Middle East during past investigations. Vehicles were few and far between, with most of the inhabitants using pack animals to carry goods around the hard-packed dirt streets.

"It should be up ahead on the left," said Harper as she pointed to a large, one-story building perched upon a rocky hilltop.

"I see it," added Kwon. "What I have not seen is a police presence or evidence of PLA activity. They must have their hands full at the border."

"I appreciate the distraction," Harper added before exclaiming, "There! See the sign?"

Kwon took a deep breath and steered the Roxor up the hill, spinning the all-wheel-drive tires on the loose gravel as he accelerated. Half a minute later, they'd gathered themselves and prepared to enter the research facility. A confident Harper led the way.

The block and stucco structure was just as plain on the inside as it was on the outside. When they entered the reception area, they found a single desk, unmanned at the moment, and multiple poster-sized photographs of the region. Behind the desk was the Third Pole Environment logo, a blue globe with a swath of white representing the massive ice cap.

Harper grew impatient as nobody emerged from the back offices to greet them. She approached an open door leading into a hallway where the sound of a man's voice could be heard. She found a young man wearing wire-rim glasses leaning against the doorjamb of an open office door, speaking with a coworker.

"Ahem." Harper forcibly cleared her throat to get attention.

"Oh. Hello," he greeted her, turning around after being startled. "May I help you?"

"Yes. I am Harp—Harris Mills." She chastised herself. *Bad start, Harper. Epic fail, you dope.* She couldn't bring herself to look back at Kwon, who was waiting near the hallway entrance. "I was wondering if you could help us."

"Sure, of course. I'm Benton. Let's step back out here." He motioned for Harper and Kwon to return to the lobby. Once they were out there, he added, "Sorry about that. We don't really get many unannounced visitors. What was your name again?"

"Harris," she replied, now settling into her new role. "Honestly, this wasn't on our itinerary for our month-long vacation through China. However, because my friend and I are faculty members in sustainability studies, we were intrigued when we learned about the work you do here."

"Oh? How did you hear about us?"

"Pure happenstance, actually," Harper replied. "The first leg of our trip began at Mount Everest many weeks ago. We're climbers and were supposed to make our first trip to the summit. Sadly, it didn't work out."

A wave of grief overcame the receptionist, and he sat in the chair behind his desk. It was awkwardly quiet for a moment, causing Harper and Kwon to exchange glances.

She continued. "Benton, um, I'm sorry if I said something to upset you."

He sighed and shook his head with his eyes closed. "We lost two of our own at Everest a few weeks ago. They died in a horrible accident."

Harper ran with it. "There was an incident that forced the mountain to be closed before we reached the top. I hope it wasn't because of the two super-nice guys who told us about working here. Their names were Adam and Trent, I believe. Funny Aussies. Did something happen to them?"

Benton grimaced and nodded. "Yes. We learned about it from the

Security Police. When our friends didn't return from the climb, our research head called the police. A week later, two men showed up and asked a few questions. They only stayed a minute or two and then left."

"I'm so sorry for your loss," began Harper, putting on her most empathetic face. "They were great guys and really funny. They spoke very highly of the importance of your work here and their contributions as drillers of some sort."

"Yes, they worked for Black Diamond Drilling based in Melbourne, Australia. They were responsible for obtaining core samples out of the Guliya Ice Cap."

Harper was intrigued. "What exactly did that entail? We never got into the details with Adam and Trent. Mostly, we traded stories about our two countries."

"They were proud Aussies. You know, mates and all that. Anyway, I'd be glad to introduce you to their supervisory research scientist, who can fill you in. It's a little hard for me to talk about."

Harper caught Kwon's eye and winked as the young man exited the reception area. A moment later, Benton emerged with a small-in-stature Chinese man who introduced himself as Professor Yang Tandong. The three exchanged pleasantries, and Harper restated what had brought them to the TPE research facility. Professor Yang offered to take them on a tour.

CHAPTER TWENTY-SIX

Third Pole Environment Research Facility
Gar County, Ngari Prefecture
Tibet, China

"It was a tragic loss for us all. Not just because these young men were in the prime of their lives, but they had just made an extraordinary discovery." Professor Yang led them through a room full of cubicle workstations, where personnel sat in front of computers, inputting and analyzing data derived from the TPE's research.

Harper continued to take the lead, with Kwon remaining completely silent throughout the interaction with the TPE personnel. This allowed him to focus on their surroundings. Harper broached the subject of the police inquiry.

"We never really found out what happened at the summit. Benton mentioned the police came by and asked a few questions. Did they suspect foul play?"

Professor Yang shook his head. "No, not exactly. I was not part of that initial inquiry. However, I did receive a phone call, oddly, from the CDC in Beijing. They asked me several questions about

Mooy and Maclaren, especially about their travels prior to their trip to Mount Everest."

Harper gulped. She had to be careful to avoid alerting the professor as to why they'd come to TPE. Thus far, he and Benton had been chatty and forthcoming. However, one question too many and red flags might be raised.

"Had they traveled anywhere?"

"Not since their arrival here more than two months prior," he replied. "Well, other than for their core-drilling responsibilities on the Guliya Ice Cap."

"I wonder what made the CDC think the guys were sick. They seemed fine to us except, well, Adam seemed to have a bit of a cold, but he was taking medicine for it."

"We don't know either," said the professor. "The CDC person asked about who the young men had come in contact with and if anyone was exhibiting symptoms of the flu. The answer was no."

"What about animal contact?" asked Harper. *One too many?* She acted like she was only casually knowledgeable on the subject. "Don't many of these diseases originate in wet markets or by coming in contact with bats and such?"

"The CDC was curious about that as well," replied the professor. "There are no wet markets in Gar County or in any part of Ngari that I'm aware of. As for bats or any other mammals, during the time Mooy and Maclaren were drilling for core samples, it was February through April. Most, if any, wild animals are found at the Qiangtang Nature Preserve many miles away from the area where the drilling was taking place. Even then, the animals are mainly horses, deer, and pangolin."

Harper stopped and turned to Kwon to confirm he'd heard the professor's statement. He provided her an imperceptible nod and spoke for the first time.

"Professor Yang, would it be possible for us to see your core samples. I'm fascinated by the work you do, and I'm most interested in the geological aspect."

The professor was glad to turn his attention back to the research they undertook at TPE. "Certainly. We have a state-of-the-art cooler designed to maintain frigid temperatures to preserve the samples. Follow me."

As he continued taking them toward the rear of the complex, he explained a little about the geological aspects of their work. "Detailed ice thickness measurements of these alpine glaciers are of high value and importance for a variety of glaciological applications. For our purposes, by focusing on the Guliya ice cap, which is one of the highest and largest ice caps on the planet, we are able to study the glacier elevation changes in terms of depth and mass. This information is then extrapolated with temperature change data to generate a model based upon existing trends."

He paused and pointed to a pegboard wall full of oversized fur-lined parkas. The full-length jackets completely covered the wearer's body from head to ankle.

"We have a variety of sizes. Temperatures are far too cold to enter the cooler without one of these."

Kwon assisted Harper with her jacket and then indicated to the professor that they were ready. He opened the door, which resembled a walk-in freezer entry in the back of a full-service restaurant. Six-inch-wide plastic strips were affixed to the interior door frame and dropped all the way to the floor covered with nonskid rubber mats. Professor Yang pulled the strips aside and motioned for Harper, and then Kwon, to enter.

The Americans immediately began to blow smoke out of their mouths as their breath condensed into tiny droplets of liquid water and ice, creating a fog-like cloud. Harper shoved her hands into her pockets, where she found a pair of gloves. She took in her surroundings. Hundreds of cylinder-shaped hunks of ice were stacked on curved-steel racks. Each was toe-tagged, as she viewed it, with a small nail, a thin wire, and a red tag containing an identifying combination of numbers and letters together with a date.

Professor Yang stepped past them and spread his arms apart. "This is what we do. You see, during the last glacial period approximately fifteen to twenty-five thousand years ago, the ice sheet gradually covered the Tibetan Plateau. As this glaciation took place, annual average temperatures worldwide dropped nearly fifteen degrees. The impact on the climate, in this region especially, was profound.

"In addition, our research team hypothesizes an enormous uplift of Tibet took place following this glacial maximum. During a remarkable stretch of glaciogeomorphological discoveries in the last month, we can now confirm the Tibetan uplift, as it is known, was accompanied by a corresponding uplift of the Himalaya chain."

Harper's eyes glazed over, but she wondered how many points the thousand-dollar word *glaciogeomorphological* would garner on a Scrabble board.

"Is this the important discovery you referred to previously? You know, the one made by Adam and Trent?"

"Well, not exactly. Their core drillings led to this theory, but what they found is far more interesting. It's wholly unrelated to our studies here, but remarkable nonetheless. I will show you."

He led them through the stacks of ice samples and turned right at the end of the last row before approaching yet another, much smaller, walk-in freezer door. This entry was not equipped with the plastic strips, and perhaps it was Harper's imagination, but the interior temps were somewhat warmer.

Professor Yang flipped on a light switch and the fluorescent bulbs struggled to illuminate. After a series of flickers and fizzes, they lit up. He walked to the back of the cooler, where a shelf contained a single object covered in a blue tarp.

"Let me introduce you to Doggo."

CHAPTER TWENTY-SEVEN

Third Pole Environment Research Facility
Gar County, Ngari Prefecture
Tibet, China

Harper and Kwon cautiously approached the frozen creature lying on the shelf, with its toothy jaws spread open. Professor Yang expanded on his introduction.

"During the process of drilling through the ice cap to obtain samples, it's not unusual for the team to unexpectedly encounter soil, rock, and decayed plant material. While we do have geologists on staff who study these samples for a variety of reasons, it's not our primary focus here at TPE. In our twelve years of operation, we have never recovered a perfectly intact animal. This creature, which Mooy and Maclaren nicknamed Doggo, came from a sample on the Guliya Ice Cap near the base of the Kunlun Mountains."

He stepped past Harper and Kwon to grasp the actual toe-tag of the specimen. Like the ice cylinders, the frozen animal was labeled with certain identification markers but was bestowed with an actual name—Doggo.

Inside, Harper was ecstatic. She could hardly contain herself as she realized what this discovery meant. For decades, research epidemiologists had pondered the prospect of microbes and viral populations being locked within the depths of glacial ice around the planet. It represented a myriad of possibilities for scientific research while posing an interesting conundrum.

Her mind raced as she asked herself—*if these ancient pathogens were discovered and later released into a world that had not built up immunities to them, invading unsuspecting species, like man, could they be stopped?*

"Has this creature's remains been maintained in a frozen state the entire time since its discovery?"

"As far as we know," replied Professor Yang. "Adam and Trent returned the core drilling samples in the same manner as they always do. It happened to be on a weekend because they were working overtime to leave on that Monday for Mount Everest. None of us were here when Doggo was brought into the coolers."

"Have you been able to determine an age?" asked Kwon.

"Based upon the ice samples taken the prior week in the area, the glaciation in this particular region took place roughly fifteen thousand years ago."

"And this is your first discovery of an animal frozen intact?" asked Kwon.

Professor Yang crossed his arms as the three stared in wonderment at Doggo. "Yes. Today, the Tibetan Plateau is a vast arid grassland, home to species like the snow leopard, wild yak, and the Tibetan wolf, the most likely descendant of Doggo although today's species are somewhat larger.

"Of course, we haven't been able to discuss the details of this with the young men, but our staff believes the sample must have come from one of thousands of frozen rivers embedded deep within the Guliya Ice cap. At the onset of the Last Glacial Maximum, it was possible some mammals failed to migrate to the south before the freeze took place."

A young woman appeared at the entrance to the small cooler. "Professor Yang, there is an urgent phone call for you."

"Please excuse me. You're welcome to stay, but I'd ask that you not touch the specimen."

"Sure," replied Harper. Then she gathered the courage to ask, "What are your plans for Doggo?"

"To be determined. Frankly, the Chinese government doesn't know about the discovery. They'd immediately take Doggo to Beijing's universities for dissection. We have a couple of options in the United States, but nothing has been decided yet. Now, excuse me for a moment."

Professor Yang and the young woman left. Kwon stepped out of the cooler to confirm he and Harper were alone. He'd barely turned around when she hit him with her idea.

"I want him, Kwon. We need to figure out a way to get Doggo on the plane back to the States. I'm so pissed that my idea for our cover identified us as environmentalists or some such. I can't tell them the truth now. They'll throw us out of here and we'll never get to see Doggo again."

Kwon walked past Harper and stood immediately adjacent to Doggo's frozen remains. He bent at the waist to take a closer look at the animal's head.

"He's been thawed. Look."

Harper joined his side, and Kwon removed the gloves provided with the parka in order to point at certain aspects of the animal's head.

"Do you see this tear along his muzzle from the flew to just below the cheek? It was torn open. The ice crystals indicate the remaining moisture in the muzzle froze differently from the rest of the body. Also, note the two broken teeth. If this happened during the dog's life, or at the point of death, it's doubtful they'd be stuck to whiskers."

"Are you saying it was thawed and then refrozen?" Harper asked.

"Very possible. Yes. If that's the case, these two men may have been exposed to something, viral genomes, perhaps, that have never been discovered."

"Creating a novel virus …" added Harper, her voice trailing off. "This is the missing piece of the puzzle. We've got to come up with —" Harper stopped midsentence as she was interrupted by the sound of excited voices coming from the main cooler.

Kwon's tone of voice was urgent. "Harper, quick. We've got to go."

She didn't hesitate although she took one last glance over her shoulder at Doggo as they exited the small cooler. Rather than return to the main walkway leading to the back of the building, Kwon ducked and ran down a parallel row of core samples. He used the cover to avoid the oncoming contingent led by Professor Yang and two other people dressed in the parkas. Kwon studied their feet as they passed them going in the opposite direction. They were wearing spiffy white tennis shoes like the professor.

He motioned for Harper to duck into an empty space that was awaiting more core samples. The three figures walked briskly toward the small door entering Doggo's cooler. Kwon grabbed Harper by the arm and began to run toward the exit to the cooler. He wasted no time pushing open the door and slinging his jacket onto the floor. Then he retrieved his sidearm from the paddle holster concealed under his sweatshirt.

In the storage warehouse area, he noticed a side emergency exit with a push-bar handle. He hoped it didn't set off any alarms, but he didn't see that they had a choice. He burst through the door, his gun leading the way, expecting to find the building surrounded by security patrol officers or, worse, trained agents of China's Ministry of State Security.

Kwon breathed a sigh of relief when he found the vehicles were parked exactly where they had been upon their arrival. Earlier, out of precaution, he'd parked to the windowless side of the building so no bored or overcurious occupants of the TPE facility could stare at it while they worked.

With Harper hot on his tail, he jumped into the Roxor and drove off the property without garnering the attention of anyone, including the two TPE scientists smoking cigarettes near the front door.

Moments after they were out of sight and driving into town, Harper turned to Kwon. "Do you have a plan yet?"

CHAPTER TWENTY-EIGHT

Gar County, Ngari Prefecture
Tibet, China

Kwon parked between two utility trucks across the street from the Gar Health Bureau. It was lunchtime and the Happy Tea House was packed with patrons. Kwon placed an order for *sha phaley*, a traditional Tibetan snack created by wrapping seasoned beef and cabbage in bread, fashioning it into a semicircular shape like a pot sticker, and then deep-frying it. He also ordered a cup of hot sweet tea for the Southern girl.

"I've never had hot sweet tea," said Harper as she hungrily chomped into the sha phaley.

"They didn't have any ice. I asked and was told ice is only available in the most expensive restaurant in town."

Harper talked with her mouth full. "So much for putting Doggo on ice for the return trip to Kathmandu. I'm guessing the temps are mid-fifties. Right?"

"Yes. Even if we're successful in securing the remains, there's no way to prevent him from thawing out."

Harper pointed toward the windshield, with the last bite of sha phaley filling her mouth. "There's our answer—the hospital."

The Gar Health Bureau, a small hospital with two entrances, one for regular patients and the other for emergencies, only contained thirty beds and probably two or three surgical suites.

"What are you thinking?" asked Kwon, who waited for the delicacies to cool before eating. He'd inadvertently bit down on his tongue during the rock ride into Tibet. His first attempt to take a bite of the hot sha phaley had caused a searing pain to soar through his mouth.

"The hospital is small, but I'm sure they have a supply of body bags. Heck, Yeshi was able to find a couple in Lhasa, and that city was taking on a lot of diseased patients. Ideally, we'd be able to find a biohazard bag large enough for Doggo's remains, and then, as an extra layer of precaution, we'll wrap him in a heavy-duty body bag."

Kwon continued eating, but asked, "Do we need both?"

"If they're available. Those red biohazard disposal bags are usually one-and-a-half mil thick and tear resistant. If we couple that with the heavy-duty PVC vinyl material of a body bag, we should be able to keep deadly pathogens in as well as the stench from when Doggo begins to thaw."

Kwon finished his food and chased it with the now lukewarm sweet tea. "Something alerted those people back at the TPE. There weren't any vehicles around the parking lot that were any different than when we arrived. Either some type of fugitive alert came out through their social media or emails, or someone recognized us from a news report. It's hard to tell. As we walked through the facility, I tried to study everyone in the building to determine if anyone took particular notice of us. There were a couple of curious sets of eyes, but nothing obvious."

"Do you think the hospital personnel may have been alerted as well?"

"Possibly," Kwon replied. "Here's the plan. We both know we have to preserve Doggo's body for our safety and the rest of the world. We don't need to make any attempt to retrieve it before we have safety measures in place."

Harper pointed across the street and then shifted her body to face Kwon. "I know what we need."

"I do, too. However, I'm the one who has to get it."

"I can help," she insisted.

"Not this time. Look around us. How many Anglos have you seen here? Outside of the TPE building?"

"I don't know. A few."

"Harper, the answer is none. I've been looking. You stand out too much, especially because of your height. I'll go in through the ER entrance, using some type of distraction for cover. I'll bide my time, and once I'm in, I know my way around an ER well enough to find what we need."

Harper sat a little taller in her seat and looked at the clock on the Roxor's dashboard. "Do we have time? If Professor Yang reported us to the security police, they'll be all over that building."

"It is what it is," said Kwon as he rubbed his temples. "We have to hope they let it go and focus on what they do there. In any event, we need to wait for dark or the building to empty, whichever comes first."

"It doesn't get dark 'til almost ten around here. We'll lose our window of opportunity. Why don't we just get the body bags and go back there right away?"

Kwon sighed. "Two reasons. First, I don't feel good about shooting up a building full of scientists and environmentalists to get Doggo."

"Who says we have to shoot up the place? Let's go in with our weapons drawn. Round them all up and lock them in the cooler while we fetch Doggo. Somebody will find them later."

"This isn't some primetime TV show. Things always go wrong when you're dealing with that many hostages. Trust me. It won't work. I'd rather wait until the building is vacated."

"And what if it's guarded by the police or those MSS thugs we've dealt with?" asked Harper.

"That's different. They knew the risks of their jobs when they signed up. In my mind, they're enemy combatants, not civilians. Everything is fair game at that point."

Harper shrugged and nodded. "That makes sense. Should we get started? Once you've stolen the biohazard bags, we can go back to TPE and find a place to stake out the building."

"Now you're thinking. Preparation. Very important."

"Yeah, yeah. By the way, assuming the place is empty after closing time, the windows all had bars on them, and the only doors we went through were solid steel with no windows around them. How do you plan on getting in?"

Kwon managed a devious smile. "The agency gave us some tools that might help. We'll set up surveillance and I'll tell you what—"

A shrill ambulance siren could be heard in the distance. Kwon didn't say another word as he immediately exited the truck and dashed in front of light traffic across the street. A minute later, he was standing in the shadows of a roof overhang, nonchalantly looking around as the sound of the siren grew louder.

Harper slid across the front seats of the Roxor to get behind the wheel just in case she needed to move in to pick up Kwon. With a nervous grip on the wheel, she watched and waited as the ambulance raced toward the ER entrance.

Kwon followed the ambulance personnel into the building as they wheeled a heart attack victim on a gurney. Two family members, a grieving wife and a wailing daughter, were close behind. Kwon blended in with the family members as he feigned concern over the overweight man who lay unconscious on the gurney.

During the chaotic scene, he gradually eased away and was soon inside the heart of the small emergency room section of the hospital. The surgeons and nurses were all dressed in light blue scrubs. They were identified by clip-on administration badges. Several hospital visitors wandered the hallways. Some milled about outside surgery suites while others stood around loved ones waiting to be treated. Each of the loved ones had a clip-on badge clearly identifying them as visitors.

To avoid undue scrutiny, Kwon set himself up to accidentally bump into a distraught young woman who was walking briskly alongside her children in the hallway. Kwon stood to the side, monitoring her progress in a convex mirror mounted above the confluence of two hallways installed to prevent two hastily moved gurneys from crashing into one another.

As soon as she was close, he abruptly turned and met her head-on. She bounced into his chest and he quickly grabbed her shoulders to prevent her from falling. He apologized profusely and even patted the children on their heads with a smile. He also, with sleight of hand, stole the visitor's badge from the young boy's shirt.

Equipped with the proverbial hall pass, Kwon then worked his way up and down the corridor outside the surgical suites. As a former emergency room physician, he knew body bags were in the highest demand where patients were most likely to die.

It only took him ten minutes of playing cat-and-mouse with hospital personnel to find the right supply closet. He located exactly what he needed, in addition to a large white laundry bag. He shoved the biohazard bags together with some medical scrubs and skullcaps into the laundry bag.

A minute later, he pushed through a utility door at the rear of the emergency room and found himself in the midst of a secured area full of dumpsters and surrounded by chain-link fencing. After determining the area was not being monitored and that no hospital personnel were present, he climbed atop one of the dumpsters, jumped to the top of the fence and over until his feet hit solid ground. If anyone had observed his maneuver, they might have described him as a Korean Santa Claus with a white cotton bag full of toys.

Kwon did not walk directly back to the Happy Tea House in case he was followed. He casually strolled across the gravel parking lot until he reached a series of office buildings. He snuck between them to avoid being seen by several physicians leaving the rear of one of the office buildings.

By the time he'd made his meandering return trip to the truck, Harper was sitting alone and exposed in the parking lot, as the end of the workday was approaching. It was time to get into position.

CHAPTER TWENTY-NINE

Third Pole Environment Research Facility
Gar County, Ngari Prefecture
Tibet, China

Harper and Kwon parked on a hilltop overlooking the TPE research facility. They waited for hours, studying the civilians who left periodically as their workday came to an end. Kwon focused on the MV3 tactical truck parked half a mile away at a small hotel. The six-by-six utility truck had arrived with a driver and two passengers an hour prior. It appeared to be unrelated to the TPE facility, but it's close proximity and the soldiers' ability to react to a call for assistance had troubled Kwon.

The Roxor was capable of traveling off-road at a speed that couldn't be matched by the MV3. However, the key to their success was remaining undetected. There was simply too large a PLA presence in the area to risk a firefight.

As they waited for the last few stragglers to leave the building, Harper asked a logical question. "We have this Garmin to guide us. And the terrain to the west appears to be a whole lot flatter than the

Himalayas. Wouldn't it be easier to dash fifty miles into one of these neighboring countries?"

"I've thought about this as well," replied Kwon. "India, Pakistan, and even Tajikistan to the north would be an option. It's the unknown that troubles me. If we're on the run, we run the risk of being captured if we make a wrong turn or the GPS leads us into a dead end. Plus, Americans aren't exactly loved by the Pakistanis lately."

Harper leaned forward and squinted her eyes. It was getting late in the evening and the setting sun began to take away their ability to see from a quarter mile away where their vehicle was parked.

"Is that a guard?" she asked, pointing down the hill toward the back of the building.

"It is. There's another one milling about the front. Not military. Maybe private security or even their own personnel in uniform. They account for those last two cars we've been waiting on to leave."

"Do they have guns?" asked Harper.

"Can't tell from here. One good thing, though."

"What's that?"

"No perimeter lighting. It's not dark enough to use night vision, but it's too dark to see details. Let's get started."

Kwon exited the truck first and moved to the back, where he gathered what he needed to pull off the kidnapping of Doggo's remains. He shoved the biohazard bags into a backpack together with a variety of tools to assist in the break-in if necessary.

Harper's role was to watch his back as he worked. She would follow his lead and keep her silenced weapon ready to shoot anyone who threatened them. She'd become hardened over the course of the trip. Her life had been dedicated to saving lives instead of taking them. It was her experience escaping the DR Congo that made her realize her life was in danger when she went into these foreign lands. It was time to adopt the same survival mindset that came natural to Kwon—kill or be killed.

They moved carefully down the rocky slope toward the TPE compound. Kwon led the way, taking advantage of the night vision to find a path with favorable footing. They reached an area of thick scrub bushes that surrounded a waist-high block retaining wall. Kwon and Harper crouched behind it as one of the guards walked casually past them toward the opposite side of the building. They'd been timing his rounds—eleven minutes to circumnavigate the building. The second guard remained stationary at the front entrance.

With the guard out of sight, everything began to move quickly. Kwon leapt over the wall, followed by Harper. They sped toward the back side of the building, where a corrugated steel roll-up door separated them from the room where the ice samples were unloaded.

Seconds later, Kwon dropped to one knee and retrieved four large glass vials from the side pockets of his backpack. He motioned for Harper to stand at the corner of the building and be ready for a reaction from the guards.

He took a final look down the side of the building facing the road and then he removed his night-vision goggles. He readied the makeshift thermite grenades. He pulled back and threw one into the center of the steel door. The vials broke open and the pyrotechnic weapon did its work.

Thermite combines metal powders that act as a fuel and metal oxide. The two vials contained measured amounts of each. When then they were combined, the result was a chemical reaction creating an enormous burst of heat and high temperature. Enough to melt the steel door.

Kwon glanced toward Harper. The silhouette of her body was illuminated by the violent effect of the thermite. She remained calm as she peered around the corner of the building. Kwon checked his side again, and it too was clear. The chemical reaction of the thermite did not produce an explosion. It simply began to melt the steel.

He assessed the damage to the door. They needed a little wider opening as well as a path to step through. He pinpointed his next target and hit the mark with the second thermite vials. In a very short span of time, Kwon was able to melt an opening in the steel corrugated door, and the thermite reaction quickly consumed its meal before burning itself out.

The entire process took a minute and, other than the brief burst of light during the thermite's chemical reaction, it was relatively quiet. He waved Harper over and the two moved inside the building's garage area. The odor of the melted steel filled the enclosed space, invading their nostrils with a charred smell.

"This way," Kwon whispered as he once again donned the night-vision goggles. As they'd rehearsed while surveilling the facility, Harper rested her hand on his shoulder and allowed him to lead her through the darkness. They were able to move quickly into a vestibule not unlike the one they'd gone through earlier when they put on their oversized parkas. This go-around, they needed their arms free and simply relied on speed to minimize their exposure to the below-freezing temperatures.

Once inside the cooler where the core samples were held, Kwon got his bearings. During their earlier visit into the TPE building, he'd focused on observing the interior while Harper engaged the professor in conversation. This proved invaluable, as it reduced the time spent inside. Kwon immediately identified the walk-in cooler where Doggo was kept, and led Harper toward it.

Twenty seconds later, they were inside and he was able to turn on the lights for them. He rummaged through his backpack and retrieved a couple of towels he'd taken from the hospital supply closet.

"Here, use this to lift the ice. It'll prevent flash freeze to your hands."

Kwon opened the red biohazard bag first, spreading it apart so they could slide Doggo into it. He looked up at Harper, who'd carefully placed the bath-sized towel under Doggo's shoulders.

"I'm ready."

Kwon used his hands under the towel to lift Doggo's rear legs and back. "Lift."

Harper was unprepared for the weight of the frozen corpse. A frozen animal weighed more than after it had thawed due to the condensed water that had frozen around the body.

"Jeez," she complained as she hoisted Doggo off the shelf and steadied the frozen remains while Kwon guided it into the biohazard bag. Once it was tied off, they lifted it into the unzipped body bag. A moment later, Doggo was secured and they were ready to leave.

"Wait here," said Kwon. "This has taken too long."

"But we were so fast," Harper countered.

"No. Be ready."

Kwon's instincts were right. He exited the walk-in freezer and donned his night vision goggles once again. The large storage cooler was still dark, and a quick scan confirmed he was alone. He moved quickly along the back wall toward the vestibule door. He could hear muffled voices on the other side of the thick insulated door. He crammed the goggles in a side pocket and readied his weapon.

Just as he was reaching for the push-bar on the back of the door, one of the guards opened it for him. It gave him an opening to surprise the guard. He kicked the door open, slamming it into the man's body, which sent him tumbling to the floor.

The other guard stood just outside the thermite-melted roll-up door. Kwon didn't hesitate. As the man raised his weapon to shoot, Kwon sent two perfectly placed rounds into the guard's chest, killing him instantly.

The other guard tried to scramble to his feet, but Kwon pounced on him. He quickly clamped his hand over the guard's mouth and hissed in his ear, telling him in Chinese to be still and quiet, or he'd be dead. The older man vigorously nodded his agreement and spread his arms wide apart to indicate his surrender.

"On your feet," ordered Kwon in Chinese. He grabbed the man's wrist and wrenched his arm behind his back. "In here!"

He wrestled the man through the vestibule into a small clerk's office. He removed the man's jacket and then tore off his shirtsleeves. He used one to gag the man. After forcing the old guard to sit in the desk chair, Kwon tied his hands and feet to the chair using the remainder of the shirt and bungee cords hanging from a hook near a locker.

"I will be leaving here in thirty minutes," Kwon lied. "Do not move or I will kill you. Do you understand me?" Kwon shoved the silenced barrel of his weapon against the man's chest. He readily agreed.

Kwon rushed out of the small office space and pulled the door closed behind him. He raced outside with his weapon drawn to check the perimeter for activity. The other guard was dead, his chest containing two clean bullet holes near his heart. Because of the darkness and lack of perimeter lighting, Kwon saw no reason to hide the body. Now they faced the arduous task of carrying the hundred pounds of frozen dead weight up the hill to the truck.

Harper and Kwon worked together, taking one rest break during the nearly quarter-mile trek up the rocky slope toward the truck. In just that brief period of time, they could hear water accumulating within the biohazard bag as Doggo began to melt.

After they stowed their gear in the back and settled Doggo on the cushioned rear bench seat of the Roxor, they slowly drove back onto the highway and headed south along Q219 toward the Nepal border, feeling relieved, but apprehensive about the next three and a half hours until they entered the Annapurna Conservation Area.

CHAPTER THIRTY

China National Highway 219
Gar County, Ngari Prefecture
Tibet, China

Kwon stuck to the speed limit plus a few miles per hour. It was imperative that they make their way back to the Nepal border before sunrise. Fortunately, the traffic on the Q219 Highway was sparse and they didn't greet any military convoys on their way south. After a brief stop to relieve their bladders and pour the last of the extra fuel into the Roxor, the conversation turned to going home.

Harper was exhausted and concerned. "Doggo's remains will began to rapidly decompose as it thaws. I don't think we can wait several days for this charter flight full of rock-and-rollers to escort us to Japan. We need a faster way back to Atlanta."

"It's gonna take a day and a half no matter how we do it," added Kwon. "A direct flight, even if it were possible, would have to total seven thousand miles."

Harper fiddled with the Garmin Aero device. She began to input the information and provided Kwon the specifics.

"Well, eight thousand one hundred miles, to be exact. Looking at commercial flight options, we'd have to fly into Qatar and then to Kennedy. We'd arrive in Atlanta thirty hours or so later."

Kwon grimaced. "Any airline is going to want approvals and waivers from the FAA and Washington to carry that thing." He pointed his thumb toward the back seat.

"What about military options? Are there any jets capable of eight thousand miles nonstop?"

"Yeah, sure. But it requires in-flight refueling using a KC-135. Our F-22s and F-35s have boom receptacles capable of hooking up with the tanker. They could have our friend Doggo at Dobbins in Marietta in a third of the time."

"What's the closest U.S. air base to Kathmandu?" asked Harper.

"Probably Bagram in Afghanistan. Harper, I know what you're thinking. You can't just call up the Air Force and request an F-35. Besides, they have limited space. They're not designed for passengers and a half-frozen wolf."

"We can fly commercial," she argued. "If they can take the extra sixty pounds or so, I'm suggesting we send Doggo straight to the CDC and let them get started."

"Okay, but still. These things are very expensive. It would take an act of Congress to make something like this happen."

Harper reached into her pocket and retrieved the Blackberry issued by the CIA when they arrived in Beijing. "That's the plan. An act of Congress. I'm gonna call Joe and get the ball rolling."

"Are you out of your mind? First, placing that call might attract the attention of the PLA cyber army who have been searching for us. Second, I don't know if Joe has that kind of juice. They like him and all, but ordering up an F-35?"

Harper was undeterred. She pressed the space bar to illuminate the display on her phone. Just as she began to dial, Kwon stopped her.

"Did you change the SIM card like the CIA told us to do?"

"What? Aw, shit. I forgot. I was supposed to after we left China and snuck into Nepal. Does that mean they might have been tracking us?"

"Well, since you haven't used your phone since we came back in, I think we're good." Kwon dug into his pocket and handed over his phone to Harper.

"I'm sorry," she apologized. "I'm still learning all this spy stuff."

"That's what I'm here for. Call on my phone, but after you talk with him, let me explain what we need, okay?"

"Roger that, admiral."

Kwon chuckled and shook his head. Harper called Joe's cell. He didn't answer, so she left him a message advising him that the number on his display was hers. She told him not to call back but to watch for her return call ten minutes later.

Ten long minutes. Harper watched the seconds tick away on the Garmin. At the precise time, she dialed the call. The conversation between them was painful because they couldn't speak openly. Neither used their names, and they couldn't relay any kind of personal information. Harper promised to explain everything in a few hours, but for now, she desperately needed his help to arrange transportation of a package. She turned the phone over to Kwon.

"Hi. Please write this down. Panther. Kilo. Tango. Mike. Then Mike. Golf. Echo. Nonstop."

Joe acknowledged his understanding and disconnected the call without another word. Kwon took a deep breath and handed the phone back to Harper. He'd used military phonetics to identify the two airport codes for the pickup and delivery destinations. Panther was the nickname used by Air Force pilots for the F-35A fighter jet.

"Hold on to this in case he calls back," he began. He pointed toward the windshield. "We're about to lose our cover."

By the time they reached the gravel road leading into the mountains, the Roxor was awash in sunshine. Kwon and Harper remained on high alert for military vehicles, especially patrolling helicopters. They were barely twenty miles from the Nepal border, but soon they'd be moving at a snail's pace due to the uneven terrain and to protect their precious cargo in the back seat.

Periodically, Harper checked the Blackberry's display for lost calls. The tall rock walls of the ridges, coupled with the mountains that surrounded them, caused their satellite cell signal to be sporadic.

Mile after grueling mile, Kwon navigated the Roxor over the rocky surface. He was able to make better time on the return trip thanks to the full sun rising over the majestic mountains to their east.

"I think we just crossed the border," announced Harper. "We're good, right?" She wanted to relax.

"Not yet," replied Kwon. "If the Chinese military wants us, they won't care about a line on a map. We're not safe until we turn onto the main road leading back to Kathmandu."

Whomp. Whomp. Whomp.

"You had to go and say it," said Harper, full of apprehension. She craned her neck to look up through the windshield. The thunderous thumping of the approaching helicopter's rotors was especially loud in the bottom of the valley.

"Roll down the window and look behind us," ordered Kwon.

Harper wasted no time cranking down the passenger window, and slowly stuck her head out to look into the skies of Tibet. Off in the distance, a Chinese WZ-10 helicopter was hovering, its stub wings pointing directly at them with four missiles mounted underneath.

"Aw, shit, Kwon. They're pointed right at us. It's got missiles and machine guns mounted on the front. I mean, he's just sitting there watching us."

Kwon glanced in the side-view mirror and then picked up the pace. The truck rocked back and forth as he gave up on trying to make the ride comfortable. He had to put some distance between them and the chopper.

"He's still there, but he's not advancing," said Harper.

Kwon managed a slight smile. The WZ-10 was waiting on orders to cross the Nepal-China border or, in the alternative, permission to release one of its guided air-to-surface missiles.

"I just need a little longer," he muttered.

He continued on the rocky trail, and then he saw an opportunity to change course. He wasn't sure where the trail might lead, but he didn't intend to stay on it long. He just needed to put the fingerlike ridge between them and the attack helicopter. He pulled between the rocks until they were too narrow to continue. Then he shouted to Harper, "Quick, out of the truck!"

Harper didn't question him. She flung open the door and ran away from the truck into the crevasse in front of them. While she ran away, Kwon opened the back door, wrapped his arms through the nylon straps of the body bag that contained Doggo, and with a grunt, lifted the frozen animal onto his back.

He trudged along the trail until he saw Harper. "Keep going! Hurry!"

Harper turned and ran. Kwon lumbered along behind her, his breathing becoming shallow and heavy. They didn't have to run much farther.

Seconds after they squeezed into a narrow split in the ridge, a thunderous explosion shook the ground beneath them. Rocks and debris rattled off the sides of the mountain, striking them on their heads and shoulders.

Using advanced technology, the Chinese variant of the Hellfire heat-seeking missile had found its mark. In just seconds after it was fired, the Hellfire dropped to just six feet off the surface of the trail and followed the path taken by the Roxor. With the precision provided by artificial intelligence, it cut the ninety-degree left turn onto the trail and smashed the truck. The Roxor exploded into thousands of pieces and sent a ball of flames and black smoke into the sky.

The WZ-10 pilot wasted no time in racing away from the scene after the kill shot was confirmed. However, all he'd managed to do was destroy the evidence of their incursion into China. Harper, Kwon, and Doggo survived the attack.

Harper leaned her head back against the rocks, her hair matted with sweat. She tilted it toward Kwon, who still had a death grip on Doggo's body bag. He stared upward, a look of determination on his face as mind and body refused to decompress.

After a deep breath and an equally noticeable exhale, she asked, "Now can we go home?"

PART III

NOW THE REAL WORK BEGINS

Do or do not.
There is no try.
~ Yoda

CHAPTER THIRTY-ONE

Office of Congressman Joe Mills
Longworth House Office Building
Washington, DC

Joe disconnected his lengthy phone call with Harper and leaned back in his chair. He closed his eyes and thanked God for protecting her. Then, for the first time since she'd left for China, he allowed his emotions to spill out. Tears of joy and thankfulness filled his eyes as he thought of holding her again. He wished he could cancel his schedule and rush back to Atlanta. He wanted to be with her. Lay in bed all day. Binge-watch Netflix or Hulu. Or just talk.

Unfortunately, neither of them was in a position to relax. The hard work was just beginning for Harper. She'd gathered all the facts from the far corners of the Earth. Now, with her team assembled in Atlanta, she had to put the puzzle together and solve the mystery. More importantly, she had to set the wheels of the pharmaceutical industry in motion.

Some of the brightest minds in the world worked for the much-maligned *Big Pharma*, as the industry as a whole was called. As a politician, Joe understood why it was easy to hate the pharmaceutical industry. Prescription drug prices were absurdly high compared to the rest of the world. Executive salaries could be stomach-churning. Lobbyists treated Washington politicians like they owned them. By all media accounts, the biomedical industry had gotten greedy and overstepped.

Joe, on the other hand, looked at this from a different perspective, one that was based largely on his experiences from his father's death and how the COVID-19 pandemic had impacted the nation many years ago.

Regardless of which side of the political spectrum a politician sat, the uncomfortable truth was that a vaccine was the only real hope for preventing a global pandemic. Furthermore, only the pharmaceutical industry had the capital, human workforce, and physical infrastructure to create one. There was a big difference between waiting four months for so-called Big Pharma to create a vaccine and four years if governmental agencies tried to undertake it. In that length of time, millions of lives could be lost and trillions of taxpayer dollars spent.

To Joe, the cost of producing a vaccine, in other words, was priceless. If it meant that he had to hold his nose while pharmaceutical companies delivered the cures and vaccines upon which Americans relied to live, then so be it. The very economic logic employed to make rapid drug development possible in order to save lives also resulted in high drug prices and fueled the constant political outrage. They were, in actuality, two sides of the same coin.

For whatever reason, whether it was the political positions he'd adopted over the years regarding Big Pharma and the relationship it had with government or his support of the CDC, Joe was being bombarded by the media as well as his political opponents during this new crisis.

Sadly, Harper had been dragged into it unknowingly. While she was racing around China in search of patient zero, he found himself defending the political firestorm. He still had the support of his newfound friends courtesy of Herbert Brittain, the international financier and businessman. But they were also exerting intense pressure upon him to get his political house in order or, in the alternative, shift the narrative away from him.

In short, Joe needed to find a bogeyman.

The logical choice was the leader of the opposite political party, who was, at the moment, the President of the United States. The two had been sniping at each other for weeks, especially since that momentous night at the Brittains' home.

A second option, one that might garner him favor with independent voters, was to go on the offensive against China for yet again failing to disclose a deadly viral outbreak to the world. The U.S. had barely recovered economically from the COVID-19 pandemic. China had received a slap on the wrist thanks to their allies at the World Health Organization, and said slap was reduced in effectiveness as a result of a backroom, handshake deal with the current administration.

Joe and his chief of staff had had an extensive conversation about this before Harper called that morning. As Andy put it, "You have an opportunity to stand tough against the Chinese while throwing shade on the president at the same time."

After Joe hung up with his wife, he was ready to go on the attack. Beijing had just released a statement on the outbreak. It was far different from their prior denials. Joe presumed Harper and Kwon's success had forced the Communist Party's hand. The two brave doctors deserved a medal for their efforts; however, it had been agreed their endeavor would have to forever be kept a secret from the public.

Joe sent Andy a text asking him to schedule a 5:00 p.m. press conference. He wanted it to be carried live by the cable news networks while giving local news stations time to receive and edit the feed for their evening broadcasts.

He sat at his desk, looked over to the picture of Harper smiling back at him, and winked to her. She was his life, and he'd take whatever political risk necessary to advance the great work she did on behalf of humanity.

He reviewed the Communist state-run media reports of the last twenty-four hours. They talked about instituting measures to counteract the spread of the disease. They used direct attacks at the U.S. for allowing the Vegas virus, as their media called it, to infect the People's Republic of China. That morning, during a speech before China's elite Politburo, President Xi Jinping announced *a people's war to prevent an epidemic and vowed to seek sanctions against Washington for allowing this highly transmissible disease to infect China.*

Joe was tired of the propaganda. He knew that eventually, just as it did in 2021, the source of the deadly virus would be revealed. He wasn't going to wait years to take the fight to Beijing. The time was now and it would be the first of several foreign policy statements he'd be making to show the American people he was more than just a congressman who inherited his seat from his deceased father. He'd earned his seat at the table.

CHAPTER THIRTY-TWO

Capitol Rotunda
U.S. Capitol Building
Washington, DC

The U.S. Capitol Rotunda was one of the most recognizable locations in Washington. The large domed circular-shaped room was located in the center of the Capitol on the second floor. Standing one hundred eighty feet tall from floor to ceiling, the Rotunda was often used for ceremonial events. In recent years, as political grandstanding became commonplace, members of Congress made arrangements to stand beneath the beautifully painted canopy and surrounded by the walls holding historic works of art as well as a frescoed band depicting significant events in American history.

Joe had taken part in press conferences in the Rotunda in the past, but usually as part of House leadership announcing a major legislative initiative. His press conference today was designed to elevate his stature politically while simultaneously taking a jab at the administration.

In order to comply with House rules requiring a certain level of importance for reserving the Rotunda, Joe had his legislative staff quickly draft a House resolution to be submitted the next day. It's sole purpose was to impose sanctions on China for their malfeasance in hiding the extent of the novel virus outbreak in their country. He knew the proposed resolution might not make it to the House floor for a vote, but it showed he was making an effort.

After a few brief words in which he outlined how the Chinese had intentionally covered up this new virus, he agreed to take questions from the pool of Capitol Hill reporters.

"Congressman Mills, how does the present situation differ from 2020?"

"There is no difference, and therefore, their actions are unconscionable. China's failure to share necessary information with our CDC representatives before they were expelled—or the World Health Organization, for that matter—prevented our nation, as well as others, from instituting containment protocols."

"What would you ask of the Beijing government?" another reporter asked.

"First of all, I'd remind them of the historic pandemic their malfeasance caused just a decade ago. The way you deal with a pandemic is you practice transparency from the beginning. You share information as it becomes available, and you accept the assistance of the many experts from around the world. When it comes to infectious diseases, we shouldn't allow geographical or political borders to stand in the way of the investigation.

"Now, and in the future, China must be called upon to share the outbreak of a new disease with global research facilities so the world can start working on developing treatments and vaccines. China, as always seems to be the case, didn't do that in the present crisis. This lack of transparency and failure to share best practices, infection numbers and statistics with global health experts prevents our country, and others, from taking the necessary precautions at the onset of an outbreak."

"Congressman, you've been openly critical of the World Health Organization as soon as the first cases were reported in Las Vegas.

The president, on the other hand, has continuously praised their efforts. How do you reconcile this?"

Joe nodded and paused to ensure the reporters were paying attention to his response. As he spoke, he could hear Andy Spangler's Southern drawl in his ear saying, "*It's awwwn now.*"

"This administration has continuously allowed the Chinese to run roughshod over Americans, related to everything from the trade deficit, tariffs, and most importantly, our health.

"For example, China has a virtual monopoly on the exporting of basic antibiotic chemicals to the United States. Our pharmaceutical companies have a genuine concern that Beijing could use their pharmaceutical leverage to block critical components and supplies from our U.S. drug companies. As an active provider of active pharmaceutical ingredients, especially the basic components for antibiotics, for example, a stoppage of the supply chain could result in millions of American lives lost. Despite my very public calls for President Taylor to address this situation, he's done nothing.

"Furthermore, the president has stood shoulder-to-shoulder with the WHO in allowing China to skirt the sanctions placed on them after the COVID-19 pandemic. Even now, the Chinese have prevented any team of outside investigators to research the outbreak, and the WHO has failed to press the issue, an indication of China's widespread influence and intimidation tactics."

"Congressman, a follow-up?"

"Go ahead."

"Sir, the president stated in an interview yesterday that the Chinese have included the European contingent assigned to their CDC to participate in the investigation. A team was sent to the northeastern section of the country as they searched for the zoonotic source of the disease. How do you respond?"

"That's nothing short of subterfuge on the part of Beijing, and the president was remiss not to challenge them. It's the functional equivalent of a wild-goose chase, but rather, they're in search of yaks. They were intentionally looking in the wrong end of the country, as the source of the outbreak was Tibet."

Damn! Joe swallowed hard as soon as he made the statement. This was not public knowledge, and even the administration was not aware of this fact. Unfortunately, the statement had been made and the press pool was now abuzz. Joe was certainly guaranteed the airtime he'd sought, but maybe not in the way he wanted it to go down. Several reporters were now trying to get his attention, including those who'd already taken a turn.

"Congressman Mills!"

"Congressman, have you been briefed to this effect?"

"Sir, has there been a new development?"

Joe raised his hands to calm down the press scrum that was pushing closer to his podium. The camera crews on scene forced their way past the reporters, holding their cameras above their shoulders to get a clear shot of Joe.

"My office has been made privy to communications from within China that the Tibetan Autonomous Region and its capital city of Lhasa, in particular, is under siege by this novel virus. The circumstances there are so dire and the cover-up so extensive that the Chinese CDC has expelled our personnel from their facility and locked them down in the U.S. Embassy. Further, they purposefully put out misinformation that the source of the virus is yak meat. To cover up this lie, they sent European epidemiologists into Northern China, and the president willingly gave tacit approval by refusing to condemn their actions."

Joe tried to deflect by staying on the offensive. He deployed a little misdirection of his own.

"Congressman, can you point to specific reporting or an investigation that will confirm the outbreak in Tibet?"

"I suggest you start with the Central Tibetan Administration, the government-in-exile that is based in India. The Communist Party's cover-up is nothing short of genocide of the Tibetan people, and it has occurred as a direct result of their cover-up. It has further hindered countries like the U.S. from instituting control measures to prevent recent travelers to Tibet from entering our borders."

"Congressman, are you suggesting the president was aware of

this and didn't inform the public or act to prevent travel between our countries?"

"All I'm willing to say is he knew, or should have known. Had he held the Communist government's feet to the fire, this potential outbreak might have been averted. The bottom line is this. If the actions of Beijing run counter to our national security interests, we shouldn't stand for it. What I'm calling for should not be viewed as punitive measures. It's not about punishing the Chinese. It's about protecting the American people and our nation's interests."

Joe thanked them and slowly walked away from the microphone. By the time the 11:00 p.m. news aired, anyone concerned about another pandemic knew the name Congressman Joe Mills.

CHAPTER THIRTY-THREE

CDC Headquarters
Atlanta, Georgia

Harper and Kwon received a hero's welcome upon their arrival at the CDC campus in Atlanta that morning. After a good night's sleep at her home in Brookhaven, where she and Kwon managed to keep their eyes open long enough for a home-cooked meal courtesy of Miss Sally, they made their way into the city.

Kwon had had extensive conversations with Harper on the flights back to Atlanta. He wanted to see this investigation to its conclusion. Despite his vast experience in dealing with infectious diseases at DARPA, he'd spent little time in the laboratory setting. In addition, he'd never observed a necropsy, especially on a specimen as unique as Doggo.

Dr. Reitherman called everyone into his office for a debriefing before the necropsy was to be performed under the supervision of the CDC's Infectious Disease Pathology Branch, or IDPB. Becker arranged for coffee from the Emory Starbucks location and picked up a couple of dozen delicacies from Duck Donuts in Buckhead on her way to work.

Harper stood at the rear of Dr. Reitherman's office as introductions were made and pleasantries were exchanged. She was the common thread between this diverse group of professionals whose personalities were as unique as the positions they held.

Dr. Reitherman had already given Harper a heads-up that Becker and Dr. Boychuck had a tendency to butt heads. Well, it wasn't really butting heads so much as the two were polar opposites.

Dr. Boychuck was all over the place, disjointed. As Mimi would say, he was *every which way*, meaning he lacked organization or the appearance of having any kind of system in approaching his job. Harper knew better because she'd worked with him, albeit briefly, in the Clark County medical examiner's office.

However, for someone like Becker, who counted out her jelly beans and made sure they were all the same color, the mere thought of working alongside Dr. Boychuck sent her screaming into the night.

Yet the two of them had forged a working relationship and, despite their personality differences, managed to become friends as well. In the short period of time Harper had observed them that morning, the two teased one another incessantly. Their interaction could make for a new spectator sport or a reality television show.

Kwon was reserved as always, but he had an aura about him that commanded respect. Jokesters like Becker and Dr. Boychuck instantly recognized Kwon's type of personality.

It was kinda like a cat that knew a human was allergic or didn't particularly like cats. Felines, like children, sensed apprehension in a person. Similar to iron drawn to a magnet, the cat will seek out that person and do figure-eights through their legs. Likewise, a child will absolutely plop themselves on the lap of the adult who dreads the thought of the little monster being around. In the end, for both feline and child, the adult human succumbs and finds that it's not so bad.

As the debriefing continued and Kwon took the lead in recounting the events in China, the trio warmed up to one another.

Soon, the conversation centered around those three so much that Harper exchanged looks with Dr. Reitherman in which they both shrugged and smiled. Now she knew how a coat rack in the corner of the room felt.

That morning, a chemistry had developed between the five people in that office. They'd been through a lot as they performed their individual tasks as disease detectives. Now they were gelling as a group. It was time to take all the evidence they'd gathered and reach a conclusion.

The IDPB's work had always been a critical component in the detection, research and surveillance of emerging diseases. As a mysterious new pathogen presented itself, their job was to generate a post-mortem diagnosis. Reaching a definitive diagnosis for a new outbreak was essential for developing control and prevention measures, as well as understanding the disease's progression and, eventually, treatment protocols.

The pathologists within the IDPB used a variety of diagnostic techniques as they evaluated tissue specimens. Geneticists, microbiologists, and molecular scientists all rely upon the reports and findings of these talented doctors. Their work this morning would take Harper and her team one step closer to identifying this novel virus.

In every murder mystery, there was a scene where the medical examiner interprets markings, bruises, and injuries on the corpse to estimate a time and cause of death. This was Dr. Boychuck's bailiwick.

The public doesn't realize there is a very similar process in veterinarian medicine. Necropsies are the equivalent of a human autopsy, performed by both primary care veterinarians and specialized pathologists dedicated to identifying an animal's cause of death.

Like a human autopsy, the necropsy posed challenges for the pathologist. They needed to determine if the changes in the animal's body leading to death were caused by an inciting disease or if they were simply incidental to the manner of death. For example, older animals will have age-related issues, such as loss of muscle mass or cysts on their kidneys. Other changes were post-mortem, a natural result of the body decaying after death.

In nearby Athens, Georgia, was one of the premier veterinary medicine colleges in the nation. The University of Georgia was known for producing stellar veterinary graduates, including a regional expert—Dr. Les Sales.

Dr. Sales was an old-school vet who was just as comfortable birthing a calf as he was glued to a microscope studying the tissue of an ailing dog. He'd been called upon by the IDPB on occasion when a zoonotic disease was suspected.

Dr. Reitherman led Harper and the rest of the group to the pathology presentation room to meet Dr. Sales and his team. They planned on using a pathology lab that was surrounded by a protected gallery. It was used as a teaching opportunity for epidemiologists and pathologists alike.

The pathology operating room was safeguarded in the same manner as the BSL-4 laboratories. Nicknamed the *gross room*, in addition to performing autopsies, the pathologists would dissect organs, a process that left a bloody mess of tissues and fluids.

The process of disease detection usually began with an initial animal host. Diseases were naturally transmissible from animals to humans. If Harper's theory was correct, Doggo was the key to the novel virus that had killed the four index patients in Las Vegas as well as hundreds in Lhasa, Tibet. Dr. Sales hoped to provide her confirmation.

"Good afternoon, everyone," Dr. Sales greeted them casually. Along with the other pathologists handpicked to work on Doggo, he lent the appearance of an astronaut prepared to walk on the moon. So he could be heard clearly, his microphone was embedded in his protective helmet and was patched into the speakers throughout the gallery. Mounted high above the operating table were four flat-screen televisions suspended from the ceiling, providing the onlookers an up-close view of the necropsy. "I'd like to briefly walk you through our process."

Dr. Sales casually strolled through the room, looking upward toward the gallery to make eye contact with his guests. He was quite the showman.

"First, we will perform an external exam not unlike what vets do at their animal hospitals. Next, we will systematically open up the body and examine all the organs while they are still in the body cavity. This will help us identify any displaced or twisted organs. Naturally, during this process, we will collect tissue samples of every major organ for analysis by you folks.

"After collecting the samples, I'll remove each organ, examine it thoroughly, and incise it to look for internal lesions. Again, throughout this process, samples will be collected and preserved.

"Now, a word of warning, especially applicable to this particular case. As pathologists, we're able to successfully reach a diagnosis about seventy-five percent of the time based on examining the body, studying the tissue through a microscope, and performing more specific tests based upon possible causes of death.

"That's not to mean the other twenty-five percent of cases are a complete failure. Certain causes of death can be ruled out. And in the case of Doggo, our task is singularly focused on looking for evidence of disease and what possibly caused it.

"Here is our challenge with Doggo. This canine might well be thousands of years old. That said, his body is remarkably well preserved. Even with the rapid decomposition that has occurred since it began to thaw, we are looking at a remarkable specimen that will provide you the opportunity to analyze and interrogate the suite of trillions of microorganisms and other creatures that witnessed his death.

"And with a little luck, his stomach contents have not been

destroyed by decay, so we can determine what this old pup had ingested before his demise.

"When I have my findings, if the disease is found to be present in Doggo's body, it will be up to you to determine how this frozen corpse passed it on to humans.

"Now, let's get started, shall we?"

CHAPTER THIRTY-FOUR

Two months prior
The Guliya Ice Cap
Northwestern Tibetan Plateau
Tibet Autonomous Region, China

Glaciers form as layers of snow and ice accumulate on top of each other. Each layer is different in chemistry and texture, especially in the Himalayas. Wet summer snow is different from winter snow, which is much drier. Over time, the buried snow compresses under the weight of the snow above it, forming ice. Particulates, dissolved chemicals, plant material and animals that were captured during this process become a part of the ice. Layers of ice accumulate over seasons, years, and centuries, creating a record of the climate conditions at the time of formation.

Trent Maclaren and Adam Mooy, who worked for Black Diamond Drilling, were specialists in harvesting ice cores from some of the coldest places on the planet. These cylinders of ice were drilled from glaciers as well as ice sheets like those found on the Guliya Ice Cap.

The Third Pole Environment program hired Black Diamond to

pull these frozen time capsules from specific areas of the ice cap so their scientists could reconstruct the climate over a period of thousands of years.

That day, the two men were on a routine job along the base of a protruding ridge. They drove a large Arctic Cat pulling a trailer with several dozen insulated boxes. Some were already carrying the cores obtained from other locations, and the last six were awaiting the last drill of the day.

Because spring was approaching, they were able to use a thermal drill, which was more effective at coring through warmer ice than mechanical drills. A mechanical drill, designed to be used in extremely cold temperatures, was basically a rotating pipe with cutters at the head. As the drill barrel rotated, the cutters incised a circle around the ice to be cored until the barrel was filled with an ice sample. Mechanical drills had a tendency to chew up things in its path until the core was contained. The thermal drill generated a much cleaner, almost flawless cylinder.

As they filled the last half dozen insulated boxes, they were unaware of the archeological find buried deep in the glacier at first. They went through their routine, secured the cylinders, and made their way back in the frigid temperatures to the TPE research facility.

When a new shipment of ice cores arrived, the insulated boxes carrying the cores were quickly unloaded by the two men into the main archive freezer. Once the new ice samples came to thermal equilibrium with their new surroundings, they were carefully unpacked, organized, racked and inspected. After racking, they were checked into the TPE inventory system.

It was a weekend when the two men pulled their last ice cores out of the Guliya Ice Cap. Because there were no other personnel working, the two men, as they'd done in the past, handled the unpacking duties. It was during this task that Mooy noticed an anomaly in one of the glass cylinders.

"Hey, mate. Check this out."

Maclaren wrapped his arms around his chest to ward off the frigid temperatures in the huge freezer.

"It's just soil, mate. Not our problem."

"C'mon, take a closer look. Have you ever seen hairy dirt before?"

Maclaren cursed and then rejoined Mooy. He rubbed the ice crystals off the glass tube to get a better look.

"I'll be damned. It's a wolf. Or a dog or something. It sure isn't dirt."

Mooy slapped his friend on the shoulder. "Come on, mate. We've gotta check this out."

"What? No, we don't. Like I said, not our problem. Let's finish up our inventory paperwork and head out for Everest early. Right?"

"Mate, listen to me. This will make for an epic snap for Insta. We'll just record this one as being compromised. Those people won't care. Hell, they won't even look at these for months. Look around you. They've got hundreds of others to work on first."

Maclaren surveyed the cavernous freezer, and then he pressed his face closer to the cylinder to get a better look. "It is cool. Come on, you mope. Grab an end. Let's carry it into the exam room."

Mooy clapped his gloves together and dutifully grabbed the back end of the heavy cylinder. They made their way across the main archive freezer and entered the small walk-in exam cooler.

"Great, it's empty!" exclaimed Mooy. After the men set the cylinder on a worktable, Mooy made his way to the digital thermostat. He turned off the freezer completely.

"What are ya doin'?" asked Maclaren.

"We gotta thaw this thing out, right? It'll take a while, so let's go get our gear ready, load up the car, and by the time we get back, we can take some selfies."

"You're a crazy bloke, but you're the best I've got," said Maclaren with a chuckle.

Two hours later, they returned to the TPE research facility in jovial moods in anticipation of their upcoming trip to Mount Everest. They'd both had a couple of beers while they gathered their gear, and by the time they entered the exam room, they were feeling good.

The temperature in the room had reached thirty-six degrees Fahrenheit. The ice around the specimen had mostly melted, leaving a wet puddle on the floor. They took a minute to sweep it into a centrally located drain. Otherwise, when the exam room was brought back to freezing temperatures, a sheet of black ice would greet the scientists when they arrived back at the facility on Monday morning.

"Can you believe this?" asked Mooy. He began to pet the wolf's lush, velvety coat. "It's been suspended in time over thousands of years. Right?"

"Probably eighteen thousand, to be exact. I heard some of those smart guys talking about the age of the most recent ice cores. You, my best mate, are looking at an eighteen-thousand-year-old dog."

"Doggo," mumbled Mooy.

"What?"

"Well, he needs a name. I think Doggo sounds good."

"Fine by me. Let's get these snaps so we can hit the road. I'm losin' my buzz in here."

Maclaren retrieved his cell phone from his jacket pocket. At the time, he didn't know the iPhone was destined to fly out of his pocket and be lost forever in a snowdrift on the Kangshung Face. Then again, he didn't know that was what fate had in store for him, either.

"Look at the mush on this wolf! Let's get a head shot." Mooy tried to force Doggo's jaw open, but it was still partially frozen. Impatient, he gave it a little too much effort and caused the animal's lips, cheek, and muzzle to tear. Also, two teeth broke off from decay.

"Careful, you mope!" shouted Maclaren.

"Yeah, yeah. Watch this." Mooy stretched Doggo's mouth open a little more, causing skin and cartilage to rip. "Get the camera ready."

Maclaren got ready to take the shot. Mooy leaned over and place his head so that his neck was in the mouth of Doggo. His friend took several photographs, and Mooy quickly pulled his head away from Doggo.

"Wow, this wolf has some stinky breath. I inhaled enough of it to barf."

"Here," said Maclaren as he shoved the camera into his friend's hand. "My turn. I'm gonna be a lover and not dog food like you."

Maclaren leaned over, positioned Doggo's now thawed tongue over the side of his jaw, and pressed his face up against it.

"See? Wolf kisses. I'll send these to my girlfriend. You know, wish you were here. That sort of thing."

"Very lame, mate. But it's a good snap."

Maclaren looked around the room. "What are we gonna do with this thing?"

Mooy shrugged. "Here, fill out this inventory tag and tie it around one of his paws. I'll set the freezer back on negative ten. When they come in on Monday, they can figure out what they want to do with it."

"Not our problem," mumbled Maclaren for the third time.

When, in fact, it had become their problem, as well as one for the rest of the world.

CHAPTER THIRTY-FIVE

CDC Headquarters
Atlanta, Georgia

"Well, look who's here," Harper began sarcastically as she entered Dr. Reitherman's office. She was the last to arrive after spending a final minute or two with Dr. Sales and followed by last-minute instructions to the epidemiologists led by Becker. She smiled at the shorter agent, who returned the gesture.

"Good afternoon, Dr. Randolph," greeted the CIA agent who'd met with Harper on two prior occasions. Each time, he'd used a different surname. Once, it was a city near East St. Louis, Illinois. The second go-around, he'd chosen a name based upon a small town east of Augusta, Georgia, that was easily recognized by Harper.

Harper couldn't resist. "You know, your counterparts in Beijing and Kathmandu are far less mysterious than you two. But, let me say, they were every bit as helpful. Listen, I never quite understand the standoffish, you-look-suspicious-to-us approach you guys take. Maybe they teach you that at Quantico? I don't know. Anyway, if it wasn't for you speaking to your superiors, Kwon and I would never have been able to locate Doggo."

"We try to help when we can," the senior agent replied. "We've spent some time with Dr. Li already. He's provided us valuable intel on this underground network of dissidents operating in Urumqi. That will be very useful to our psyops people."

Since the Korean War, the Central Intelligence Agency had engaged in psychological operations designed to convey selected information to citizens in foreign countries to influence their emotions, motives, and objective reasoning.

Likewise, in the present day, the Russians and Chinese were extraordinarily adept at manipulating the American public and its government officials. The advent of social media and its users' reliance on news reports posted to sites like Twitter, Facebook, and Reddit made Americans especially vulnerable to disinformation campaigns.

By the time Facebook became the largest social media network in the world with more than one billion users in 2012, there were signs of moral decay and societal collapse. During 2020 as the nation was battling the deadly COVID-19 pandemic, animus was so high, pundits and historians alike wondered aloud whether the U.S. was headed for a second civil war.

Harper asked, "Can we use those people to get the word out in Tibet and Xinjiang about this virus? Many in Lhasa are aware of what's happening, but those in the countryside are kept in the dark. The same seemed to be the case in Xinjiang."

"Absolutely," responded the senior agent. "Obviously, the agency uses psyops to effectuate regime changes in dictatorships around the world, but we also have humanitarian motives. Your experiences in China are very valuable to our approach and to the nation's foreign policy."

Dr. Reitherman glanced at his watch. A conference call was scheduled with the mayor of Las Vegas in thirty minutes. "These gentlemen wanted to get your final take, or at least your educated opinion, on any bioterror component to this."

"I know that was a concern of yours early on. Truthfully, the facts don't support it. I firmly believe the disease originated with the canine host—Doggo. However, that doesn't mean it wasn't studied and manipulated by their scientists. It's still too early in the outbreak, at least in our country, but a telltale sign to watch for in the future is whether this novel virus mutates.

"Because it is so new, mutation is to be expected. If it doesn't, then there's a chance it was engineered by the Chinese scientists. The next logical conclusion, of course, is that they used human carriers as weapons to introduce the virus onto our soil."

"But not with the four soldiers whom we confirmed to be part of their elite Siberian Tigers unit?" asked the younger agent.

Harper replied, "No. They just happened to be at the wrong place at the wrong time. Due to their lack of experience with handling disease-infected patients, they easily contracted it from patient zero, or each other."

"Anything else, gentlemen?" asked Dr. Reitherman.

"No, sir," replied the senior agent. He managed a smile. "Dr. Randolph, it was a pleasure to work with you and I trust you'll keep us abreast of your findings."

"I will."

The other agent spoke up. "Also, will you please send my regards to your husband. I'm sure he wouldn't remember me, but before I joined the agency, I was with the Secret Service assigned to the Longfellow building where his office is. We crossed paths many times in the hallways and he always took the time to say hello. I can't say that for most of our elected officials."

Harper beamed. She loved to hear nice things said about her husband. After they'd spoken last night before bed, she'd googled his name to see what kind of news stories were written about him. She was furious within minutes after scanning the headlines and ended up tossing her iPad across the room into an overstuffed chair. Politicians and the media disgusted her most times.

The two agents left and Kwon excused himself to check in with his superiors at DARPA. After he left, Dr. Reitherman gestured for Harper to get comfortable before Dr. Boychuck arrived.

"Do you realize this is the first time you and I have been alone all day?" he asked.

Harper scowled and thought for a moment. "You know what, you're right. It's been a helluva day."

"Tell me about Kwon."

"He's an aberration. He's part robot, part supercomputer, part warrior, part human. In that order."

Her description drew a laugh from Dr. Reitherman. "He was brutally honest and detailed about your time in Beijing. Had I known you'd be going through all of that, I would've strapped you to that chair and fed you through a tube to keep you from leaving for China."

"I haven't told Joe everything. Might not for a long, long time. Then again, I suspect he knew I'd be facing trouble, which is why he chose Kwon to come with me. He pulled me out of the line of fire more than once."

"I heard. Kwon also said you had to use a gun. He didn't provide details, but it was clear you shot and killed people. Are you okay?"

Harper averted her eyes and shrugged. She really hadn't had time to think about it. "You know, everything happened so fast and we were constantly on the run defending ourselves. Look, the way my brain processed everything, it all was simple. I didn't want to die, so I had to make the person trying to kill me die first. I believe it would be different if I tried to walk up to an innocent human being and shoot them. I doubt I could pull the trigger in that case. Over there, it was almost second nature."

Harper had a déjà vu moment during which some recognition of those words seemed familiar. It wasn't that she might have said them, but possibly she'd heard them before.

"Well, I bring it up because I know you will start to get back to a normal life, at least for you anyway. If you find yourself having difficulty with, you know, that part of your investigation, we have people on staff to talk to."

Harper shook it off. "Nah, I'm good."

There was a gentle knocking at the door, and Dr. Reitherman's secretary stuck her head in the door. "Doctor, that charming Dr. Boychuck is here to see you."

From the reception area, the eccentric pathologist could be heard. "Yes. Yes. Yes. Charming, suave, and debonair!"

Harper chuckled. If Becker had been there, her eyes would have rolled right out of her head.

CHAPTER THIRTY-SIX

CDC Headquarters
Atlanta, Georgia

"Woolie, please come in." Dr. Reitherman heartily greeted his new friend. In the short time Dr. Boychuck had spent on the CDC campus, he'd made quite an impression with his knowledge of forensics and pathology. Certainly, the CDC's own team of pathologists were top-notch, but Dr. Boychuck brought a level of street smarts with him because he'd examined so many different kinds of cases.

"Thank you, good doctor." The eccentric medical examiner was in a jovial mood. He turned to Harper. "Ah, Harper. I must say the unearthing of that ancient animal was quite an accomplishment. Watching your talented pathologists work alongside Dr. Sales was a real treat. He has promised me an opportunity to perform a necropsy with him in the future if the situation arises."

"I hope it yields the results we need. Doggo's discovery by the two Aussies may have been a zooarcheologist's dream, but it has turned into an epidemiologist's nightmare."

Dr. Reitherman gestured for them to take a seat. They still had a few minutes before the mayor was supposed to call in, so he initiated some small talk.

"Harper, are you aware that Woolie and I both have roots in the Old Country?"

"Which one?" she asked innocently.

"Germany, of course," replied Dr. Boychuck. "My family was originally from the Bojko mountains in Western Ukraine. When the old Soviet Union forces overran Ukraine in the early 1920s, my family fled across Poland and settled in Bavaria outside Munich."

Dr. Reitherman joined in. "My great-grandfather lived in Munich, where he raised four sons. As Hitler began his rise to power in the early thirties, the entire family emigrated to New York. He saw the threat posed by Hitler's brand of nationalism and left the country they loved."

"Yes. Yes. Yes. A very smart decision, indeed. My family, as Ukrainians, only knew oppression and overbearing government. The Soviet influence over Ukraine prior to our leaving for Bavaria was becoming unbearable. As we Americans say now, the Boychucks jumped from the frying pan into the fire. Two of us died in World War II, ironically, on the Russian Front in Poland."

Once again, Harper marveled at how the people from seemingly different backgrounds and personality types came together for a common goal—fighting disease. She had a question about those last days of Hitler's reign of terror when Dr. Reitherman's secretary buzzed in. Mrs. Mayor was on the phone.

Dr. Reitherman placed the call on speaker. "Good afternoon, Madam Mayor. I'm Dr. Berger Reitherman. Thank you for calling."

"Well, now," she began. "It appears my diplomatic emissary has fallen down on the job. Woolie, are you there or at least partially present?"

He laughed. "Yes. Yes. Yes. I am here, Mrs. Mayor."

She briefly chastised him. "Why have you not instructed this nice doctor to refer to me as Mrs. Mayor? Hmm?"

Dr. Boychuck began to stammer. Mrs. Mayor had an effect on him that Harper couldn't quite place her finger on. She wondered if they had some kind of history other than that of mayor and coroner.

"Yes. Yes. Yes. Of course, Mrs. Mayor."

Dr. Reitherman was enjoying watching Dr. Boychuck squirm. "Mrs. Mayor, my apologies. Woolie did tell me this and I forgot."

"Hmmm. Well, you're excused, but Woolie is not. That will be determined by this phone call."

"Hi, Mrs. Mayor! Dr. Randolph here."

"Harper, you lovely young woman, it's good to hear your voice. I want you to know that I ripped a new one in that overweight, windbag governor of ours in Carson City over the way you were treated while in our fair city. When this is over, I hope you'll be my guest sometime. I've seen your husband on television. He's quite the firecracker. We need a passel more like him in DC, I'll tell you that."

"Thank you, Mrs. Mayor. I'll tell Joe he's got your vote." Harper inhaled as if she were trying to draw that last statement back into her mouth. It was such a common phrase as it related to politicians. She doubted—no, she hoped the others didn't place a broader meaning to it.

"Count on it," she said. "Anyway, I've got the governor on the run as it pertains to his stupid lockdown maneuver with the National Guard. People in the valley, from dishwashers to casino operators, are up in arms. Not just the ones working the Fremont Street casinos and hotels. This had a chilling effect on our entire economy. Tourism dropped seventy-five percent immediately. Despite our best efforts, we couldn't convince people to come back."

Dr. Reitherman took the lead during the conversation with the somewhat cantankerous mayor. That was fine by Harper, as she hadn't fared so well in a prior conversation with a politician while in Las Vegas.

"We understand, Mrs. Mayor. How may we help?"

"Can you issue a statement to the effect that there is no cause for panic or concern? We need the CDC to quieten down the frightened mob."

Dr. Reitherman glanced at Harper, who remained silent. While she agreed the National Guard presence on Fremont Street had been premature, it was also impossible to declare an *all clear* at this juncture.

"Mrs. Mayor, the investigation has developed rapidly over the last twenty-four hours, but there is still work to be done. Once our final determination is available, there are channels to follow. In this case, the director of the CDC will be in communication with the White House."

"He started this debacle! You know that, right? That fool in Carson City doesn't take a crap without Taylor's approval. Just the other day, he was interviewed on the local news demanding everyone stay six feet apart and wear masks practically twenty-four seven. Lo and behold, some locals snapped a picture of him maskless at the Bella Vita down in Henderson, yuckin' it up with some of his political cronies. Busted!"

Dr. Boychuck burst out laughing and Dr. Reitherman's face broke out into a huge smile.

Harper covered her mouth to stifle her laugh. She instantly imagined Ma, Mimi, and Mrs. Mayor having tea in the ladies' parlor at Randolph House. Those three would send the ghosts to the neighbors' for a few days.

Dr. Reitherman continued. "Mrs. Mayor, if you could hang tight for a few more days, we might be able to issue a statement one way or the other. Might I suggest a few measures that aren't too restrictive but might also provide your visitors a level of comfort?"

"Yes, absolutely."

"You know, they are pretty extensive. I'll have Harper's assistant email them to you by the end of the day. Implementing things like thermal temperature cameras, plexiglass shields at the gaming tables, and having EMTs on site go above and beyond the expected safeguards like disinfectants, social distancing, and free face masks."

"I'll take all the advice you can give us. We need people's fannies back in those casino seats."

Dr. Reitherman continued. "Mrs. Mayor, I have a request if it is okay with you."

"What would that be?" she asked.

"May we borrow Woolie for a little while longer? We have more presumptive positives being sent to us from around the country, and I'd like him to be a part of each autopsy. He has an eye for detail that will help expedite our investigation."

She began to laugh. "You can keep him as long as you'd like, but you have to feed him!" She burst out laughing as she finished her statement. Dr. Boychuck sat a little taller in his chair, attempted to suck in his protruding belly, and shoved a half-eaten Snickers bar into his lab coat pocket.

"You've got a deal. Thank you, Mrs. Mayor. I look forward to speaking with you soon."

"T-T-F-N," she said as she disconnected the phone.

Both men in the room had a perplexed look on their faces, so Harper explained, "T-T-F-N. Ta-ta for now."

She'd heard Mimi say it a million times, and Tigger did, too.

CHAPTER THIRTY-SEVEN

CDC Headquarters
Atlanta, Georgia

Harper stole away from her coworkers for the first time all day. Everyone was assigned a task and she was the quarterback, roaming from floor to floor of the main building, asking for updates and giving direction. This was crunch time. That critical period where all the facts came together and the CDC was prepared to make its official determination.

So many questions ran through her mind as she sat on the floor of a vacant conference room with a can of Red Bull in her hand. *How lethal is this virus? Whom does it kill? Why are some spared? Are the new patient counts accurate—and, if not, are they overstated or understated?*

Estimates derived from their early cases indicated a lethality slightly higher than influenza. Becker's most recent numbers pointed to an infection fatality rate as high as one and a half to two percent. A death rate in that range meant this novel virus might kill more than six million Americans.

Naturally, Harper knew that even under the worst-case

scenarios some people would never be exposed, and others might develop a natural immunity, preventing them from being infected at all.

Calculating fatality rates was complex, and the numbers were almost always skewed early on in an outbreak because seemingly healthy, asymptomatic patients don't get tested for a disease even though they were carriers. Harper had observed this with the COVID-19 pandemic.

Some people who were infected had no symptoms or only mild ones. Even those with more severe symptoms resisted going to the hospital due to lack of insurance. Many of those recovered on their own. Others didn't fare so well.

With the data received thus far, Harper was comfortable that she had a clear view of the tip of the iceberg—those seriously infected patients who required hospitalization. The troubling number, the unknown, was the number of Americans who had mild or hidden infections. She referred to them as the *a-syms*, for asymptomatic patients. Like the silent but deadly pathogen within them, the a-syms walked among healthy people, wholly capable of spreading the infection to others.

Harper buried her face in her hands for a moment and then pulled her hair back behind her ears. In her mind, she was already preparing a statement for the press. People who were already showing symptoms—such as fever, cough, or difficulty breathing— could be identified, isolated, and treated.

First and foremost, she had to stress a containment strategy for those patients who presented with symptoms. She imagined a busy city sidewalk or a grocery store in which a-syms walked around spreading the virus to others. This was determined to be the case with COVID-19. For years after the pandemic was declared over, scientists continued to gather data. It was determined that the coronavirus was transmitted on average 2.55 days to 2.89 days before symptom onset. For days, a-syms comingled with healthy patients and shared the virus, infecting everyone they came in contact with.

Years of study revealed the hidden part of the COVID-19 iceberg was huge. Many people who were infected with SARS-COV-2 didn't even know it. When the final tallies were made, the CDC determined the actual fatality rate of COVID-19 to be 0.26 percent of people it infected or about one in four hundred. The COVID-19 fatality rate turned out to be far lower than the seasonal flu. In the meantime, the economic damage to the world economy had been done.

Harper shook her head as she pushed off the floor to stand. She drained the last of the Red Bull and dropped it into a wastebasket in the corner. The lesson learned from 2020–21 was a simple one. *Fear and panic are more dangerous than the disease itself.*

She emerged from the conference room and immediately ran into Becker in the hallway. She was dressed in all white scrubs with a mask dangling under her chin. The safety goggles propped on her forehead completed her mad scientist look.

"There you are. I've been looking all over for you. We have some preliminary results from our geneticists."

"That's exciting," quipped Harper.

"Yeah, no doubt," Becker said with a laugh. "Talk about boring. Whew! Anyway, do you mind walking with me while I explain?"

"Lead the way, Doc Brown," replied Harper.

"Who?"

"You know, Dr. Emmett Brown, the loony scientist from the *Back to the Future* movie."

"Before my time," said Becker dryly.

"C'mon, Becker, it was before my time, too. Don't you watch classic movies?"

"Sure, just not that one. Do you wanna hear about this or not? It really is fascinating."

Becker opened a file folder she was carrying and thumbed through the pages until she found the report she was looking for. She continued.

"Okay, so, Woolie and I have been puzzled by the known patient profiles. The victim's ages, demos, medical conditions, etcetera absolutely defy logic. We needed to know why the virus is provoking only mild symptoms in some people while severely sickening or killing others."

"I take it you have an answer."

"Taking into account we are very early in this outbreak, we've started to form a hypothesis based on two commonalities. One is a person's blood type. Patients with Type A blood had a fifty percent greater chance of suffering severe symptoms that required oxygen or a ventilator."

"That's odd," muttered Harper. She was focused on Becker now, putting aside all the other aspects of the investigation that were running through her mind.

"Yeah, a real head-scratcher. Our working theory is that the location on the human genome where blood type is determined also contains a stretch of DNA that can trigger strong immune responses. The genetic variations associated with Type A blood seems to lead to an overreaction in the immune system, causing extensive inflammation and lung damage."

Harper asked, "Tell me about the demographics of the known cases. Is there a trend based upon race?"

"Thus far, this disease has proven to be an equal opportunity bug. Despite the fact that the Type O blood patients, typically non-whites, seem to be catching a break, the patient counts reveal there is no definite trend across racial lines."

"Viruses don't discriminate," added Harper. "What's the second common factor?"

"The eggheads have homed in on six genes in the genome that could be influencing the course of the virus. They're not sure which one is controlling the virus's ability to attach to cells."

Harper abruptly stopped in the middle of the hallway. "Becker, where are we going?"

"I think you need to go talk to the eggheads."

CHAPTER THIRTY-EIGHT

CDC Headquarters
Atlanta, Georgia

Nearly two centuries ago, scientists used a live virus from another animal species to combat smallpox, one of the most lethal human pathogens ever known. In the intervening years, science had provided the tools to intentionally produce in the laboratory other live viruses capable of protecting against their more lethal siblings. Through the use of genetic engineering, mutations in viral genomes were created to battle the misery of human infectious disease. Despite these leaps in scientific study, the efforts designed to eliminate infectious diseases from impacting society could not outpace emerging novel viruses.

Harper stood among the geneticists who were gathered in a small conference room with walls made entirely of whiteboards. Dr. Sanjay Chandra, a molecular biologist and former professor at Oxford, had the floor.

"Welcome, Dr. Randolph," he greeted her with a smile and a nod.

"Thank you for allowing me to listen in. I understand you've made some progress."

"Yes. You're just in time. Let me explain."

Dr. Chandra turned to the whiteboard and began to make scribbled notes using several different colored markers. He lent the appearance of an out-of-control orchestra conductor as he furiously wrote on the whiteboard. After a moment, he turned to the group.

"We have learned, as is always the case, that viruses attack cells they recognize. This novel virus identifies specific receptors that are present on the body's cell surfaces.

"Now, this virus, like so many others, evolved by borrowing and modifying cellular genes. Like other pathogens, it depends on specific cellular functions for its replication and survival in its hosts, both animal and human. Some of these functions required for viral replication are expressed in most cells, although there are exceptions not pertinent to this case.

"The human body has its own defense mechanisms. We have learned that this virus forms two groups, those that infect organs at or near a portal of both entry and exit, such as body orifices. This group multiplies efficiently and eventually yields to the body's immune response. However, the second group is more powerful and potentially deadly. It remains after the infection and remains in a passive state for the life of the host. This second group leads to herd immunity, a critically important stage required to burn out a pandemic.

"I've been told Dr. Randolph went to extraordinary lengths to answer the question of where this virus originated. Our specimen, *Canis lupus*, the wolf known as Doggo, has now been confirmed as the intermediary host of this virus. Genome studies confirmed the disease was passed along to Doggo from the source animal.

"Our first suspect was *Rhinolophus*, the common horseshoe bat. We compared the genome sequence of Doggo's remains to RATG13, the coronavirus commonly found in horseshoe bats. The genetic markers were insufficient to make a determination. We then conducted an analysis of other viral groups known to the region, including Western China, India, and Pakistan. One has to remember, this creature's remains are fifteen thousand years old based upon our estimates. The world was a different place then.

"First of all, we learned bat genomes can be ruled out. We ran hypotheticals, genetic marker comparisons, and even took into account the intrusion of other animals that may have been in the region at the time of Doggo's demise, such as civets and camels. None created a match."

Harper fidgeted. While she was interested in the science behind Dr. Chandra's conclusions, she was a bottom-line kind of gal, as was Becker, who leaned into her boss and whispered, "Just land the damn plane already."

Harper allowed a slight smile and nodded. Dr. Chandra continued as he prepared for landing.

"We then looked to animals prevalent on the other side of China and found a genetic match. On the basis of our genetic analyses, we've determined the original host was none other than the scaly ant-eating pangolin. Today, this long-snouted mammal is rarely found in Western China, so it was initially overlooked as a culprit.

"Our conclusion, based on the genetic comparison of viruses taken from Doggo and from humans infected in the early stages of this outbreak, is that the genetic sequences are ninety-nine percent similar. We are now able to publish our report and formally pass this data on to Dr. Randolph."

Spontaneous applause erupted among the geneticists. Harper and Becker glanced at one another before joining in the celebration. From this point forward, rather than trying to solve the mystery of this virus from the most recent patient to its beginnings, Harper's team was capable of rapidly filling in the blanks.

She thanked Dr. Chandra and the other molecular biologists in the room. She turned to Becker and nudged her arm.

"While they finish their report, let's see what we can do about treating these patients."

CHAPTER THIRTY-NINE

CDC Headquarters
Atlanta, Georgia

Harper and Becker made their way to the den of epidemiologists. More than a dozen disease detectives worked alone, or collaborated, on various aspects of the investigation. As soon as they entered the laboratory, heads turned and she was given a hundred percent of everyone's attention.

"How's it goin', guys?" she asked casually.

The senior-most epidemiologist, who had remained in Atlanta while a much larger contingent of the Epidemic Intelligence Service had been dispatched to Las Vegas and Los Angeles, left his desk and greeted the new arrivals.

"As a matter of fact, Dr. Randolph, we have the invisible enemy in our sights. Would you like to see?"

"Damn straight," she replied with a laugh.

He motioned for her and Becker to join him at a single workstation containing a large electron microscope. She rolled a chair in front of it and offered it to Harper, who chose to stand.

"It's a phenomenal image of a dying cell infected with the virus. Take a look."

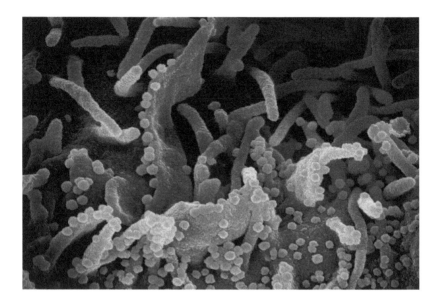

"It's amazingly crisp," commented Harper.

"I like to generate images to convey that this is a living entity in an effort to demystify it, making it tangible for people," the CDC's leading electron microscopist explained.

"It's a creature," muttered Harper, echoing Dr. Boychuck's words when the two first met in Las Vegas.

"Yes, in a way, it certainly is. It has purpose, although not conscious like most creatures. We often refer to it as the invisible enemy because it is during the early parts of our investigation."

Harper stood back and allowed Becker to take a turn at the microscope. "It's devouring the cell."

"Indeed, it is. You're looking at a world that people can't get to see. This particular image represents a sample ten thousand times smaller than the width of a human hair. It's one-billionth our size."

"It's difficult not to be awestruck," Becker added as she stepped away from the microscope.

The microscopist agreed. "Despite the deadly nature of the viruses, I've come to appreciate the beautiful symmetry in many of them. They're elegant and not malicious in and of themselves. They're just doing what they do. Devour."

Harper asked, "What can you tell us so far?"

"This particular virus has an elaborate biological structure, but it also has weaknesses that can be exploited. It's these weaknesses that will lead you to developing a treatment protocol and a vaccine.

"In the example you just viewed, the larger folds and contusions represent the surface of a diseased kidney cell from one of your Las Vegas index patients. The dozens of small spheres emerging from the surface are the virus particles themselves."

He waved to get the attention of a member of her staff.

"Yes, sir?"

"Please bring up the image taken from Doggo's kidney, and give me a side-by-side on the center wall monitors."

The epidemiologist nodded and scampered back to her desk. A moment later, a second image appeared. It was similar to the first except the virus particles were more clustered.

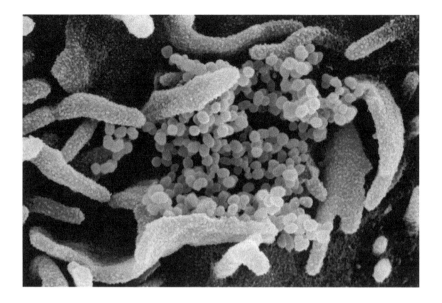

"The difference between the two represents the stage in which the hosts were under attack. Doggo's sample, revealing the close cluster, indicates the wolf had been infected a relatively short time before his death. While he might have been exhibiting symptoms, it was not likely the cause of death."

Harper turned to Becker. "Do we have a final necropsy report from Dr. Sales yet?"

"Nothing official," replied Becker.

"Unofficially?" Harper asked.

"He drowned. There was evidence Doggo's body was deprived of oxygen, resulting in damage to the lungs and brain."

The microscopist continued. "The image from the index patient gives us a window into how devastatingly effective this novel virus appears to be at co-opting a host's cellular machinery. Just one infected cell is capable of releasing thousands of new virus particles that can, in turn, be transmitted to others."

"Are you prepared to classify this virus?" asked Harper.

He nodded and then explained, "Of course, we look at four primary characteristics in classifying a novel virus. We consider their nucleic acid, whether RNA or DNA, as well as its strandedness, whether single or double. Then there's the protein shell, the replication method, and other lesser details to consider."

Once again, Harper was waiting for the plane to land.

The microscopist walked past Becker and retrieved a notepad from his desk. "Preliminarily, I have confidence in this designation." He showed them the notepad with a series of numbers and letters scribbled on it. The final conclusion was circled at the bottom.

"Type A influenza?" asked Harper.

"Yes, specifically, antigen Type B because it is apparent the virus changes by a more gradual process of antigenic drift." Antigenic drift is an abrupt, major change in an influenza virus, resulting in new proteins capable of infecting humans.

He continued, pointing to his notes as he explained, "At this time, I'm declaring the host of origin to be a pangolin rather than the canine. Based upon my conversation with Dr. Sales and thanks to the remarkably preserved stomach contents of Doggo, we're confident in our hypothesis." He paused and gathered his thoughts before continuing.

"The geographical origin is the Tibetan Plateau or the Himalayas. World Health will have the final say on this. Very political, you know."

Harper nodded. No nation wants a deadly disease associated with its name.

He continued. "Because there is no evidence of an avian or swine relationship, it appears there was the entry of bat influenza into the pangolin's mammalian cells. Therefore, the appropriate designation is H17N12, a truly novel virus."

Becker solemnly repeated the designation. "H17N12."

The microscopist added, "The long form is Virus Type A, Tibet, Strain Number 05, Year 30, Virus subtype H17N12."

Harper furrowed her brow and walked toward the images displayed on the wall. "Now that we know who you are, let's figure out how to beat you."

CHAPTER FORTY

CDC Headquarters
Atlanta, Georgia

They stopped by Becker's office to drop off the goggles and mask; plus both of them needed a much-needed chocolate break. Stress relief was best achieved with a handful of M&M's properly parceled out, of course. A text message notification was heard, so Becker quickly retrieved her cell phone from her lab coat.

"It's Woolie. He and Kwon need to meet with us in the Bergermeister's small conference room as soon as possible."

Harper looked down to her perky assistant. "Does he call Dr. Reitherman, Bergermeister, too?"

Becker laughed. "No. Those two get a kick out of speaking to one another with phony German accents. They constantly refer to one another as *Herr Doktor.*"

Harper shook her head in disbelief. "I never looked at Dr. Reitherman as having that kind of sense of humor."

"Your pal, Woolie, has that effect on people. You know his real name is Wolfgang, right?"

"Yeah. Which do you like better?" Harper asked.

"Woolie makes the most sense. Actually, and don't tell anybody, but he's the second person I've met recently that I can't come up with a better nickname for."

"Really?" asked Harper.

"Yup. Can you imagine calling that eccentric cadaver carver anything besides Woolie?"

Harper was clearly entertained, enjoying the lighthearted moment. "No, I suppose you're right. Um, wait. You said he's the second person you can't apply a nickname to. Who's the other?"

Becker quickly responded, "Kwon."

"Why's that?"

"Too scared."

Harper continued laughing. "Becker, you don't have to be afraid of Kwon. He's one of us."

"How would I know? He's barely said two words to me." She reached into her lab coat several times until she'd retrieved three like-colored peanut M&M's.

"He's not much of a talker," Harper said reassuringly.

"Not true. He talks to you. And Woolie. And the Bergermeister. But not me."

Harper looked away from Becker because she wasn't able to make the statement with a straight face.

"Becker, maybe it's you who intimidates him."

By the time Harper turned toward Becker to gauge her reaction, she was gone. Harper stopped in the middle of the hallway and swung around. Becker was standing with her hands on her hips ten feet away.

"Shut up," she said teasingly. "He's not even human. I've always wondered what the military is doing with all that new technology. He's like the Terminator. You know, *I'll be baaack.*"

"Come on, Boom-Boom. I don't have time for your silliness."

"Shhh, you can't call me that in the office. People might get the wrong idea."

Harper continued toward Dr. Reitherman's office suite while Becker scampered to catch up. When they were next to one another again, Harper whispered, "Be nice to Kwon or I'll tell them all about your stripper-pole days in college."

"It wasn't like that. It was, um. Hey, I paid my way through college with unconventional methods. Nothing illegal or compromising."

"Salacious?"

"Not illegal," she shot back.

Harper gave Becker a playful shove as they entered the double doors of Dr. Reitherman's office suite. They could hear the rest of the group talking among themselves.

"Sorry we're late," said Harper. "We were on the other side of the building, looking at H17N12."

Dr. Reitherman's secretary exited the conference room and closed the door behind her. He turned to Harper.

"So we have a name?" he said inquisitively.

"We do, and a source," replied Harper.

"Not Doggo?" asked Kwon.

Harper purposefully hesitated. She wanted to force Becker to interact with Kwon. She picked up on Harper's pause and answered his question.

"According to the preliminary necropsy, Doggo's stomach contents revealed partially digested remains of a baby pangolin. Several, in fact."

Kwon scowled. "I didn't know they were mammals. Their scales suggest the reptilian family."

"The diseased pangolins carried a novel strain of influenza resulting in the H17 designation," added Becker.

Kwon tilted his head. He impressed Harper with his breadth of knowledge of infectious diseases. "Isn't H17 reserved for bat transmissions?"

Becker responded, "Yes, and there are traces of a bat's viral genome based upon microbiologists' findings. Because the intermediary hosts aren't swine or avian, they chose H17."

"Well, that's good enough for our purposes," interjected Dr. Reitherman. "Everyone take a seat so Woolie and Kwon can reveal what they've confirmed from the pharmacological perspective. Woolie?"

"Yes. Yes. Yes. Unfortunately, it took many more patients and deaths to reach this conclusion."

Kwon interjected, "And confirmation from Dr. Zeng's case in Urumqi. The earliest case, the Australian, Adam Mooy, was studied by Dr. Zeng and a pathologist at the university hospital. They recognized that this virus signaled the cytokine molecules to mobilize in a war against H17N12." He looked to Dr. Boychuck to continue.

"Yes. Yes. Yes. Through our own pathology, we have learned the body overreacted in its fight against the virus. As a result, widespread inflammation occurred. The natural result of these overactive white blood cells was a flooding of soldiers, who began to fight among themselves, taking the patient's vital organs down with them."

"Similar to avian flu," added Becker. "With a little HIV/AIDS thrown in the mix."

"A deadly cocktail," said Dr. Reitherman.

"As H17N12 sweeps through the body," began Kwon, "the cytokine storm is triggered, resulting in severe infections of the central nervous system and vital organs. It appears the lungs are the first to go."

"How do we slow the process?" asked Harper.

Dr. Boychuck responded, "It is a most unusual set of circumstances determined by studying all the confirmed positive cases in Las Vegas. The vast majority of elderly survivors were taking a medication designed to dilate the patient's blood vessels, which increased the amount of blood flow to the heart."

"ACE inhibitors," said Harper. She glanced at Becker. "Do you remember Wallace? At the Gold Palace? He had a cough and claimed it was caused by his lisinopril."

"Yes, I remember. That is a common side effect."

Dr. Boychuck interrupted. "There is a Wallace on my patient list from Las Vegas. Donald, I think."

"That's him," said Becker. "He was very heavy. Did he get sick?"

"Yes. Yes. Yes. However, he is recovering. His weakened heart and excessive weight complicated his recovery, but he is still alive."

"Dr. Zeng was onto this," said Kwon. He glanced at Harper. "The angiotensin-converting enzyme 2 attaches to the outer membranes of vital organs, especially in patients whose immunities are compromised for other reasons."

She nodded in agreement. "This accounts for the deaths of patients with weakened immune systems."

"Unless they were taking an ACE inhibitor like lisinopril," offered Becker.

"Exactly," said Harper. "The healthy individuals, like the Olympic athlete in Austria, didn't take a drug like that, but it's most likely his parents did."

"Yes. Yes. Yes. All has been confirmed. We cannot find a fatality in which a patient routinely took an ACE inhibitor medication."

Harper summed it up. "The virus uses the ACE2 receptors to enter the lungs in a mechanism similar to SARS. Using an ACE2 receptor blockade along the lines of lisinopril disables the viral entry into the heart and lungs while rendering an overall decrease in inflammation."

The room grew silent and Dr. Reitherman leaned back in his chair and clasped his hands behind his head. "In my career, I cannot think of a time when a commonly used medication was unknowingly instrumental in warding off a virus. I think we can have our people begin their work with health care specialists to formulate the basis of a treatment protocol."

Everyone nodded their agreement.

CHAPTER FORTY-ONE

CDC Headquarters
Atlanta, Georgia

Over the next forty-eight hours, Dr. Harper and her team worked virtually nonstop to tie up any loose ends and to reconfirm their working hypothesis. By the time Friday afternoon was upon them, every single new case, both recovering patients and deceased ones, fit perfectly within their models.

Around the world, other leading scientists and epidemiologists took the data generated by the CDC's efforts and applied it to their own H17N12 cases. In a first, the previously obscure pangolin made world headlines as the media refused to use the official designation, Tibetan flu, in favor of pangolin disease. In addition, the vast majority of news reports failed to mention that the offending pangolin had walked the Earth fifteen thousand years ago.

In wet markets across China, the pangolins, which were considered a delicacy in China and in high demand throughout Asia for their medicinal qualities, were being destroyed.

Harper was dismayed at the amount of misinformation being spread via all forms of media. Dr. Reitherman, like his superiors, was anxious to make his formal statement to the press to dispel the inaccuracies and fearmongering.

His statement to a full house in the CDC's media center took about fifteen minutes. The questions he was bombarded with lasted the rest of the hour until finally he was pulled away from the podium. He was exhausted by the time he returned to his office suite. His mood lifted when he found Harper in the conference room together with Becker, Dr. Boychuck, and Kwon.

"Congrats, Dr. Reitherman!"

"Yeah, boss. You crushed it!"

"Well done, *Herr Doktor*!"

Kwon simply extended his hand to shake. That was the extent of his enthusiasm for just about anything.

Dr. Reitherman was appreciative. The head of the CSELS removed his jacket and draped it over a chair. "Thank you, all. I wish I could have mentioned each of you by name, but amazingly, nobody has leaked Harper and Kwon's excursions into China. Personally, I believe the administration doesn't want to admit your success." He patted them on the back as he walked by.

"Unsung heroes was the term you used," said Becker. "I'll take it."

"Yes. Yes. Yes. None of us need a new line item on our résumés. It is the results that count."

"Absolutely, sir," added Kwon. "For me it was an honor to work with each of you. I have to say, this rivals any mission I undertook on behalf of DARPA."

Harper raised her hands in the air. "Hold on, everybody. This conversation sounds like it might be leading toward goodbyes. I have an invitation for you all."

The ever-jubilant Becker began a happy dance. "Party at Harper's house! Woo-hoo!"

"Wait, not quite. I've got a better offer than that."

"We're all ears," said Becker.

"Earlier today, I had a chance to speak with Ma and Mimi. They expressed how proud they are of us and are naturally appreciative of our efforts. They've invited everyone out to

Randolph House for a weekend of rest, relaxation, and down-home Southern cookin'."

Becker was the first to accept her invite. "I'm in! Hubba-Hubba is in Chicago on business for a few days. One of his clients is the Chicago Zoological Society and the Brookfield Zoo. My schedule is wide open."

Kwon nodded. "I've read about a Dr. Boone and her work with primates."

"Yeah, my husband likes swinging with the monkeys, too."

They shared a laugh, and Harper turned to Kwon. "Are you in?"

"I don't see why not. I honestly can't say I've had any of the Southern dishes I've heard about."

"Great," said Harper, turning to Dr. Reitherman and Dr. Boychuck. "Gentlemen?"

"Yes. Yes. Yes. Thank you for this kind invitation. Berger?"

"Well, my wife is also traveling, so I'm a bachelor feeding on takeout for a few days. If you're sure they wouldn't mind."

Harper laughed and waved off his statement. "Y'all have to understand. They are used to putting on the biggest soirees in town. The five of us plus Joe, hopefully, will be a walk in the park for those two."

"Will Joe be joining us?" asked Dr. Reitherman.

"I hope so," Harper replied. "He has some kind of meeting scheduled outside the city, but he's sure he can get there by midmorning tomorrow."

"When do we leave? And who's driving?" asked Becker.

"Just a moment," said Dr. Reitherman as he excused himself and left to speak with his assistant. Less than a minute later, he returned.

"Everything okay?" asked Harper.

"Oh, sure. You see, I promised Kwon's employers I'd give him a ride back to Virginia. I just made arrangements to do that first thing this evening."

"But, sir, he wants to go with us," protested Harper.

Dr. Reitherman raised both hands to his waist in an effort to assuage Harper's concern. "I didn't say how long it would take. We'll all meet at DeKalb-Peachtree by seven. I'll have the CDC Learjet ferry us over to the county airport where your home is. If I recall, we've picked you up there before, am I right?"

"Yes, sir. It's a fairly long, lighted runway at four-to-five thousand feet."

"I thought so. Anyway, can everyone make that work?"

"Heck yeah!" shouted Becker. "Um, now?"

"Now, Elizabeth. Scoot!"

"You don't have to tell me twice!" she exclaimed as she hurried out of the office without so much as a see you later.

Dr. Reitherman turned to Dr. Boychuck. "Woolie, I'll run you by your hotel and get you checked out. My place is on the way to the airport, so we can just knock it out together."

"Yes. Yes. Yes. This is very nice of you, Harper. Thank you for including me in all of this."

"We couldn't have done it without you," she said with a sincere smile. "Kwon, let's saddle up. It's time for another adventure."

Kwon smiled. "I can only imagine."

"It'll be safer than the last one, I promise."

None of them hesitated to make themselves scarce.

PART IV

INDEFINITE DOUBT

It's always too late no matter what we do.
~ Dr. Harper Randolph, on hunting viruses

CHAPTER FORTY-TWO

Randolph House
Heard's Fort, Georgia

The group chatted continuously during the short flight across North Georgia to the historic community of Heard's Fort. Established in 1774 by Virginia colonist Stephen Heard, the settlement had served as the temporary capital of the new state of Georgia after it ratified the Articles of Confederation in 1778.

When most Americans thought of Georgia and its history, visions of a mid-nineteenth-century, war-torn South as portrayed in Margaret Mitchell's *Gone with the Wind* came to mind. Certainly, Georgia was a major theater of the Civil War, with major battles fought in nearby Atlanta. However, many are unaware of the strategic importance this part of Georgia played in the American Revolutionary War.

The Battle of Kettle Creek was fought about ten miles from Heard's Fort. The British had begun their southern strategy by sending expeditions from New York to capture the strategic port located in Savannah. Thereafter, the British forces moved up the

Savannah River, captured Augusta just to the southeast of Heard's Fort, and established a garrison there.

The Southerners would have none of that. The Georgia Patriot Militia led by Colonel John Dooly teamed with South Carolina militia leader Colonel Andrew Pickens to conduct guerilla tactics against the British.

In early February of 1779, British forces moved deeper into the state in an effort to recruit loyalists and establish outposts, one of which was near Kettle Creek. British Lieutenant Colonel John Boyd led a company, unaware that he was being stalked by the Georgia Patriot militia.

Both Colonel Dooly and Colonel Pickens flanked the British forces. Despite being greatly outnumbered, they had the strategic advantage of knowing the Kettle Creek area. They maintained the high ground and were able to pin down the British forces. During the battle, the British commander perished and the Loyalist line was broken, with all of its men being killed, captured, or chased back toward Augusta.

This battle was an important turning point in the Revolutionary War. It proved the British were unable to engage the loyal patriots and were ineffective in their attempts to take and hold the interior of America.

Just over a decade later, in 1795, a home was built in Heard's Fort that, after several expansions, became known as Randolph House. Harper had been born in this historic home and, from her early childhood, was raised there by her grandmother and great-grandmother. It had always been her safe place. A home that provided her refuge from the outside world. One that, like the two women who raised her, had always wrapped its loving arms around her when she needed a hug. On the occasion of this trip, she was there to celebrate with her friends, both old and new. Her good spirits reflected in her talkative mood.

One of the locals had an SUV that doubled as a taxi service. The town didn't have a need for a full-time taxi. It was barely three miles from one end to the other. As they drove to Randolph House,

Harper directed everyone's attention to the many points of historical interest along the way.

This area boasted more antebellum homes per capita than any other part of Georgia. Heard's Fort had managed to avoid the wrath of Union General William Tecumseh Sherman during his famed March to the Sea. While his task was to disperse the few remaining companies of the Confederate Army, he was remembered by many in the South as a cruel military leader who burnt homes and crops of the Georgians, forcing them into poverty and starvation.

He'd given his men free rein to take or destroy food, horses and livestock. The federal troops, *Bummers* as they were called, routinely violated orders along the march to Savannah. History has shown their scorched-earth policy was intentional to make the Southerners feel the cost of the war, or *to make Georgia howl*, as Sherman once wrote.

Heard's Fort was just north of Sherman's route and was spared the destruction and suffering of others. As a result, several homes, such as Randolph House, still stood today.

It was just after dinnertime when the group poured out of the SUV near the dining room entrance of the stately home. After everyone grabbed their bags, Becker was the first to make her way toward the dining room entrance.

"Becker, wait," said Harper. "Ma and Mimi would skin me alive if I took you guys through one of the side entrances. I'm sure they're waiting to greet us at the front."

Harper led her guests around to the front of the house. Dr. Reitherman was the first to comment.

"What year is it again?"

Harper laughed. "For this weekend, you can pretend you're back in 1795. Consider this. Randolph House was built when George Washington was president. Just let that soak in for a moment."

"It's amazeballs," quipped Becker. "Hey! We have a welcoming committee."

Everyone picked up the pace as they strode up the front steps. The hand-carved wood door slowly opened. Ma and Mimi emerged dressed in their everyday, yet Sunday-best for most, cotton dresses and heels.

"Ma! Mimi!" shouted Harper, echoing the exuberance she'd shown as a child. She burst ahead of the others and lovingly embraced the genteel women.

Soon, the group was exchanging pleasantries in the shadows of the forty-foot Greek Revival columns. Both the American flag and the Betsy Ross flag, with its five-pointed stars arranged in a circle representing the thirteen colonies, were hung proudly from the second-floor porch.

"Come in, everyone. We have a few treats for our weary travelers."

Dr. Reitherman and Dr. Boychuck offered their arms to escort the elderly women through the home's grand foyer. Once the door was closed, the aromas from the kitchen filled their nostrils, but the history of the home permeated their senses.

"If only the walls could talk," muttered Dr. Reitherman as his eyes examined the original horsehair plaster walls and vintage crystal chandelier.

"Oh, but they do, of course," said Mimi in her soft, frail voice.

Becker's eyes grew wide. "It's haunted?"

Ma, who stood nearly six feet tall like Harper, gently patted Becker on the back. "Don't you worry your little head none, dearie. Haunted is such an ugly word. It leaves the impression of something mean-spirited. That's not at all the case here. Of course, we have relatives of the past who still reside in Randolph House, but they are incapable of haunting."

Harper laughed out loud. "No, the Randolph family is full of partiers, both past and present. Let me show you."

They glanced into the ladies' parlor on the right and the men's parlor on the left before entering the grand ballroom. The fifty-foot-wide, eleven-hundred-square-foot space was made for dancing.

"Wow!" exclaimed Becker as she dropped her bag and immediately danced across the room as if she were Tchaikovsky's sugar plum fairy. She happily skipped away, raising and lowering her arms like a bird preparing to take flight.

Dr. Boychuck was impressed with the wood detail of the grand ballroom. "Two fireplaces?"

He'd escorted Ma into the room, so she took him up to one of the fireplaces with matching mantels. "These are quite historic. They were originally installed in the old Heard House that was built in 1824. In May of 1865, Jeff Davis held his final meeting there with his cabinet before the Confederate States of America was dissolved. When the building was raised to make way for a new courthouse, our ancestors acquired these beautiful mantels and surrounds to install around the fireplaces in the ballroom."

Harper discussed the building history of Randolph House. "Back in the day, homes often started out small. In fact, in 1795 when this was originally built, it was a simple two-story with a kitchen and a single bedroom above it. At the time, it faced east toward the street we drove in on."

Ma continued. "Then in 1820, Miss Maria Randolph—who, by the way, is a lineal descendent of Pocahontas—expanded the home. She was an elegant lady and the center of the social scene at the time. All the Randolph women share her genetics, as Miss Maria stood over six feet tall."

"Her name is pronounced like Mariah, but it was actually spelled like Maria," added Harper.

Ma wandered through the ballroom and gestured as she spoke. "Over the years, the east and west porches were enclosed to become the morning room and the dining room. The exterior porches to the rear of Randolph House were enclosed to include a downstairs master suite, an oversized kitchen, and more storage. Other than that, she's stood proud for over two centuries."

"Yes. Yes. Yes. Proud and beautiful like her hostesses."

Mimi, who'd been attached to Dr. Boychuck's arm the entire time, squeezed him a little tighter. "You are a most interesting man, Dr. Woolie. Perhaps we could share a brandy in the parlor after supper?"

"Oh, man. Watch out, Woolie. My Mimi doesn't take no for an answer."

Mimi swatted at her great-granddaughter. "You hush, Harper Randolph. Don't you have some homework to do?"

The group burst out laughing. Harper's family had become their family. The only one in the group who hadn't spoken other than during the introductions was Kwon. While Ma and Mimi led everyone to the dining room for supper, Harper pulled Kwon aside.

"Hey. Are you doin' okay?" she asked.

"Yeah, I'm good. More than good, actually. It's just, well, this is a little overwhelming. This is a world that I thought only existed in the movies."

Harper understood. "Time stands still here. You look around and see homes like this one built in the 1700s with many, many more built prior to the Civil War. Unless you've spent time in the Old South, you wouldn't believe a place like this could possibly exist."

"How old are Ma and Mimi?"

"Ma is seventy-four and Mimi is ninety-two."

"You come from an amazing gene pool, Harper."

She furrowed her brow and a wave of sadness came over her. She'd grown close to Kwon and felt she could trust him with an aspect of her personal life she rarely shared.

CHAPTER FORTY-THREE

Randolph House
Heard's Fort, Georgia

"Every time I return to Randolph House, memories are everywhere. There are those from adulthood, such as when Joe and I got married in the backyard. But childhood memories, both good and bad, are the most prevalent."

"Harper, there's no need to talk about anything uncomfortable if you don't want to," interrupted Kwon. "I shouldn't let my mood force you to go to a place that's—"

"No, please. It's fine. Listen, you and I risked our lives together. You saved my life more than once. I'm okay, you know, spillin' my deep, dark secrets."

"It's up to you."

Harper nodded and motioned toward the sunroom. Tonight's meal was a potluck-style, take-what-you-eat-and-grab-a-seat type of gathering. Ma and Mimi wouldn't pressure her to join right away. Besides, from the sounds of laughter and excited voices emanating from that side of the house, it was apparent the two of them had not been missed.

"My father, Jack Randolph, was a special agent with the Georgia Bureau of Investigation. I'm an only child, the apple of his eye and the son he never had, all wrapped into one. To call me a daddy's girl would be an understatement." Harper paused and sighed. Kwon reached for her arm, but she smiled and nodded.

"It's fine. Daddy was involved in a lot of things for the GBI. When I was a kid, meth houses began to spring up around Thomson, which is down the road about thirty miles. He and his partner were constantly busting the houses, arresting the bad guys, and destroying the product.

"It wasn't long before drug dealers out of Atlanta moved in to fill the void. But, instead of meth, they were pushing heroin, which made a comeback about that time. As they became successful pushing horse all the way into Augusta, organized crime got a sniff of the action and took over.

"In any event, they didn't take kindly to the war on drugs being waged by Daddy and the other GBI agents. One Saturday, the start of a weekend when he was supposed to be off, he and I went hunting. It was the end of the day and he got a call from his supervisory agent. They'd gotten word of a drug deal going down in Thomson and they needed him.

"He took me home, hurriedly got his gear together, including his vest, and raced down to Thomson. Because he was late to the raid, he wasn't fully briefed on the mechanics of the takedown. In fact, he was only supposed to be in a support role, but that's not how my daddy did his job. He was one of those cops who ran toward the gunshots, not cower behind a wall."

Harper gulped and fought back the tears. She gathered herself and continued. "The raid went bad because the GBI was outnumbered. Plus, the people they were up against weren't the usual gangbangers. They were trained and heavily armed. Daddy, while trying to help another agent who was taking on fire, was killed. His Kevlar could only cover up so much, you know?

"I was only nine and my mom had just turned thirty-four. We had Ma and Mimi to help support us, but it wasn't enough. My mom slowly descended into the abyss. Over time, a psychosis took over, leaving her completely unaware of her surroundings. Ma and Mimi tried psychotherapy. Nothing worked, and eventually her dissociative amnesia became so severe that her doctors said she was no longer safe outside a long-term mental health care facility."

Kwon exhaled. "Is there any chance for improvement?"

"No. They've tried everything. For a while, I tried visiting her, but her lack of recollection only made her frustrated and then increasingly violent. My last visit didn't end well. Not at all."

"I'm sorry, Harper. I don't know what to say."

Kwon reached out and hugged her as she fought back tears.

"You know, I don't either, anymore. I feel terrible for her. Ma and Mimi do as well. We had our own lives to live, so we've moved on. The memories hit me again before I arrived at DARPA. Mom is in a residential treatment facility in Virginia, just south of Richmond."

"When was the last time you saw her?" Kwon asked.

"It's been a long while. As I said, it went horribly wrong, with her hurting herself in a tirade and me running out of the facility bawlin' my eyes out."

"If I can ever do anything for you, please tell me."

"I will. I thank God that Joe introduced us."

Becker bellowed across the ballroom, loud enough to stir up some of the apparitions who wandered the home at night. "Food's getting cold and Woolie has practically scarfed down all the mashed potatoes."

Harper and Kwon laughed. "Aren't we a bunch of misfits?"

Kwon agreed. "Is it possible to create a comedy show about a bunch of misfits, as you call us, who search the planet for the next deadly disease?"

"Yeah, I firmly believe this group can generate enough material to make even that subject laugh worthy."

Kwon led her across the ballroom, where they joined the boisterous bunch around the dining table. Glasses of wine were filled. Bellies were protruding over waistbands slightly more than when they arrived. And laughter filled the air as everyone enjoyed the moment.

For Harper, this was just what the doctor ordered, except Joe wasn't there.

CHAPTER FORTY-FOUR

Randolph House
Heard's Fort, Georgia

The group slept well during the night except Becker. All five of the bedrooms upstairs had their own full bathrooms. Harper slept in her old bedroom known as *Nestle Down*. It was the original bedroom when the house was first built. When she was a very young child, she'd adopted it because it was smaller and cozier than the other four guest suites, known as *eighteens* because of their size—eighteen feet by eighteen feet, plus the bathroom.

Homes were square and boxy during the turn of the eighteenth century. They were often designed in a two-over-two style, meaning two upstairs windows on each end of the house directly above two downstairs windows. Toward the latter part of the 1800s, especially in rural communities, additions and wings were added to accommodate growing families or loved ones who couldn't afford their own home.

That night, Becker's experience was different from the guys'. She slept in what Harper used to call the scary room although she'd never say that out loud to anyone. It was the master bedroom of

Archibald Colley, an Army colonel who was the bunk mate of General George Patton at West Point. Colonel Colley served in World War I alongside *Georgie*, as his friend had been called since their days in college.

After the war, he left the service and married into the Randolph family. As was customary during that point in time in the South, he and his wife, Mary, slept in separate bedrooms although they loved each other dearly. When she died of smallpox, he was heartbroken and lived out his days at Randolph House, angry at God for taking his beloved wife.

Harper was convinced Colonel Colley's spirit remained, and over time she came to accept why he was angry. To pacify him and ease his pain, she set up a shrine, of sorts. The original writing desk from the 1920s that Colonel Colley used to write letters was still in the room. She traveled to an antique store in Augusta one day and found a copy of the 1909 West Point Howitzer, the U.S. Military Academy's yearbook. Photographs of Colonel Colley and General Patton graced the pages, extoling their accomplishments in literary studies and sports.

She found other items in Ma and Mimi's storage boxes full of Randolph House memorabilia. Over time, she created this shrine in his room, and the ghost of Colonel Colley seemed to relax. Harper guessed that Becker's high energy must've stirred him up somehow.

While everyone heartily ate the homemade biscuits and sausage gravy, scrambled eggs, and sausage links, Becker seemed to be in a daze due to lack of sleep. Harper recognized the look. Until she built the shrine, she'd had it, too.

"Say, Becker, how'd you sleep?" Harper couldn't resist. Everyone kept eating, but Dr. Reitherman glanced at Harper and then over to the weary epidemiologist, who hesitated to answer.

"Okay. I had a lot on my mind."

"Like what?" Harper asked, trying to hide her teasing intent.

"Um, who's Mary?"

Mimi snickered and Ma elbowed her mother.

Harper responded, "She was a Randolph. The grandniece of Miss Maria. Why?"

"I kept hearing her name last night. "But it was a man who was saying it. And he was so sad."

Harper speared a sausage link and bit off an end. She spoke with her mouth full. "You were probably dreaming."

"No, I was wide awake. I heard a sound, kinda like a chair moving across the room. But it wasn't in my room. It was in the front bedroom where Woolie was sleeping."

Harper knew what that was, too. For years, she was the sole inhabitant of the spacious upstairs. For fun, she'd take turns sleeping in the different bedrooms. Ma and Mimi didn't mind as long as she made the beds back proper. She'd heard the chair sliding across the floor when she'd slept in that bedroom as a child. She'd try to downplay the ghostly activities to calm Becker's nerves.

"It's an old house that creaks and cracks. It's just your imagination."

Becker pursed her lips and looked around at the others. "Just the same, um, Kwon? Would you mind changing rooms with me?"

Kwon's eyes darted from Harper to Ma and Mimi. "Sure, if it's okay with our hosts."

"They'll be okay with it, right, you guys?"

Harper burst out laughing. "Three weeks ago, I watched Becker go toe-to-toe with National Guardsmen armed with automatic weapons. She was like the Tasmanian Devil. Also, she crawled through an air-conditioning duct trying to help us escape the lockdown. Something goes bump in the night, and she's done."

The group had a hearty laugh at Becker's expense. In the end, she got her way.

"I'd like to take a walk around the town," said Dr. Boychuck.

"Me too," Dr. Reitherman chimed in.

"Okay, I'll be your tour guide. Before we head out, I'd like to show you where Joe and I got married. Also, a special garden I made with Ma and Mimi."

Everyone helped the ladies clean up but were eventually run out of their kitchen. The two old biddies, as Joe referred to them, were very territorial about the kitchen, especially when guests were in residence. Nobody was allowed to lift a finger unless they were prepared to suffer their wrath.

After Kwon and Becker made the guest room swap, they all met by the carriage house located behind the circular driveway to the rear of Randolph House.

"Thirty-some years ago, Ma and Mimi ran Randolph House as a bed and breakfast. It filled their need to host events while supplementing their income. For several reasons, they chose to focus on themselves and family. As you can see, a lot of the entertaining aspects of the place are still here.

"In the 1800s, this carriage house was once used to keep their horse-drawn buggies and horses. When Colonel Colley bought his first car, he converted it to a garage. Ma and Mimi later enclosed it to be used as an indoor gathering place in case it rained."

Kwon pointed at two large white columns positioned in front of an enormous magnolia tree. "What are those for?"

"They used to host weddings here, including mine."

"You and Joe were married out here?" asked Becker.

"Yes, we were. It was fabulous. It was in May and the flowers were in full bloom. Mimi, who was Belgian, speaks excellent German in addition to her native French. She used to say, *die Blumen sprechen*, which translates *to the flowers are speaking.*"

"This is incredibly beautiful," said Becker.

The group slowly walked toward the magnolia tree full of white flowers. Dr. Boychuck was the first to notice a trend.

"All of the flowers in this area are white."

Harper couldn't resist. "Yes. Yes. Yes."

Dr. Boychuck laughed. "Very funny, young lady. I promise, after you send me back to Las Vegas, you will always remember this part of me."

Harper hugged the aging medical examiner. "I will remember everything about you. Squishy, too. I'm sorry he missed all the action."

"Yes. Yes. Yes. I can assure you we will have many evenings to converse about my days in Atlanta with you nice people."

Dr. Reitherman led the way past the magnolia. "It's a moon garden."

"Very good," said Harper. "How did you know?"

"My grandmother had one in Munich. Being in Bavaria, she lived in a much cooler climate. Many of her flowers bloomed late in the day."

Harper nodded her agreement. "It gets very hot and dry here in the summer. Many of the night bloomers don't like the stifling Georgia heat the afternoons bring."

"Well, it's remarkably well-maintained, Harper. This, just like the rest of the place, is a real gem."

The SUV taxicab slowed as it passed them. It turned through the block columns at the east entrance to Randolph House. Harper stood a little taller, and tears began to stream down her face. Before the vehicle came to a stop, the passenger door swung open and Joe began to step out. He was met with the force of an NFL linebacker as Harper crushed him with a much-needed embrace.

For more than a minute, the two held one another, tears flowing down their faces. A couple with that kind of deep love should never be apart, but it was the life they led. It made for some very happy, tearful reunions, especially after the last few weeks.

The rest of the group stayed in the moon garden, allowing the loving couple to enjoy their moment. After they broke their embrace and laughed at themselves in embarrassment, Joe paid the driver and left his bags in the driveway. He joined the rest of the visitors and introduced himself to Dr. Boychuck.

As they spoke, Becker's phone received several notifications for both emails and texts. She casually walked away from the group to scroll through the messages. Harper squeezed her husband's hand before releasing it. She chased after Becker.

"Is something wrong?"

"No, not really. Yeah, maybe."

"Spill it, Becker."

"I'm not the one who spilled it. Somebody in the White House did."

"Whadya mean?"

"I guess President Taylor demanded to know how we were suddenly able to produce conclusions so quickly when just a week ago we were sort of floundering, as he put it."

"We discovered Doggo, oh—" Harper caught herself. "The White House wasn't fully informed about how that happened, were they?"

"Nope," said Becker as she curled her lips and sucked them into her mouth as if she'd just tasted a very tangy pickle.

"Let me guess, Taylor knows I was involved."

"Yup."

Harper rolled her eyes and thrust her hands on her hips. "And it hit the media."

"Of course. It's his weapon of choice."

"Geez lou-freakin'-ise!" Harper exclaimed loud enough to draw the attention of the others. Their conversation stopped and now all eyes were on the two of them. "Is there any blowback on Joe?"

Becker had been scrolling through the media reports. "It's hard to read out here in the glare. I've seen his name mentioned as being your husband."

Harper turned around and waved the group over to join them. "Hey, guys. Why don't you go inside with Becker? There's been a development. I need to talk to Joe for a minute, and then I'll be along."

Everyone but Joe asked what was going on. Becker explained as she herded them toward the house, leaving Joe and Harper alone.

She turned to Joe with a concerned look on her face. "Joe, um, I'm sorry. Something has happened and it's hit the news."

Joe gave Harper a reassuring smile. "Darling, I know all about it. I'm the leak, not the White House."

"What? Why?"

"It was necessary. I had to get you fired."

CHAPTER FORTY-FIVE

Randolph House
Heard's Fort, Georgia

Joe led the way through the dining room door and immediately peeled off into the kitchen to greet Ma and Mimi. They loved him like a son and were especially appreciative of how he cared for Harper. While they reunited for a moment, Harper entered the parlor with a little extra spring in her step. She was immediately approached by Becker, who had been pacing the floor, a sign that the young epidemiologist was stressed.

"What's wrong?" she asked, her blue eyes probing Harper's in an attempt to take a peek inside.

"Nothing. Why?"

"You're too cheery. I'm always suspicious of the cheerful."

"Aw, shit, Becker. I have my husband with me. No worries."

"I worry. It's my job."

Harper draped her arm over Becker's shoulders and whispered, "Not today. Rest. Relaxation. Remember?"

Becker shrugged and exhaled. *The girl is too wired.*

Joe entered the ballroom with a Randolph matriarch on each

arm. He had a way of turning on the charm when he was with the two old biddies, a moniker he borrowed from *The Grinch* movie. The three had a mutual admiration and respect for each other, one born out of a common denominator—their love for Harper.

"Guys, I'm told we've got a couple of hours before dinner. I wonder if you'd mind giving us non-doctor types a rundown on where we are with this disease."

Harper tilted her head to the side. She realized she hadn't discussed this novel form of influenza with Ma and Mimi, nor had they asked. Their lives centered around each other, Randolph House, and their small town. Beyond that, they generally didn't care unless it directly affected them. In a way, that made life simpler and more tolerable.

"Sure, it'll be like story time, right, Mimi?" asked Harper.

"Yes, dearie. You never wanted to go to sleep on time. You'd read books, and when you finished them, you'd turn to us to make up a story."

"You guys were always so creative. Well, I've got a story for you that started at least fifteen thousand years ago."

Ma laughed. "Honey, we'll have dinner ready in a couple of hours. Fifteen thousand is a lot of years."

The group laughed. Dr. Reitherman came to the rescue. "That is a lot of years, but she'll be able to fast-forward. You'll see."

Joe helped rearrange the furniture so that Harper could sit near one of the fireplaces as she spoke. He gave her a kiss on the cheek and plopped himself on the sofa between the two elderly Randolphs.

"Ma and Mimi, this is gonna start out like a horror story, but I promise, it will have a happy ending. Okay?"

Mimi waved her hand in front of her. "At my age, I've seen or heard my share of horror stories. Go ahead, dearie."

Harper took a deep breath and began. "You know, in our world, seemingly natural acts can end up having a profound effect on humans. Fifteen thousand years ago, when the Earth was on the verge of experiencing a prolonged period of colder temperatures, animals sensed this climate change and tried to adapt.

"In Western China, the gradual onset of this cooling resulted in ice and snow buildup occurring along the base of the Himalayas. As a result, food became scarce for every critter up and down the food chain. Our story is about a wolf that was later named Doggo.

"Doggo did his thing every day. He hunted for large, hoofed mammals like deer, elk, and moose. However, as the days grew colder, those animals were some of the first to migrate south to avoid the coming cold. So Doggo turned to smaller mammals like beavers, mice, and rabbits. They also fled the cold, leaving him with fewer and fewer options.

"China was the home to an interesting creature that, at first glance, looks more like a reptile than a mammal. It's called a pangolin."

"In a way, this cute creature, which is the size of a house cat, looks a little like a dragon with a pointy nose, retractable claws, and lots of scales for protection. In fact, when it feels threatened, it curls up into a tight ball, giving it the appearance of a large artichoke."

Becker interjected. "Imagine a walking pinecone or an artichoke with legs."

"Or even a friendly crocodile that curls up into a ball," added Dr. Reitherman.

Harper continued. "Pangolins wander around, minding their own business, foraging for ants and other insects for their meals. They dig around streams, rock outcroppings, and at the base of trees in dense, dark forests.

"The places where this cute little mammal foraged were also frequented by horseshoe bats—the planet's number one culprit for passing infectious diseases. Most likely, the pangolin, while foraging for insects, ingested bat guano or excrements and became infected with a virus.

"But that's not how the pangolin died. You see, wolves like Doggo have a keen sense of smell and taste. Back then, like today, pangolins were considered quite the delicacy. Doggo probably hunted this creature and ate him, or might have even found a nest of softer-shelled baby pangolins, which had the virus in their bodies. Either way, Doggo became an intermediary host of this pathogen.

"Last night, I got an email from Dr. Sales with his necropsy results. Doggo died from drowning, but his body was coursed with a deadly virus. He probably was feeling the effects of the disease, causing him to fall into a stream or get swept away by a river. After Doggo died, his body was consumed by thousands of years of ice and snow.

"Now, here's the fast-forward part, as Dr. Reitherman mentioned. Fifteen thousand years later, with our advanced technology, man is conducting archeological expeditions and scientific experiments around the globe. One of these research projects is underway in the region where an ice cap was formed during the period of intense cooling fifteen thousand years ago. And it happens to be where Doggo died.

"Two guys, Australians, worked for this research facility conducting core drilling in the ice. Their job was simple. Go to a designated spot, drill deep into the ice, and extract the samples for study. However, they came across something unexpected—Doggo's frozen remains."

Harper took a deep breath and glanced at Kwon. "Kwon and I traveled to China in search of patient zero, the first to be infected by the disease. We knew it would be a crap shoot to be able to identify him, but it had to be done. One thing we never expected to track down was the intermediary host. In this case, Doggo.

"Our investigation led us to the research facility in Western Tibet, where one of the scientists was kind enough to give us the nickel tour. He showed us Doggo lying on a shelf in a darkened cooler.

"Kwon was the first to notice Doggo's appearance. He pointed out evidence that the wolf had been thawed and possible tampered with. Here's what I think happened. As we learned during our investigation, these two men, Mooy and Maclaren, were fun-loving, attention-seeking partiers. I believe they allowed Doggo to thaw in order to get a closer look. Possibly, they tampered with his mouth by prying it open, ripping the frozen skin and breaking a few teeth of the wolf in the process. During these shenanigans, the virus was transmitted from Doggo to the Australians. And that's how these things begin."

"Just like that," muttered Ma.

Dr. Boychuck smiled at Ma. "Yes. Yes. Yes. An innocent, albeit irresponsible act, can result in a global pandemic in a matter of months."

Joe asked, "How did these two infect others?"

Harper replied, "According to their supervisor, they were alone in the facility over a weekend because they were scheduled to take time off. They were both climbers, one more experienced than the other. An item on their bucket list was to climb Mount Everest. Because they were in China, they were able to drive up to the North Face, cutting off a couple of weeks compared to those climbers who began in Nepal. From what I've learned, the North Face was the more dangerous and challenging route of the two.

"Perhaps what happened next was because the two men weren't

sufficiently experienced to climb the northern route or the fact they disregarded warnings against alcohol consumption. In any event, a horrible accident occurred.

"As they neared the summit, from what we learned, Mooy was the first to collapse. In his attempt to hold on to the tether line, he snapped it, creating a whipsaw effect. He tumbled over the edge of a rock face and died soon thereafter. Maclaren, like many others in their climbing group, lost their balance and fell thousands of feet to their deaths. It was a horrific scene."

Harper paused, so Joe asked a question. "Was Mooy's body recovered?"

Kwon replied, "Yes. It was the only one of the dead they could reach. The PLA sent an elite tactical team called the Siberian Tigers to Everest. Using a highly skilled chopper pilot, the four-man team was able to drop down to Mooy's location and retrieve the body. They immediately left Everest and returned to Lhasa, the capital city of Tibet."

"Those four soldiers became our index patients," added Becker. "Apparently, they were granted leave to travel to Las Vegas for a poker tournament. During the brief period they spent with Mooy's diseased body on the helicopter, they became infected. By the time they arrived in Vegas, they were contagious and spreading the love to others at the Gold Palace Hotel and Casino."

"I take it you've been able to narrow it down to a list of suspected viruses?" asked Ma.

"Better than that," replied Harper. "In a whirlwind forty-eight hours, everyone in this room and our coworkers at the CDC were able to identify the disease, sequence its genome, and identify key traits of its victims to help protect those who are most susceptible to contracting the disease."

Mimi, who'd begun to nod off during Harper's discussion, recovered just in time to ask, "What's it called? Sin City disease?"

Everyone laughed. Harper leaned back in her chair and smiled. She loved Ma and Mimi.

"Well, I'm sure Mrs. Mayor would have a fit with that. Whadya think, Woolie?"

"Yes. Yes. Yes. The new name only offends the government responsible for hiding the disease from the world."

"What is it?" asked Joe.

Dr. Reitherman replied, "Most likely, the media will label it the Tibetan flu, at least initially. There will be a scrum between World Health, the Chinese government, and my bosses until they all agree on something. The scientific name is H17N12."

Harper looked at her watch and wondered if it was too early for a beer. She shrugged and announced, "I'm parched."

Joe helped Ma and Mimi off the couch. Ma asked, "Honey, would you like an Arnold Palmer? We brewed sweet tea and I have lemonade, too."

"Thanks, Ma. But I'm on vacation and we've all had a stressful month. I was thinking something a little more, um, potent."

"Beer it is," she said disapprovingly, not because of the drinking but because of the early hour. "You know where to find them."

As the two ladies of the house moseyed off to the kitchen, Joe turned to the group. "Listen, I need to speak with all of you. Why don't we move into the men's parlor so the ladies don't overhear us? Plus, our good Catholic hosts keep the bar stocked, so we can all have a celebratory cocktail."

Dr. Reitherman said, "I don't know if there's much to celebrate now. Becker shared the media reports with me before you came in. I'm probably out of a job."

Joe lowered his eyes and shoved his hands in his pockets. "Let's go talk."

CHAPTER FORTY-SIX

Randolph House
Heard's Fort, Georgia

Joe ushered everyone into the parlor. Harper showed everyone their drink options and retrieved a couple of beers for her and Joe out of the built-in refrigerator. Dr. Reitherman was the first to speak.

"This leak came straight from the White House. They're probably pissed off because I snuck Harper and Kwon into China. But you know what? I'd do it again. I'll say the same thing to the director of the CDC when he fires me."

"They can't fire you," said Becker. "It was your decision that led us to the truth. Their beef should be with China, not your methods."

"Yes. Yes. Yes," agreed Dr. Boychuck.

Joe tried to assuage everybody's fears. "Hold on, I need you to hear me out. Please get comfortable and let me explain. I'm the source of the leak."

Dr. Reitherman continued standing and a scowl came over his face. "Joe, why? I mean, this may tank my career."

"Not necessarily, Berger. Careers don't end, they simply transition."

"What does that mean?" Dr. Reitherman asked.

Joe approached him and gestured for him to sit. Dr. Reitherman reluctantly obliged.

"Berger, as you know, I have been active in Washington, funding and defending the CDC. There are personal reasons for that beyond being married to Harper. The threat of deadly infectious diseases has always been a part of my political platform. The COVID-19 pandemic opened my eyes a lot and strengthened my resolve to do something about it. This new threat opened the door."

"The door to where?" asked Dr. Reitherman.

"Listen, the facts have always been there. The vast majority of these diseases arise in Asia, namely China. Also, of course, in Africa. The challenges in third-world countries are different from China. In Africa, as Harper can attest, you are dealing with ignorance, superstition, and lawlessness, in addition to fighting deadly outbreaks.

"In China, the Communist Party rule poses an entirely different set of issues. Beijing's misinformation and secrecy has made the viral outbreaks harder to control. Their failure to make cultural changes to prevent the spread of disease is causing a greater risk to the rest of the world because we are kept in the dark. If you won't change the way you live, at least change the way you cooperate."

"That was the reason COVID-19 was so deadly," interjected Dr. Reitherman. "Had they disclosed information from the beginning, it's likely the spread could've been contained to their own country."

"Politics and economics played a factor," added Kwon.

"Yes, exactly," said Joe. "Our nation, heck, any country, should not be blindsided by these diseases. If there is anything that should bring us together, it's a common enemy like a deadly pathogen."

"We've always offered our assistance with the best of intentions," began Dr. Reitherman. "They turn us down and, of course, they publicly claim we never offered. This outbreak was no different."

"Actually, this time was worse," interjected Harper. "They intentionally violated their sanctions by expelling our people from their CDC. Then, to compound their wrongdoing, they took the

European contingent on a wild-goose chase as far away from the epicenter of the outbreak as possible."

Joe took a sip of his beer and nodded. "This is what we can come to expect in the future. Fighting infectious diseases will no longer be done in a spirit of cooperation. There will always be secrecy based on geopolitical interests and economic ones. There will also be national security matters to consider. If China can hide a naturally occurring outbreak from us, how do we know they're not expanding their biological weapons program?"

"This is what concerns us at DARPA," said Kwon. "Bioweapons in anyone's hands, whether a nation-state like China or a terrorist organization, can have deadly consequences for America. We are always the number one target of terrorists. At DARPA, we investigate a number of scenarios, including those in which our adversaries like China equip terrorists with bioweapons."

The room fell silent.

Joe finished his beer and set it on the bar. "All of which brings me to what I want to tell you."

CHAPTER FORTY-SEVEN

Randolph House
Heard's Fort, Georgia

Joe sat in a chair and crossed his legs. His face became serious as he looked each of them in the eye. "I have been contemplating all of this for years. Berger, I think you'll agree. At times your hands are tied when it comes to your investigations. Think about it, to investigate and solve this one, you had to overstep your authority to arrange for Harper and Kwon to get into China."

"You're right, Joe. You've had to listen to me piss and moan about it for years. The CDC is a massive bureaucracy in which the higher you climb on the organizational chart, the more fearful you become of losing your job because you stepped on the wrong politician's toes."

Joe turned to his wife. "Harper, I know you love what you do, but you've also complained many times about the CDC's lack of resources due to budget constraints or even questionable spending priorities."

She expanded on her position. "Joe, don't get me wrong. The CDC does the best it can with what it has to work with. The budgets continue to get slashed, and those at the top, present company excluded, seem to allocate resources to pet projects beyond the CDC's core purpose, which is to protect Americans from communicable diseases."

Joe sighed. "I've set something in motion without consulting you. The window of opportunity was very narrow, and I had to make certain assumptions. Over the last three days, I've been in constant communication with the acting director of DARPA. As Kwon knows, Alicia Saffras is a temporary placeholder until the Senate confirms the president's choice for the position. Fortunately, at least in this particular case, partisan politics didn't get in the way of nominating Dr. Peter Kingman to provide a young, new perspective to DARPA's leadership team."

"I know Peter well," interjected Dr. Reitherman. "We worked on projects together at BARDA and had several opportunities to interact while he's been at the National Institutes of Health." BARDA, an acronym for Biomedical Advanced Research and Development Authority, was the research arm of the government focusing on chemical, biological, and nuclear events, as well as naturally occurring diseases.

"He speaks very highly of you, Berger. You too, Kwon. My colleagues in the Senate expect him to sail through confirmation next week and be sworn in as early as Friday. Not that it was necessary for his approval by the Senate, I pledged my support and willingness to assist him in any way I could."

Joe turned in his chair and addressed Harper again. "We ended up meeting for dinner the other night, and he inquired about you. Because I've known him for years and trust him, I disclosed what this group has been up to. His response couldn't have fit my goals any better."

"What did he say?" asked Dr. Reitherman.

"He asked my opinion. Basically, his proposal was this in not so many words. If he could make a place within DARPA to combat these diseases outside the internal political constraints and bickering between rival nations, would anyone be interested? He didn't name names, but simply threw it out there.

"As our conversation continued, I confided in him about the frustrations Berger and Harper had with the CDC. I also told him of Kwon's answering the call of duty to assist Harper in her quest to find patient zero in China." Joe took a deep breath before continuing.

"The bottom line is this. Peter sees you three as the nucleus of a covert team that will fight diseases before they hit American soil. Off the books, operating in the shadows in much the same way as Kwon has been doing for years. The difference will be that you're fighting this unseen enemy that is every bit as deadly as a nuclear bomb, if not more so."

Joe sat back to gauge everyone's reaction. Harper had been aware of the proposal before she entered the house with Joe earlier. She'd had to pry it out of him, but he didn't dare spring it on her like he was the others.

"How do I fit in?" asked Becker.

Joe quickly responded, "The wheels I set in motion will most likely result in Harper's termination, especially since the Taylor administration knows it will potentially harm me politically. I have a plan for that, and her firing will backfire on the administration if they try to make political hay out of it. That being said, her getting fired will play right into our hands because then she becomes a free agent. When she joins DARPA, if that in fact becomes public knowledge, it would be seen as a logical landing place.

"As for Berger, he won't be fired, formally, but I suspect he'll be forced out through an unplanned early resignation. Again, this works in our favor. He will be the public face of this new covert operation within DARPA. Because of his connections to the agency already, plus with his relationship to Peter, this won't raise eyebrows.

"Now, as for Woolie and Becker. It's tempting to bring Woolie on board as a staff pathologist, but DARPA doesn't have the facilities for that. However, they do have influence over counties and municipalities especially when it comes to their virtually unlimited budget. You can expect some fancy new equipment and an upgrade to your facility in Las Vegas. We can even orchestrate it to provide a feather in the cap for your mayor as well as Clark County governmental officials. We'll get the necessary concessions enabling you to assist with our autopsies from time to time."

"And me?" asked Becker nervously.

"You'll have an important role as the eyes and ears within the CDC. The DARPA team will provide you valuable investigative information, and you can keep them abreast of your work. I imagine, with this secretive relationship, you'll fast become a rising star within the EIS ranks. Does that sound good to you?"

"I'm in!"

"Woolie?" asked Joe.

"Yes. Yes. Yes. Please, I would be honored to be a part of this team in any way possible."

Joe turned to Dr. Reitherman. "Berger, I'm sorry I couldn't discuss this with you in advance. I've known you for as long as I've known Harper."

"You know her a little better than you know me," he said with a chuckle.

"Can't argue there. Here's the thing, your abilities are squandered working as an administrator while people with less talent critique your every move but take the credit for your successes. Make no mistake, you'll not be on the front page of any newspapers, but your ability to save American lives will be enhanced."

"That's all that matters to me," said Dr. Reitherman. "You can count me in, too."

"Kwon?" asked Joe.

"If this is where my country needs me, then I'll be proud to serve."

Joe rose out of his chair and quickly pulled two more beers out of the refrigerator. He handed one to Harper and smiled. She winked in response.

"What are we calling this new operation?" asked Dr. Reitherman.

"The killer Bs," suggested Becker. She gestured to each member of the group as she spoke. "I'm Becker. Then you have Boychuck and Bergermeister."

"Wait, what?" asked Dr. Reitherman.

"She calls you Bergermeister behind your back," replied Harper.

"You do?"

"It's all in fun. Now that I don't work for you anymore, I can call you Bergermeister to your face."

Dr. Reitherman shook his head and smiled before he turned to Joe. "When will this take effect? I need to know how much longer I have to make this young woman suffer while she is still in my employment."

Becker backpedaled. "Hey! I was just kidding!"

The group laughed and Harper moved to rescue Becker from her boss's wrath.

"Okay, Becker, what about Dr. Li Kwon? How do you make him a, quote, *B*?" She used her fingers to generate air quotes.

Becker furrowed her brow as she thought of an answer. "Oh, that's easy. Kwon is a badass. That's your B." She pointed at him. Kwon nodded and managed a smile.

"And," Harper began, stretching out the word, "*moi?*"

A devious grin came over Becker's face. "Well, B also stands for …" she teased with her voice trailing off.

"Don't you dare go there, Becker!" protested Harper.

"Boss!" Becker exclaimed as she burst out laughing. "What did you think I was going to say?"

As everyone joined in the laughter, it was Joe who came up with the perfect title for this new operation.

"Virus Hunters. That's what you are. Disease detectives who search for these microscopic organisms, deadly killers that never stop seeking out human beings to destroy."

"I like it!" exclaimed Becker.

"Yes. Yes. Yes!"

"Virus Hunters. Has a nice ring to it," added Dr. Reitherman.

Harper leaned over to Kwon. They exchanged fist bumps and subtly nodded to one another. With Kwon by her side in the field, she'd never face the same kind of restrictions identifying and studying deadly viruses like she had in the past.

She stood and raised her beer. "Virus Hunters. Cheers!"

Glasses clinked and congratulations were exchanged. Suddenly, Ma entered the room.

"I see y'all have found reason to celebrate. There's nothing better than a good old Southern dinner to share the love of family and success. Join us in the dining room, please."

CHAPTER FORTY-EIGHT

Randolph House
Heard's Fort, Georgia

Ma and Mimi had pulled out the fine china that had been in the Randolph family since the turn of the nineteenth century. Dinner plates were already placed in front of each guest, containing certain garnishes, including pepper jelly, pats of locally churned butter, and pickles from Ma's garden. All across the table, serving platters and bowls were filled with ham, both yams and white sweet potatoes, mashed potatoes with gravy, a variety of farm-to-table vegetables and freshly baked bread. The ladies of the house pulled out all the stops for their guests, as they sensed this home-cooked meal might be their visitors' last for a while.

Once everyone was settled in their seats, Mimi, a devout Catholic like Ma and Harper, said grace. They preceded the blessing with the Sign of the Cross, and then recited in unison:

"Bless us, O Lord, and these, Thy gifts, which we are about to receive from Thy bounty. Through Christ, our Lord. Amen." They crossed themselves once again.

"My goodness, ladies," began Joe. "I haven't seen a spread like this since Christmas dinner last year."

Dr. Boychuck rubbed his hands together. "Yes. Yes. Yes. The aroma is delicious in and of itself. I can't wait to partake."

The platters of food were passed around, and everyone loaded up on their favorites. Ma addressed the group. "Now, don't be shy. We made enough for seconds and thirds. There's a reason we have that big kitchen. Right, Mimi?"

"We've fed a lot more than this bunch," she replied as she served herself a generous portion of fried okra, her specialty.

Harper reached across the table and snatched Becker's pickle spear off her plate.

"Harper Randolph!" exclaimed Ma. "Don't you dare reach across my table and take this young lady's food!"

"But, Ma, she always lets me have her pickles."

Becker defended Harper. "That's right. I can't touch them. Pickles give you warts." She said it so matter-of-factly it caused uproarious laughter at the table. Ma forgot all about her effort to teach Harper some manners.

Throughout the meal, the guests came to know more about each other, and soon it sounded very much like any family dinner around America on a weekend.

Dr. Boychuck and Mimi chatted continuously about Las Vegas. She quizzed him about the drive-thru wedding chapels and Elvis sightings.

Becker discussed her food aversions with Ma, which included her dislike for coleslaw and, as she put it, unidentifiable noodle salads. Ma questioned whether Becker had sought psychiatric help for this abnormal behavior.

Dr. Reitherman and Kwon compared notes on who was still at DARPA since the last time the soon-to-be-former CSELS director had spent time there. Dr. Reitherman found that he and Kwon had several mutual acquaintances. Their conversation turned to places to live, and Kwon offered the services of a Realtor he knew who would be discreet. DARPA employees were known to keep to themselves. Kwon reminded Dr. Reitherman that their social lives revolved around others within the building, and even then, people tended to hang with those they worked most closely with. It helped foster a tight bond.

As for Harper and Joe, they held hands under the table, admiring the dynamic they'd help create. Different people from varied backgrounds had come together as a team to fight a deadly disease. The war was far from over, as there was always another battle brewing out there somewhere.

Harper leaned over and kissed Joe on the cheek. She whispered, "Thank you."

He nodded and kissed her back. "Virus Hunters."

Harper smiled and studied her new team again. She made eye contact with them, and they returned a knowing nod, smile, or wink. She lifted her wineglass to each as a silent toast.

She leaned in to Joe. "That's what we do. Um, that, and save the world, of course."

Joe chuckled. "My god, what have I done?"

That statement earned him a playful elbow to the ribs and another kiss. She repeated the words again before finishing her wine.

"Virus Hunters."

THANK YOU FOR READING THE VIRUS HUNTERS!

If you enjoyed this trilogy introducing the Virus Hunters, I'd be grateful if you'd take a moment to write a short review (just a few words are needed) and post it on Amazon. Amazon uses complicated algorithms to determine what books are recommended to readers. Sales are, of course, a factor, but so are the quantities of reviews my books get. By taking a few seconds to leave a review, you help me out and also help new readers learn about my work.

And before you go ...

SIGN UP for my mailing list at BobbyAkart.com to receive a copy of my monthly newsletter, *The Epigraph*. You'll also learn about special offers, bonus content, and you'll be the first to receive news about new releases in the Virus Hunters series.

VISIT my feature page at Amazon.com/BobbyAkart for more information on the Virus Hunters or any of my other bestselling survival thrillers listed below which includes over forty Amazon #1 Bestsellers in forty-plus fiction and nonfiction genres.

WHAT'S NEXT?

Not all things lost in the Bermuda Triangle
are lost forever.

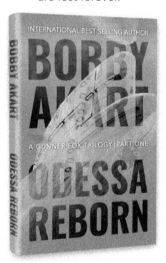

Gunner Fox and the Gray Fox team face off with an enemy
thought to be extinguished nearly a century ago.
In a race against time, they follow clues from Berlin to Buenos Aries
and across three continents to stop the heinous plot.

AVAILABLE ON AMAZON

A NOTE FROM THE AUTHOR

First, let me take a moment to thank you for reading my first series featuring Dr. Harper Randolph and the Virus Hunters! These characters and their story have been planned for three years since the success of my Pandemic series published in May 2017. During the course of my research, I became thoroughly convinced that our world was wholly unprepared for a global pandemic. Here's why.

In the mid-twentieth century, a new weapon, the atomic bomb, shocked the world with its ability to destroy the enemy.

For centuries, another weapon has existed...

One that attacks without conscience or remorse...

Its only job is to kill.

They are the most merciless enemy we've ever faced...

And they're one-billionth our size.

Be prepared to become very, very paranoid.

WELCOME TO THE NEXT GLOBAL WAR.

Over the past half century, the number of new diseases per decade has increased fourfold. Since 1980, the outbreaks have more than tripled. With those statistics in mind, one had to consider the consequences of a major pandemic and now we're living the nightmare.

Death has come to millions of humans throughout the millennia from the spread of infectious diseases, but none was worse than the Black Death, a pandemic so devastating that uttering the words the plague will immediately pull it to the front of your mind. From 1347 to 1351, the Black Death reshaped Europe and much of the world.

In a time when the global population was an estimated four hundred fifty million, some estimates of the death toll reached as high as two hundred million, nearly half of the world's human beings.

This plague's name came from the black skin spots on the sailors who travelled the Silk Road, the ancient network of trade routes that traversed the Asian continent, connecting East and West. The Black Death was in fact a form of the bubonic plague, not nearly as contagious and deadly as its sister, the pneumonic plague.

Fast-forward five centuries to 1918, an especially dangerous form of influenza began to appear around the world. First discovered in Kansas in March 1918, by the time the H1N1 pandemic, commonly known as the Spanish flu, burned out in 1919, it took the lives of as many as fifty million people worldwide.

A hundred years later, in 2020, the COVID-19 pandemic swept the planet destroying lives and the global economy. As of this writing, the death toll is still climbing as a treatment protocol hasn't been established; there is no vaccine, and testing is in short supply.

Why does the history of these deadly pandemics matter?

Because it has happened before and it will happen again and again—despite the world's advanced technology, or because of it. People no longer stay in one place; neither do diseases. Unlike the habits of humans during the Black Death and the Spanish flu, an infection in all but the most remote corner of the world can make its way to a major city in a few days. COVID-19 has proven that.

Terrible new outbreaks of infectious disease make headlines, but not at the start. Every pandemic begins small. Early indicators can be subtle and ambiguous. When the next global pandemic begins, it will spread across oceans and continents like the sweep of nightfall, causing illness and fear, killing thousands or maybe millions of people. The next pandemic will be signaled first by quiet, puzzling reports from faraway places—reports to which disease scientists and public health officials, but few of the rest of us, pay close attention.

The purpose of the Virus Hunters series is not to scare the wits out of you, but rather, to scare the wits into you. As one reader said to me after reading the Pandemic series in 2017, "I now realize that humans can become extinct." Not a comforting thought.

This series is also designed to give you hope. You see, the stories depicted in the Virus Hunters novels are fictional. The events, however, are based upon historical fact. Know this, there are those on the front line of this global war. The burden lies on the CDC and their counterparts around the world who work tirelessly to protect us. This series is dedicated to the Virus Hunters—the disease detectives and shoe-leather epidemiologists of the CDC's Epidemic Intelligence Service who work tirelessly to keep these deadly infectious diseases from killing us all.

Lastly, for many years, I have lived by the following premise:

Because you never know when the day before is the day before, prepare for tomorrow.

My friends, I study and write about the threats we face, not only to both entertain and inform you, but because I am constantly learning how to prepare for the benefit of my family as well. There is nothing more important on this planet than my darling wife Dani and our two princesses, Bullie and Boom. I've always said, one day the apocalypse will be upon us. Well, sometimes I hate it when I'm right.

Thank you for supporting my work and I hope you enjoy the future novels featuring the Virus Hunters.